SHAPES IN THE MIST

Dilys Gater

CHIVERS
THORNDIKE

This Large Print book is published by BBC Audiobooks Ltd, Bath, England and by Thorndike Press®, Waterville, Maine, USA.

Published in 2004 in the U.K. by arrangement with Anecdotes Publishing.

Published in 2004 in the U.S. by arrangement with Anecdotes Publishing.

U.K. Hardcover ISBN 0–7540–9921–0 (Chivers Large Print)
U.S. Softcover ISBN 0–7862–6263–X (General)

The text of this Large Print edition is unabridged.
Other aspects of the book may vary from the original edition.

Set in 16 pt. New Times Roman.

Printed in Great Britain on acid-free paper.

British Library Cataloguing in Publication Data available

Library of Congress Control Number: 2004101111

Thanks to Simon Tansley for taking me to see the Bridestones and for his stimulating conversations, arguments and allowing me to share his impressions, experiences and knowledge.

Thank you to the following people who provided help, inspiration and background information:

Doug Pickford for his interest, his talk on 'Sex, Drugs and Old King Cole' and for kindly allowing me to quote from his book *The Bridestones* (Bawdstone Press, 1998)

Kevin Kilburn FRAS for information on new discoveries in astro-archaeology

Mr & Mrs Goodfellow of Bridestones House for kindly allowing me access to their garden

David A. Hunt for taking me to see Thor's Cave

Ray Poole for his enthusiasm about local history

As always, with love and gratitude to Prospero the Magician.

1

We'd had our first read-through of *Hamlet* that day—the day Loz announced he was going to join a coven.

Now though I am as starry-eyed as the next would-be actress, I do try to be realistic about my acting ability and I hadn't seriously expected to get either of the female roles. Not heavyweight enough for Gertrude, possibly not sweetly fey or drop-dead glamorous enough for Ophelia either. So oh, the thrill when I found I had landed the Player Queen! Only a small part true, yet a real part, something meaty I could get my teeth into and definitely not one of the also-rans, hangers-on and court ladies.

As we theatre folk know, there are no small parts only small actresses! And since I fully intended to be Big—with a capital B—it was thus singled out, marked as a future star that I was glowing all over when I got back to the flat after classes that afternoon. Loz rather put my news in the shade, though. I mean, if one is studying at a Theatre School it is generally accepted that one will be indulging in a little acting—possibly even getting a part—but it's not every day you make up your mind to join a coven.

'You mean you want to be a witch?' I

1

queried. Loz looked doubtful.

'I thought it was just women who were witches. Aren't men warlocks or something?'

'Uh-huh,' I shrugged, to show I didn't know. Some melodramatic hamming it up in *The Crucible* during my last year at school had been my only connection with witchcraft during a comparatively sheltered life.

'There are no such things as warlocks. It's a popular fallacy, they're all called witches. But what on earth has persuaded you to convert to Wicca, Loz?' asked Miranda crisply as she came in from the kitchen with our evening meal laid out temptingly on a tray.

We always refer to Miranda as 'Randy' and not for the obvious coarse and indelicate reason, since she has never had a close man-friend even though she is a cool, poised twenty-eight with stunning blonde 'English Rose' looks. She has a couple of prohibitive degrees and holds some kind of administrative position in the offices at Harrods—something to do with accounts—and she is a sort of distant relative of mine.

It was her presence (and the existence of her flat) that had been the deciding factor in my family's decision to allow me to come to London to study as an actress. It is old-fashioned if you like, but I'm afraid I don't belong to one of those liberated families where you're grown up at twelve and considered to be free and independent, encouraged to go and do your own thing, whatever that may be. My family is deeply protective and traditional. My relatives still look on me as an innocent child who needs guidance and a hand to hold when venturing into the big wide world outside the county of Staffordshire and the wooded hills round the village of Rudyard, near where I have always lived.

My grandmother, who has the final say on these matters, didn't know about Loz though, when I was making arrangements to come and live with Randy. She would probably have accepted him without a qualm mind you, but my various 'Aunties' and 'Uncles' might, if she had mentioned his presence in the flat to them, have expressed a certain amount of trepidation. Even in this age of world travel, many of them have never ventured beyond the borders of their own county let alone been to London, and they would almost certainly have regarded Loz as something in the nature of a visitor from Mars.

Loz is actually a sweetie. He is a pet, everything delightful you can think of. But he is unemployed—and according to Randy, probably chronically unemployable—so it is fortunate he has some sort of small private means, though it is from a Trust Fund and he can't touch the capital. He is twenty-six and describes himself as a 'professional dilettante'. He leads a tortured, Byronic kind of existence that is remarkably sexless considering it is

3

mainly involved in trying to sort out his sexual identity satisfactorily. His relationships are fraught with heavy Freudian (or possibly Oedipal?) overtones. He lies awake worrying about it at nights. Sometimes I wake up and see the light on in the living room and I take pity on him and sit drinking hot chocolate, sharing his midnight vigil as he paces the floor. His life is filled with weighty problems of this sort as well as 'art' with what Loz considers a capital A.

His sudden announcement that he was going to turn witch however, caught both Randy and me off guard. Loz had never given any indication during the months I had known him that he was cut out for coven life—though I admit, I had no idea what that entailed. But Randy has an infuriating habit of knowing something about everything: it comes from serious reading of *Reader's Digest* and *The National Geographic Magazine* instead of *Cosmo* or *Vogue,* or even *Woman's Weekly* like any ordinary girl. She would have been sure to notice. Loz had been lodging with her for over two years.

'I must do it! I have to deal with something that's—well, I can only say it's been deeply traumatic. It's really shaken me,' Loz uttered desperately and I was fascinated to observe that he was actually speaking through clenched teeth. You don't often come across such behavioural clichés in real life.

4

Randy and I both looked up. She had made us spaghetti Bolognese and I was hungry, but Loz's tone implied that something more than just ordinarily awful was involved. We waited. Then Randy said encouragingly:

'Yes, well?'

'I can't possibly tell you,' Loz declared in a rush. 'They swear you to secrecy, you see. It's a secret society, an Order of some kind, world-wide and immensely powerful.' He blinked at us like an indecisive owl. 'I'm scared out of my wits, quite frankly. I mean, if they decided to hunt me down they'd easily be able to find me with the resources they've got, so that's why I need to work on some sort of power of my own to be able to protect myself.'

We stared, dumbfounded.

'It can't be that bad, surely. You're making it sound like—I don't know, the Mafia or the Ku Klux Klan,' Randy began bracingly. I enquired with a sudden spurt of interest:

'What did you do that was so terrible? I can't believe for a minute you'd ever get involved in any heavy stuff, it just isn't possible. I don't think you've got it in you, frankly Loz,' I added quickly. 'You're too nice a person, I mean.'

He turned his attention to his spaghetti, relaxing a bit.

'Well, no, I didn't actually do anything, you're right,' he admitted cautiously. 'That's the trouble, you see, I defied them. I turned them down. I said no.'

'To what, for heaven's sake?' Randy demanded, her beautifully arched brows lifted almost to her hairline. 'Come on, tell Momma.'

With an air of relief Loz dropped his mysterious pose. As we ate the whole stark and naked truth was laid before us. In his most dignified manner, he explained that in his eternal quest to find himself and establish his identity satisfactorily once and for all, he had answered an advertisement in *Loot* that had apparently been placed by a Dominant Woman who wanted to meet a Submissive Man. On reflection Loz considered it was possible he might be quite happy living a life of submission to some strong-willed woman who would take care of everything for him. He had written off and waited for a reply with an increasingly hopeful picture of the unknown 'Mistress Emma' building up in his brain, certain she would provide the answer to all his problems.

'And then the envelope came—an SAE I'd sent,' he told us, dramatically white-faced. 'And I opened it and—Well, look, I'll show you.'

Burning his boats now, he rose from the table and went to find the art briefcase he affected as part of his dilettante image, while Randy and I carried on with our meal in speculative silence.

*   *   *

Mealtimes were formal affairs at Randy's. The table was situated in an alcove next to the sweep of long green velvet curtains that covered almost the whole of one wall from ceiling to floor, hiding the patio doors. In the summer we had them open onto a tiny terrace with flowers in urns, and there was a lawn and a tangled garden down some ancient mossy steps beyond.

Randy's flat was on the ground floor of a block of about twenty purpose-built flats set in the grounds of what had once been a rambling early Victorian house in North London. The combination of old-established gardens and modern flats with all mod cons could not have been bettered, and from what I had seen of some of the others Randy's was the best of the block. It was cool in summer with the patio doors, warm and cosy in winter, while the garden beyond gave the impression that we were in the depths of the country. In addition, the flat had spacious bedrooms and there was an impressive hall with a feature recess that boasted a Pompeian-type mural and statue that looked like marble. Randy swore she had purchased the flat on the strength of that rather quirky touch alone, without looking further.

In the enormous living-room the three of us could have sprawled about quite easily without

7

getting in each other's way—not that there ever was any sprawling in this efficiently run establishment. Randy had invested in a dark leather chesterfield—Harrods paid her well—with matching club chairs. She believed in formality at all times and there was no slopping about with TV dinners on our knees. The table where we ate our meals and snacks was always exquisitely laid with silver and napery, with candles at either end. I had really taken to this kind of sophisticated living since moving in with her and it came naturally to Loz, or at least that was the impression I'd got.

But the two most aristocratic members of our household (who, lured by the prospect of free food were now condescending to amble in from the kitchen to join us) were four-footed. Dick, the orange Persian, could not help but make an entrance wherever he went, though he underplayed his personal magnificence with the laid-back air of a boss-cat who doesn't have to prove a thing to anyone. Dick conducted a constant running battle with two moggies who lived on the other side of the building, but apart from getting away with the occasional few clawfuls of orange fur they never seemed to do *him* any harm, though they often limped home themselves with bitten ears and scratches. We were rather proud of Dick's prowess, though the owner of the moggies not surprisingly held quite the opposite view, and complained bitterly to anyone who would listen about what a monster he was.

Nobody would ever have dreamed of saying anything that wasn't entirely complimentary about our little black and white kitten Turpin, however. He was a recent addition to the household, a stray Randy had adopted—she is very soft hearted under all that blonde Harrods cool. Since Dick was already called Dick and the new kitten was mainly white but had a black 'highwayman's mask' across his little furry face, it seemed inevitable that they should team up as a double act so Dick and Turpin they instantly became. And while Dick stalked majestically, throwing his weight round, Turpin climbed onto people's knees with immense cunning or made himself at home in nests of their best sweaters. The trouble was that I never had the heart to scold him. He could get away with murder.

I was feeding him the remains of my spaghetti—or at least the Bolognese sauce, though he'd eat anything—when Loz re-emerged from his room grimly clutching the envelope that had brought him such dire tidings.

'Just *read* it,' he mourned. 'I tell you, I was utterly petrified. And I still am. I mean, at the thought that things like this are allowed to go on in a civilised country! It's unbelievable. If these people should ever catch up with me— uhhh! I don't even want to think about it.'

Randy took the envelope and briskly

unfolded the papers it contained. She read a page, showing no emotion, and when she put it down and went on to the next I couldn't repress my curiosity. I picked it up and ran my eyes interestedly over it.

'YOU ARE ENTERING THE ARSKAYA ACADEMY'

was starkly emblazoned across note-paper decorated with sketches of stiletto shoes with heels so high that they would have had their wearers walking round horizontally, thrown forward parallel to the ground. A few grim-looking iron-studded collars, leashes and whips were also in evidence and when I glanced unbelievingly down the typed page I saw that there was a curlicued (duplicated) signature in purple ink at the bottom which claimed to be that of Loz's dream girl, 'Mistress Emma'. Rather taken aback, I began to read.

'The Arskaya Academy is a Secret Order run by Dominant Women for those despicable inepts whose role in life is to try ineffectually to serve. It has its Headquarters in Kent, England, in the country retreat of our Foundress, a member of the French nobility unselfishly dedicating her life to the domination of lesser beings who actively need to be disciplined and

10

corrected. All our members are similarly dedicated to upholding and furthering her work in this important and time-honoured tradition.

'YOU ARE WITHIN THE ARSKAYA ACADEMY!

'It is housed in a unique building with the distinctive façade of an Establishment guaranteed to appeal to the lover of Pain, the interior retaining the elegant antiquity of the wonderful de Sade era. For we are noted for our devotion to the association of pain, terror, humiliation, togetherness and trust so exquisitely described by our Foundress as 'Exploitational Caring'.

'SURRENDER YOURSELF TO US!

'We will use you as you need to be used. We will treat you as you deserve . . .'

I had begun to read with the slightly supercilious tolerance of youth, prepared to be amused. This was so ludicrous it had to be a joke. But I turned the page onto a few unexpectedly bizarre details that gave me a physical jolt that actually made me feel slightly nauseous.

I might claim to know all about the secret obsessions and dark extremes of behaviour that went on in the claustrophobic and violent Jacobean tragedies we studied in the course of our dramatic education but I had been brought up in what is commonly called a

11

'decent way'. I found it rather shocking to actually encounter such extremes of behaviour so matter-of-factly in the course of my everyday living. Feeling suddenly very young and innocent, I let go of the page as though it had burned my fingers.

'Pathetic if it wasn't so pathological,' pronounced Randy coolly, flipping through the other papers that had been included. 'I was aware of course that there is a bondage and domination scene around but I never realised this kind of sick scam could get past the law. I don't blame you for reacting the way you did Loz, it's not only offensive it's blatantly criminal. Obviously a con—including the demands for instant payment for getting involved. I hope you weren't silly enough to part with any money.'

Silence, then:

'You mean, you don't believe it?' Loz demanded, blinking at her even more owlishly. 'You don't think these people are real?'

'Oh, hardly, darling. The most debased, sad kind of fantasy, that's all,' said Randy with conviction. She added after a moment (during which she had obviously been searching her memory for reports of related exposés in *Reader's Digest* or some of her other informative sources): 'Probably all dreamed up by a couple of foxy-faced crooks skulking in a dirty little office above a betting shop.'

Loz remained unconvinced. His jaw was

12

tensed and his fingers clutched whitely at the envelope.

'But didn't you read the testimonials? And the threats if I didn't register *promptly* and pay up?' he asked, with an air of bravado that I knew hid an inner trembling. He seized a sheet and began to read aloud.

'I have wrecked my life searching everywhere for the cruellest woman in the world. It was in vain until I found Mistress Emma. She has fulfilled my wildest dreams and made everything worthwhile. I shall be her slave for always. She has made me suffer so much that for the first time ever—Um, well, never mind the rest,' he added, stopping hastily and clearing his throat. His fair skin went ruddy as he glanced towards me in sudden recollection of my presence.

Because my family had asked her to and because I was so much younger—a mere innocent at eighteen—Randy had assumed a kind of moral responsibility for me right from the start. She wielded an alert censor on what I could and could not be allowed to know of what went on in the wicked world, and Loz usually enjoyed participating in helping to keep me unsullied. On this occasion, however, both of them had been too preoccupied to recollect that I was sitting at the table with them.

'I am so sorry, Tania,' Loz said now with such genuine distress that I knew he meant it. 'I wasn't being fair to you. I shouldn't have

13

said anything or shown you these papers. I apologise.'

He reached across awkwardly to take the sheet I had dropped, the picture of guilty embarrassment. I tried to lighten the atmosphere.

'Hey, don't mention it. I have been to school you know, and learned about the existence of—um—well, whatever you call this sort of thing. Though I do have to admit I can't see much to get turned on about in the prospect of—what was it I was just looking at?—being gagged and blind-folded and shoved into a skin suit to be whipped. And—uh—well, the rest of it. Sorry Loz, the imagination doesn't even begin to boggle, I suppose I'm not broad-minded enough. Quite honestly it just seems rather desperate and icky to me.'

'Oh, what a sensible child! How absolutely sane you are, Tania,' Loz sighed in some relief. He shuddered. 'Perish the thought. But don't you see this is why I must save myself at all costs and get some power to my elbow. I mean, I know you're right, Randy dear, it's probably nothing but fantasy, yet all the same I can't help myself. I'm being positively haunted. Hunted! I can't sleep for horrific visions. Gangs of fearsome females determined to get me, screaming at my heels like—well, like the Harpies or the Amazons—'

'The Ride of the Valkyries?' Randy suggested, allowing herself the well-schooled

14

flicker of a smile but Loz was too lost in dreadful contemplation to notice and simply nodded agreement.

'Oh, how true. And whoever really sent these little nasties, well—,' he added piteously, 'it isn't just them. It's the prospect behind it all. Women! Gangs of women—powerful secret societies—! Speaking for myself, entirely personally and no offence intended, I do find aggressively assertive women can be very frightening at times, you know.'

Randy could not repress her amusement, but at the sight of Loz's pained face she quickly recovered her self-possession.

'It does leave a bit of a loofah taste in the mouth,' she allowed briskly. 'But you needn't worry about any gangs or secret societies or even ordinarily assertive women hounding you Loz, I promise you. Tania and I will protect you.'

'Even though I did pay the 'Out' fee?' Loz admitted after a moment in a very small voice.

'Paid the 'Out' fee? Oh, Loz—' Randy regarded him sadly. 'You were never anything like 'In'! You should have told me, I'd have been only too delighted to call their bluff. Still, never mind, at least you're rid of them now. They won't bother you again.'

Loz was still dubious as he replaced the papers in the envelope.

'Mmm, maybe. All the same, I think I might be happier if I was to join a coven. Then I'd be able to—to work spells and things myself. And I'd have the other witches—and the warlocks, if there are any—to protect me.'

Randy raised her fine brows expressively in my direction but said nothing more as she rose to clear the plates and bring in slices of lemon meringue. Best to let it lie. We both knew that Loz could be extremely stubborn if he ever got an idea into his head and even I could see that he had been really frightened. Surely though, I thought, nobody in their right mind would ever take that kind of warped joke seriously—

But then what did I really know about pain and fear? The sort of anxious torment that made Loz's life so difficult for him? The sort of compulsion that drove people down their dark and desperate avenues of behaviour, the guilty secrets that might haunt them?

For a moment, just for a moment I was aware of gates opening within my mind. I was aware of myself hovering between levels of understanding that, though I sat in the comforting normality of Randy's living room, turned it for an instant into somewhere else, an unfamiliar terrain. For the first time in my life I faced and had to acknowledge the existence of prospects unknown, of presences looming that could be frightening and hostile.

There was a big world out there. And somewhere, a mentality that might embody very different and diametrically opposed truths to the ones I regarded as good, the ones I lived by. There might be choices made, freely made, to take pleasure from the barbs of cruelty and humiliation and pain inflicted—to actively delight in the prospect of suffering—

I was lost, naked and shivering. The levels of the world were turned upon each other so that I was neither in space nor time. I was an object, an abject dead flesh that had its only reality through the contact of the pain inflicted by the living flesh that lifted it, bound it with bonds that cut deep to bring forth the salt taste of blood. I had the freedom of the whole air and yet I could not move. I was held immobile in a living death, suspended helpless between earth and sky and knowing neither of them for comfort.

There were voices keening in the wind that blew cold from the sea, the voices of souls lost and beseeching their way. The first heavy drops of the storm that gathered itself together out there in the darkness stung my flesh like knives. And I knew without knowing how I knew that they were the forerunners, that even the grass was bending lower before the tempest that would come, crouching itself ever deeper and lower against the sand, blurring the line of the shore so that all was grey, all shapes in the mist, no substance, no difference between earth and sky, sea and land—

*'I know that I hung on the windy tree
For nine whole nights,
Wounded with the spear, dedicated to Odin,
Myself to myself.'*

Who can say when anything begins? Did the story really begin then, at the precise instant when I consciously became aware of those other realms and accepted their existence and the existence of weakness and the evil which, being nothing in itself, feeds on weakness? Or did it begin at my birth, or even further back at some moment lost in the mists of the past?

All one can say about beginnings is that once they have happened then inevitably must follow either progression or ending. It was all too much, too soon for me, and the vision that had for a moment seemed so clear retreated from my groping and fearful grasp. But the path had been laid before me without my knowledge or consent, and once I had consciously set my foot on it there could be no going back.

Nothing had changed in Randy's comfortable living room. Loz was still frowning over his envelope and Turpin was still purring in a satisfied manner at my feet as he washed his face after clearing the remains of my Bolognese. Hardly a minute had passed since I had allowed myself to explore those random thoughts about the possible reality of entering willingly into suffering—had experienced the terrifying flashing vision of being strung up, bound and helpless—

Yet I had an uneasy conviction deep within me that something *had* happened. Some step had been taken that was irrevocable. And somehow—in some way I did not understand—things were never going to be the same for me again.

2

I could hear a cheerful clatter from the kitchen where Randy was stacking the plates and setting out our slices of lemon meringue on the serving tray. In her super-efficient way she believed in doing the housework herself and never expected us to muck in at all except to keep our rooms tidy. Since she was a wonderful cook and a wonderful housekeeper —let's face it, a wonderful everything really—I could see her point. Why put up with my messing around or Loz's well-meaning but inept efforts when you could do it yourself in half the time?

While we ate our fluffy, tangy dessert in a reverential silence, I pondered on what had just occurred. That vision. Those words. It hadn't been that I had actually seen anything, or even heard a voice *as such*. It had been more like an awareness of the vision and the words, a kind of *thought*. As though I had actually undergone the experience at some time, known the words once but forgotten them until now, like suddenly remembering a poem you learned years ago or recalling some fragment of conversation you'd overheard without realising it.

It was more than odd. I had to admit I found it quite disturbing. I would have sworn I had never visited any such wild seacoast, certainly never been treated to terrifying violence or so far as I knew ever heard about scenes of the kind that had just manifested themselves to me. I had no idea where or when I might have suffered those moments of painful awareness nor where I might have heard those words—those penetrating, haunting words of the lament that had come keening on the wind. I had no idea at all what it meant, and now when I tried to identify the words I found I couldn't even remember them, only a sort of impression of what they had conveyed.

Despair. Desolation. Loss. A sense of such utter and complete devastation that my mind prickled with a coldness I had never felt in my life before and quickly pushed away. It was not pleasant to think about.

As Randy carried out the plates I got up and went across the room to sink into the comfort of the leather chesterfield, sitting as close as I could get to the fire. Turpin immediately materialised on my lap, where he proceeded to curl up while Dick leaned his weight against my feet and gazed as though hypnotised into the fake gas flames. I started to feel better.

'Well, I've got things to do. I should be learning my lines,' I said, speaking with unnatural brightness in a conscious effort to break the silence and change the subject to something safer. ('Safer?' I thought dazedly. Just exactly what was going on here?) 'Did I tell you I've landed a part—a real part—in *Hamlet?*'

'Ophelia?' Randy cried from the kitchen.

'No, the Player Queen. But on the whole I'm not sure I'd have wanted Ophelia anyway,' I declared. 'She's always difficult to play. I've seen videos and old films and things but I've never yet come across a convincing performance of the mad scene from anyone. Marianne Faithfull was the nearest, amazingly enough, in some ancient version from the Sixties or Seventies. Or at least, that's my 'umble opinion. I wouldn't have minded having a go at Gertrude though—quite fancy myself as the sexy, experienced older woman— but of course there was no chance. I look far too young.'

Across the room, Loz smiled and said precisely: 'You *are* young.'

Obvious, but like so many obvious remarks this was something that suddenly struck me with a relevance I hadn't been aware of before. I was still hearing the echo of those snatched words I couldn't identify going round in my head, as well as feeling very lazy (the sybaritic influence of Randy's lemon meringue). I sat back to ponder on Loz's unexpectedly pertinent comment.

*   *   *

Yes, I supposed I was young in many ways, younger possibly than other girls of my age. And yet instinctively I knew I was older too, with some kind of subtle maturity of spirit they did not possess. I wasn't sure how this had been acquired. It had been instilled into me somehow as a result of my upbringing.

I might have been said to have grown up in a kind of time-warp, a backwater where time had stood still. And in spite of my wide and extended family I had the sense of having grown up alone. My mother, who had died at my birth, was only a name to me and though my father was alive I hardly ever saw him. He had some kind of high-powered job in the oil industry, and went round the world to different oilrigs or oilfields when summoned to put out fires or sort out problems, my grandmother said.

His home base (rather surprisingly since he was English) was in Copenhagen. He had a long-standing Danish girlfriend with whom he shared a luxury apartment and he spent any free time he had there—going to the Tivoli Gardens and the theatre and so on I supposed when I ever thought about it. I imagined he led quite a sophisticated lifestyle, though I had nothing to complain about materially, since both Gran and I were more than handsomely provided for.

It was my grandmother who had brought me up, and she had done it in a less flamboyant, more traditional manner than my high-flying father might have done, in the country house situated near the village of Rudyard in the Staffordshire Moorlands, which had been my mother's family home.

I lounged on the chesterfield lost in my thoughts while Randy briskly assembled and filled our coffee mugs. She had made that concession to informality even though she had a lovely coffee set with tiny *demi-tasses* ringed with gilt stored away in a box somewhere.

I could not just ignore what had happened. I had to try and make some sense out of it so to the accompaniment of the percolator bubbling away comfortingly in the kitchen, I allowed— or rather, deliberately forced myself—to consider the situation as honestly as I could. I had come a long way in the last few months, mentally as well as physically, from my strangely reclusive country childhood and girlhood to this moment, to revelations in a classy London flat and the world of Dramatic Art.

Part of the training of an actor, we had learned, involved the application of a kind of on-going personal psychoanalysis. This helped you to understand yourself as well as others better, enabling you to use the natural instruments of mind and body to the full in your art. You had to examine yourself, your feelings, actions and motivations in depth so that you could learn how to control them. Self-discipline, we were told repeatedly, was the basis of everything—any creative artist must first apply himself to acquiring practical skills and techniques before he could achieve the true freedom of expression that would allow the inspiration of greatness, even genius, to work itself through.

In many ways I had been familiar with this kind of thinking all my life, so I found nothing odd in devoting any spare moments I happened to have to consciously examining and evaluating the various aspects of the status quo. With my mug of coffee in my hands and the weight and warmth of Turpin companionable on my lap, lulled by the comfort and familiarity of my immediate surroundings, I proceeded to do it now.

*   *   *

The hills and woods of that lovely little backwater where I had grown up had not only been timeless but curiously lacking in spatial boundaries. They might have existed at least partly in some mysterious dimension of myth or fairy-tale: the woodland might have been the woods where the lost Babes wandered, where birds and small forest creatures covered them with leaves and watched over them as they slept. As a child I might have wandered unknowingly into—and thankfully, also out of—the deep fastnesses of a haunted forest more times than I knew.

My home too had something of that ghostly quality. It was small but very old, with low ceilings, ancient oak beams and a 'priest's hole' that Gran prudently used as extra storage space. I had always taken its history for granted, as well as its specially magical atmosphere that lingered almost like some forgotten fragrance on the air. It was just my home.

If I had thought about the subject at all I would probably have put any suggestion of other-worldliness down to prosaic, physical things. The fact that there was always a subtle perfume lingering about the house for instance, that provided a persuasive pot-pourri very evocative of past times, past days. There were herbs in the tiny knot garden and scented flowers outside my window. Drifts of lavender and the old roses that bloomed every summer not only smelled, but looked as though they might have come from some exquisitely illuminated mediaeval Book of Hours.

25

Perhaps, I suddenly realised in a flash of blinding clarity, I had always been conscious without actually being aware of it, of other voices like the one I had just heard outside the range of my hearing, presences and realities beyond the comfortably familiar. More than one door seemed to have opened in my mind in the last few moments. In an instant I had grown new perceptions. I felt light-headed, aware of a kind of freshness, a brightness to my thoughts as though a veil had been lifted. At last—at long last—I was seeing everything clear.

For instance, just as I took my home for granted, I had always taken it for granted too that my grandmother was not like other people. She was not, but in what way she was different I had simply never queried. Now though, I could see the difference—and see even further than that.

Gran was in her early sixties and in some ways looked her age, having typical grandmotherly white hair (gold gone to silver-grey, actually) and a figure stunted by the arthritis that plagued her. Yet often when I looked at her I seemed to see her take on some other form. Sometimes she was a kind of elderly crone, bright eyes shining tolerantly with depths of ancient wisdom. Sometimes she was a beautiful girl who looked as young as me.

It had never seemed strange to me that Gran had this ability to appear in different guises, but I had always assumed, if I considered it at all, that it was something she was responsible for herself. She could do it because she was special, because I had been particularly blessed with a grandmother who was not like other people's grandmothers but was unique. Suddenly though, as I sipped meditatively at Randy's efficiently fragrant and flavourful coffee and stared along with Dick into the flames of the gas fire, I seemed to see things from quite a different point of view. It was almost as though they or I or all of us had been turned completely upside-down. And what I saw staggered me so much that for a moment my throat contracted and my heart started to bang uncomfortably fast in my chest.

What if all the time, I had been looking at it from the wrong angle? What if Gran actually *was* like other people and it was myself who was different? What if *I* was actually the one who was in some way special and unique?

*   *   *

It might have been the work we had begun to do on Hamlet, the doorway that we were expectantly regarding as open onto another world where a ghost could return from beyond the grave to revenge his murderous death. It might have been the prospect of a reality where everything was actually part of a much greater 'play' and had as little meaning as the posturings of the players on Will Shakespeare's stage at the Globe. Or maybe (and I knew in my heart that this, however gratuitously it had presented itself to me, was the real answer) it was the prompting of those words which had come into my head silent and voiceless as the wind blowing through my mind, and that image travelling subtle as thought through the ether. Whatever the catalyst had been, I was consciously alive and aware for the first time I could remember, power surging through me as though I had suddenly discovered how to function on all engines.

Great insights and revelatory visions do not happen accompanied by streaks of lightning, I can tell you that. They seem to be so obvious that you wonder how you could ever have been so dumb you missed them. With a kind of simple inevitability, I saw it all now. I saw it quite clearly. The indisputable truth.

It wasn't Gran who was able to shape-shift (and how did I know that was the right term for it, I wondered darkly, nevertheless certain that I was correct). It was in fact me who had the ability to see other aspects of reality that took on different physical form. It was me who had been granted the gift, whatever it was, not Gran.

*   *   *

This idea was not entirely welcome, though as soon as the thought occurred to me I knew with complete conviction that I was right. The realisation that it was me who was different seemed to remove me at one stroke, lift me and set me down somewhere far away from everything I had always been able to regard as familiar. I hadn't changed, I was exactly the same—but everything else had changed. The world around me appeared to have been subjected to some kind of earthquake and suddenly it took on all sorts of new contours.

My awareness even of those nearest to me seemed to shift round, take a half-turn as though a gigantic hand had jerked me eighty degrees further on than them. Gran, for instance, who had always seemed so much older and wiser—particularly since she was two generations removed from me, not just one. How was it I had never realised before that age and wisdom bear little relation to the passing of seasons and years?

Now as I thought of my grandmother I could see again that young, lovely girl who had always seemed to be hovering in the shadows behind the arthritic elderly lady or the ancient crone. Was this the real presence that existed behind my grandmother's familiar image, was this the true person I had yet to come to know?

As I pondered I realised that actually, I did already know her in an odd sort of way, the ghostly girl-woman. I had always known her, she had been as much a part of my growing up as I was myself and I could have described every detail of her appearance. About eighteen—my own age now—with delicately sweet features and soft flaxen hair, simply combed from a side parting into loose waves that framed her face, she wore a dress of lilac crepe that hung in clinging folds to her slim body.

She was not just a figment of my imagination. She had been a real person, really lived in a time I had only been able to glimpse in old black-and-white movies I had seen of Ginger Rogers and Fred Astaire. She had been Gran's mother, my own Great-Grandmother, who had grown up in the Nineteen Thirties— ancient history to me—in those far-off days when Fred was putting on his 'top hat, white tie and tails' and sweeping Ginger off into a carefree rendering of the Piccolino or the passionate intensity of *Let's Face the Music and Dance*.

Gran kept all the old family snapshots stuffed away in a suitcase and the girl-woman was there, immortalised for ever on a hand-tinted square of paste-board. Someone had clicked their little Kodak box camera on a summer afternoon and frozen her in time at a moment when she had been young and in love. Smiling, she stood clasped in the embrace of a dark-haired man whose laughing eyes teased, mocked and beguiled. He was the man she would later marry—the man who was destined to become my Great-Grandfather.

Ever since I could remember, that girl in the lilac crepe dress had haunted me. The tinted picture of her and her young lover was my favourite of all the family snaps in the box. It had been taken in the halcyon days of their courtship just before the Second World War, and the garden in which they were standing was one I knew well, since it was the garden of the house where I too had grown up. It had hardly altered over the years, though it seemed to have been extra green and somnolent in the lush richness of that long-gone, far-away summer.

Somehow you could almost feel the warmth of the sun, catch the fragrance of pinks and hear the lazy hum of bees. Behind the girl-woman and her lover, the sky glowed luminously soft and blue while just visible through the trees, gold-etched, lay a dazzling patch of silver light. The shining waters of Rudyard Lake dreamed secretively in the eternally still, hot afternoon.

As I sat in Randy's flat, seemingly a part of the accelerated pace and life of London, I realised how mistaken I had been to think that I was free, independent, a modern girl in a modern world where all things were equal. For they held me fast, those unsuspected ghosts of time and place. I was not free. I had never

31

been free. I was bound and helpless as I had been in the vision I had just experienced, a prisoner suspended in air yet tied to the earth, at the mercy of whatever unseen links held me to the past, and to the countryside where I had been born.

*   *   *

My maternal roots are sunk in the county of Staffordshire in the English Midlands. The village where my mother's family has lived for generations is very old. According to the local history books it existed as far back as Saxon times, when it was called Rodehyerd (or sometimes Rudierd). When the Domesday Book was compiled it was the new King, William the Conqueror, who was listed as tenant of all the surrounding land.

Even now you can get a sense of that ancient wildness and feel you are far removed from reality, but in those days it was really isolated pioneer country, wasteland and thick woods. Later on this area belonged to the Bishop of Chester and formed part of his huge hunting estates.

At that time the lake did not exist and the village was just a tiny hamlet. It was not until several centuries later that Rudyard really put itself on the map, so to speak, during the dawning of more modern times when Staffordshire started to boom in a Wild

Western, frontier territory sort of way. It was raw and brash, rough and tough, humming with the new industries that would bring prosperity to the Five Towns of North Staffordshire and their people and give the area the name it is generally known by—the Potteries.

In spite of the smoky gloom and grime of the Industrial Revolution that smirched sooty fingers across the stained-glass colours of mediaeval England, scarring it for ever, a good deal of the countryside remained—and still remains—quaintly rural. In the North Staffordshire Moorlands where my home is situated, visitors can enjoy wandering in the sort of scenes that belong on a picture postcard. Rudyard village itself clings partly to the side of a green, steep valley, very much away from it all. There are trees and flowers. There is space and a sense of timelessness. Sky. And there is water, the water of the lake that gives the place its claim to fame—though perhaps it would be more realistic to admit it was the English writer Rudyard Kipling who made this beautiful village a household word. Rudyard was not named after him, he was actually named after it! His parents, with romantic nostalgia, christened their son in memory of the spot where, in 1863, they had first met at a picnic party!

If you go further afield you come to the miles of wild, high moorlands that stretch not far away. They are picturesque places of sweeping sky and massing cloud against looming horizons, far vistas of green valleys drenched in sunburst, bent trees, rocky outcrops and crags and the lonely companionship of grazing sheep in the mist. The importantly bustling little market town of Leek—just far enough away to make a trip there into 'an outing' in more leisurely times—boasts ancient ecclesiastical roots into the past: there was a Cistercian Abbey called Dieulacres here, founded in 1214. And there are impressively rich connections still to be seen with the silk industry, with William Morris, the Arts and Crafts Movement and the Pre-Raphaelites.

Artists like to paint in this area, walkers can lose themselves in the remoteness of the landscape and be alone with nature. There are tales of all kinds of ancient superstitions while echoes of witchcraft, occult practises and ghosts swarm on every side from the Headless Horseman who will snatch you up and carry you off on a grim and jolting ride to death, to the Mermaid who lures travellers into the depths of Black Meer on Morridge Moor.

The famous 'huge tremendous cliffs' called the Roaches are a mecca for climbers; the spa town of Buxton entices with its old-world charm and the cosmopolitan hospitality of its hotels and Opera House; while the ruggedly pictorial enticements of the Peak District of

Derbyshire are all not far away to the north. The former 'dark Satanic mills', now updated into museums and historic showplaces of the Pottery towns immortalised by Arnold Bennett, lie a few miles to the south.

*　　　*　　　*

Rudyard Lake (which covers some 164 acres) was actually man-made, created originally as a reservoir to supplement its waterways by the Trent and Mersey Canal Company in the final three years of the Eighteenth Century. It was a picturesque spot, the village consisting of a scattering of farms and cottages with several large, imposing country houses in the vicinity, many of which—like my home—still exist in some form or another today. But with the coming of the railways in 1850 the pace of life accelerated in this peaceful backwater. Interested and entrepreneural locals were keen to make sure they cashed in on the opportunities that were now open to them.

The Industrial Revolution had brought country folk flocking in thousands to the towns and cities where there was work and once they were settled there, a new industry chugged smartly into being to organise and exploit their activities during any opportunities they might have to get away from their working environment. Tourism was triumphantly born, the people's leisure promising to become a potential source of profit as well as pleasure.

Large numbers of Staffordshire pottery workers and town-dwellers were encouraged to escape into the country round Rudyard on excursions and holidays on a regular basis. Cordially invited to enjoy all the pleasures and relaxations the lake and its environs could offer, they took to the idea with the greatest enthusiasm, and for the next eighty years or so Rudyard positively boomed. Its little railway station saw huge numbers of visitors arrive and depart—at Bank Holidays the eager day-trippers ran into thousands.

The local gentry (as one might have expected) protested vigorously against this invasion of their privileged environment. Philistine hordes thronged, trampling through the green peace of the hills and valleys. They indulged themselves in boating on the lake and refreshed their various appetites in the many tearooms and similar establishments that sprang up like mushrooms to cater for them. Resourceful Rudyard was quick to promote events like the Grand Aquatic Fete of 1877, where the famous Captain Webb, who had swum the Channel two years previously, gave a demonstration of how this feat had been achieved. Another favourite of the visiting crowds was the 'intrepid high-rope walker' known as the great Blondin, who on several occasions entertained large numbers of awestruck spectators when he balanced his way along a rope stretched over the lake for two hundred yards at a height of a hundred feet!

*　　　*　　　*

I had grown up with the past, my mind filled with visions that were so much a part of me that I accepted them unquestioningly. Skating parties on the lake, sunny-shady summer picnics. The old traditions of Well Dressing and flowery rituals. Assembly balls and even more ancient festivities where the sound of fiddles and—somehow—the echo of flutes, bells and strangely primitive drums accompanied the figures that moved in their patterns of advance and withdrawal, attack and retreat.

These were all inherent in my own being. There was stillness and graver beauty too in a myriad other images of life. Lantern-light as carols sounded through snowy winter dark, the hush of deepest woods and lonely places that were cool even in the most blazing noon of long-past and idyllic childhood summers.

Some of these were my own impressions and memories of course but many, I now realised with my new awareness, were not. They had come from outside sources, memories and minds that were not my own. Some had been handed down through the family snapshots, through local histories and superstitions and books, through the tales I had heard from my large and extended family of 'Aunties' and 'Uncles' of a way of living that extended far further back than my own eighteen years.

But some of them were even older, reaching into pasts that were lost in the tangled wildness of time forgotten, time out of mind. As I sat drinking my coffee, I had to face and accept the real truth of the matter. That like the vision I had just seen, the words I had just heard, much of my awareness had come from another world, the shadowy world of ghosts.

*   *   *

I must have been unusually quiet. When I looked up, Randy was staring at me curiously and I ostentatiously rummaged in my bag, put on my glasses. I felt overwhelmed, unable to share my revelations with anyone just then, even her, so I buried my nose deep in the pages of *Hamlet*. But I wasn't registering the Player Queen's lines, those precious lines that were going to give me my first chance to impress the London theatrical world and hopefully storm barricades in the West End— or at the very least, in provincial rep.

I was thinking back with an inexplicable pricking sense of loss, as though something had slipped away for ever, thinking about my carefree childhood. About Gran, who had until this moment always seemed so much older and wiser than I. About my Great-Gran, the girl-woman in the lilac crepe dress. And about the unseen, unknown mother who had died at my birth when she was eighteen.

Eighteen. A significant age. The age of initiations and rites of passage.

My own age.

*   *   *

In those days all men were the children of Mother Earth, for this was anciently, before the time of the other gods. Then Great Nerthus alone cared for her people and was known to them. She would come among them in her holy wagon, as a mother to her children, and all men laid aside their weapons and forgot their wars and did her reverence when she came.

When the sacred oxen were seen pulling the cart in which the goddess sat screened from the view of vulgar eyes, then there was feasting and friendship each to the other, and the halls were open to all. Always when great Nerthus came to us, the women gathered flowers such as they could find, for the land was bare and even in summer the wind was rough from the sea so that the grasses in the dunes grew aslant, clinging to the Earth.

We sang in her honour and bowed ourselves before the priest who alone might look behind the screens of the cart upon the goddess. And we

39

laid garlands round the necks of the oxen and twined grasses in the horns of the patient beasts, and the harpers sang until dawn and the young men of our people danced, but with joy and not in berserk wildness such as Odin taught his followers when he came.

I had a father then, and a mother. I had a name to which I answered. But I forgot them, forgot them all, forgot my name and my family and my tribe after Nerthus reached out to touch me.

There might have been tears, I do not know, when I left them. Certainly there was pride when I was called. The harpers began to compose songs in my name when the wagon left my father's hall. I was honoured for my calling. Yet I walked behind the wagon in submission, as befitted a chosen daughter of Nerthus, with my head bowed for I could not look upon my great Mother.

I walked even thus as the wagon made its journey across the land, linked as the kine were linked in my dedication, silent with the mystery of my calling. Because Nerthus had given me the gift of speech that needed no words, thus I communicated only with her, for what was there for me to say to any other?

When great Nerthus touched me and named me as her daughter all was said. I was hers and I had always been hers, like the hound who knows his master but knows not the how of it . . .

40

Our production of *Hamlet* was something of an innovation. Normally we first year students could hardly have expected to be involved in full-scale Shakespeare at all, let alone during our very first term. But the project was linked to an investigative study of street theatre and theatre history in general, as well as the work of the Bard and also (possibly far more meaningfully to the directors of the Theatre School) to local public relations. Not only would our performance be presented out of doors from a cart, in the style of the players of mediaeval times, but we were to perform in the inspired setting of the forecourt of the Civic Hall!

Our production was being featured as one of the jewels of the local council's forthcoming 'Elizabethan Christmasse Fest'—roast chestnuts, frumenty and syllabub, mulled wine, groups of revellers playing Elizabethan instruments and singing madrigals and all the local traders capering round dressed in farthingales and ruffs. It promised to be the most enormous fun for everyone—though of course as theatrical performers, we were taking our London debut *very* seriously indeed.

Ted, who was directing *Hamlet*, was a former pupil of the Theatre School where I was a student. He had gone on to work in repertory but had made his name (wouldn't you guess) when he struck gold in one of the soaps on television. He was not a regular member of the staff but had been roped in as 'Guest Director' for our play, the powers-that-be having decided that his name, now the equivalent of a household word, would pull in the *hoi poloi*, who might not otherwise have been very interested in the emotional problems of an obscure Danish nobleman as presented in the style of the Elizabethan theatre. We had been reassured to discover that as a director, Ted was very good, something you do not always expect to find when a person is over-night famous and naturally gifted with looks that are devastatingly dark, lean and hungry.

For this production he had decided to go right back to the roots of folklore and legend. He had set our version of *Hamlet* in the Sixth Century or thereabouts. It was difficult to be certain, he told us, as apparently if you are not an *aficionado* of Danish history it is difficult to differentiate some details of the Sixth Century from the Fifth—or even the Seventh. At any rate, it was long before the more familiar Viking era, which actually started in about the Eighth Century. At this very early period, on a par with the Dark Ages in English history, the original story of the Danish prince Amleth (on which Shakespeare's play is based) seemingly emerged from the collective consciousness of history and myth in Denmark and found a focus.

*   *   *

The earliest surviving literary account we have of the Hamlet story was written by a character called Saxo Grammaticus in the Twelfth Century and published in England in 1514. There is another version, with different details, in Francois de Belleforest's *Histoires tragiques*, which was actually written (in French) during Shakespeare's lifetime and then translated into English.

And for those who are not familiar with Shakespearean sources, it is believed that his immediate inspiration and possibly even the basic framework for his own play, was actually a play by another dramatist called Thomas Kyd, author of a popular crowd-puller of the period called *The Spanish Tragedy*. This document, long since lost, is referred to by scholars as the *Ur-Hamlet*.

Having filled us in on the historical background—or some of it, anyway—Ted went on to reveal his concept of the play. The overall theme for our production, he announced, was to be myth-like, swirlingly vague and symbolic. Hinted at, rather than stated. The designer was even now in the process of bringing this idea to life, costuming us in a mixture of Gothic, furs and homespun.

The atmosphere we were aiming to create had dark elements of the supernatural mingling with the shifting mists to reveal glimpses of armed warriors and lovely women in gold crowns, their cloaks gleaming with gems against a background of prehistoric trappings of the sort found in ancient burial mounds. We were thrilled because it looked as though we were going to have the best of all worlds—brutal realism for the macho types among us, yet softened and overlaid by sloshy *Idylls of the King* sentimentality so that the tender-hearted were satisfied as well.

What we loved even more about the production was that it had been carefully slanted towards those members of the cast who were not among the principals—and that was most of us since *Hamlet* doesn't have big flashy roles for many people. Ted had decided to incorporate a kind of Greek chorus effect and in this, the most exciting and innovative version of the play that anyone had ever heard of, the castle of Elsinore was to be crammed to overflowing with spirits and ghosts.

Dim figures of the students who played 'other parts' were to double everywhere, picking up on the more familiar appearance of the Ghost of Hamlet's father and haunting the action relentlessly, stalking the main protagonists throughout in a variety of cunning guises. The result—highly gratifying for an ambitious Thespian, I have to admit—was that we were all on-stage nearly all the time.

Ted gave us incredible confidence. He held in-depth sessions on the various literary and historical sources of the play alongside the practical sessions of blocking and interpretation. Mime and dance-drama sequences were included for the ghosts and spirits. It was all heady stuff. We got high on it and I particularly liked the idea of being able to name-drop in an off-hand, intellectual kind of way, proceeding to try out my newly acquired expertise on Randy one dark and frosty evening that also happened to be the night of Halloween.

On this, the traditional eve of partying and revels, we were both cosily at home and inclined to stay put in the warm. I had been rather surprised to discover that Randy rarely indulged in the kind of high-powered dating and clubbing I would have expected someone so blonde and beautiful to carry on as a matter of course. But it is actually amazing how many of the gorgeous girls in London lead quite staid and domestic lives. Randy was first and foremost a shrewd career woman but she was also a home bird who loved her own space. She was happy in her own company, a very undemanding and restful person to be around and the ideal audience for me to show off to.

'Did you know that Shakespeare was a fraud?' I asked her idly from the depths of the chesterfield, where I was practising my breathing and voice exercises lying on my back.

Though the flat was fully equipped with TV, DVD, video and hi-fi equipment of the highest quality (even, in the corner of Randy's bedroom, her electric harp, which she played quite often) she believed in fostering traditional social behaviour, which included the art of intelligent conversation. Consequently we rarely had the television on in the living-room in the evening and watched what we wanted to see individually on our portables in our own rooms.

'I was amazed. Seems the greatest dramatist of all time was a real con merchant when he came to write his plays. He nicked all his ideas from other people, and sometimes he even pinched their play-scripts as well,' I told her, expecting her to be impressed. But she immediately put me in my place with no trouble at all (courtesy, I assumed, of the *Reader's Digest* or something similar).

'So far as I know, nothing has ever been proved either way when it comes to the authorship question,' she said briskly. She was working on an intricate *petit-point*, her needle flashing efficiently in and out of a lush pattern of fruit and singing birds. 'Though when it comes to 'Who Really Wrote Shakespeare?' I did favour the Earl of Oxford at one time—the evidence is very persuasive. But on the whole I think I'm inclined to prefer the Marlowe theory.'

'Ah,' I said. She'd lost me.

'Christopher Marlowe,' she explained kindly. 'He probably wrote most of the plays that are attributed to Shakespeare but since he'd been a government spy, a kind of Elizabethan 007 and was officially dead by then, he obviously couldn't own up to being the author so they had to be performed under another name.'

While I digested this, Randy went on: 'The real William Shakespeare's job was actually as a sort of editor with the company, you know. He never really claimed to be an original author at all, he just polished up everybody else's scripts for performance on the stage.'

'Oh,' I said, after a moment. 'Ted didn't tell us—quite—all that.'

Randy gave me a dry look.

'Didn't he? Ah well, Ted doesn't need to be an academic, does he?'

'How do you mean?' I asked warily.

'One can hardly avoid noticing that you seem to have a lot to say about him, Tania. It's "Ted this" and "Ted that" every time you open your mouth. You hardly ever mention your Rowan.'

'*My* Rowan? Just because I've had coffee with him a few times,' I said, dismissing Rowan as I turned onto my stomach. It was true that I had been out a few times—well, sort of—with

Rowan, who played the Ghost in our production, but I hadn't realised Randy had taken our outings as anything serious. Although to be fair to her, I supposed she might have found my evenings in Rowan's company significant simply because I hadn't 'been out' as such with anyone else since I had arrived in London. Nobody had asked me particularly, but I wasn't especially interested in anyone else anyway just yet.

Rowan had made a good impression on Randy when I introduced him to her though her opinions were difficult to predict and I could never understand, for instance, why she didn't seem to be very interested in my reports on Ted's innovative ideas and always ended up asking what Rowan thought. I put it down to the maternal role she had decided to assume towards me. Obviously she regarded Ted as a dangerous exotic—a threat to her innocent little chick—but it was impossible to take exception to Rowan. The word that sprang to mind when you looked at him had to be 'steady'.

He was a few years older than the rest of us, more marked by life experience. Six foot three of muscle (since apparently he'd trained for some years as a dancer) he had the sort of quiet presence you could mistakenly dismiss as weakness rather than strength; and contrasted to Ted's TV profile, Rowan's face was more the sort you could have confidence in. His voice was the first thing I had noticed about him. It was steady and deep with a Scots accent and that, together with his sudden flashes of dry wit, had jolted me into growing appreciation of his company in spite of myself. He *was* good company but that was as far as it went, and I said so to Randy.

'So we're back to Ted, are we,' she commented. 'Well, I suppose it had to happen sooner or later. You're waiting for the moment when Ted turns round to the Player Queen and sees you in that gold and blue flounced velvet affair you're going to wear, with your hair loose and wild in Cretan crimping like some kind of sophisticated Botticelli nymph—and your glasses off, of course. He'll do a double take and breathe: 'My God, Tania—you're *beautiful*!' And then, of course, Rowan will never get a look in, and questions like whoever actually wrote Shakespeare's plays won't matter.'

'Ted sees me with my glasses off all the time,' I protested. 'I only wear them for close work, you know I do. And the same goes for my hair—not that I only use it for close work, but I often leave it loose—though not in Minoan crimps—.'

Then I glanced at her face. She was smiling.

'Poor pet, I'm teasing you. But you do seem to have got it bad. First love, unrequited passion *and* a father figure complex all in one. Relationships can be hell, can't they? That's what made me decide not to bother with men. It makes life much easier.'

'I don't know anything about relationships. I've never had any,' I admitted after a moment, surprised at her unexpected revelation. Randy's parents (distant 'Aunt' and 'Uncle' to me) had so far as I knew been very happily and traditionally married for forty years. Assuming my psychiatric role out of habit, I wondered briefly how she had come to acquire such a cynical view of wedlock herself. Did it spring from disillusion within her personal experience, or was it a more general fear of commitment? Randy was constantly revealing unexpected depths.

'I think Gran considered that twenty-five would be a good age to introduce me to the birds and the bees, and I've some way to go yet,' I added, trying to make it sound flippant, but Randy lowered her embroidery and regarded me seriously.

'You mean you've never had a real boyfriend? At nearly nineteen? I find that quite surprising, Tania. You really are lovely, you know, glasses for close work or not.'

I shrugged, nibbling on a fourth after-dinner mint. Loz had not turned up to share our evening meal with us, and since Randy always set out two mints each, I had appropriated his as well as my own.

'I've never had many friends at all, I suppose, even girl friends,' I said reflectively. 'I hadn't thought about it before, it just didn't seem relevant. I've known a lot of people but never missed that sort of closeness. Even now that I'm in the middle of the most luvvying sort of atmosphere you could possibly imagine—and all actors need approval like they need air, I suppose—oh, I enjoy it, but I could get along without the other students or an audience if I had to. I don't think I'd miss them, not really. Ted's a bit different, of course—.'

'Oh, of course,' Randy agreed, straight-faced.

'He really is special. He's practically a genius, almost like an icon, a kind of mentor,' I said, trying to sound reproving, but my heart wasn't in it. I was more interested in considering the point she had just raised. 'It is odd, I suppose. You know, although nothing has ever actually been spelled out, I think Gran instilled in me a sort of conviction that I have to save myself for a higher destiny—no, don't laugh—.'

Randy was regarding me unbelievingly, her lips curling upwards in spite of her efforts to stop them.

'Maybe I'm going to be—oh, what? I don't know, the actress of my generation, or something,' I said.

It was a little embarrassing to appear so youthfully naïve but I stood my ground doggedly. 'Gran is quite solemn about these things. I admire her for it though, for having values and trying to teach me to have a sense of values too. I think they matter. And even though maybe I never really believed in this great destiny in my secret heart, at least a sense of discrimination has probably saved me from making a fool of myself.'

'Wise child,' Randy commented, turning back to her work. My cheeks were red but I felt as though I had scored a point, been let off some kind of hook. 'Sometimes you can be unexpectedly old, Tania.'

'Well, what about you?' I countered, not sure how to take this barbed remark but interested all the same in Randy's romantic secrets. 'I haven't noticed you thinking it's strange to be celibate—if that's the right word. What's the feminine version of celibate?'

'Virgin, I suppose,' she said, amusement crinkling her eyes though her voice was appropriately grave. 'But let's face it, who's got the courage to admit to being a virgin these days? It's become practically obligatory never to have been a virgin since you were about ten—if you ever were one at all—to be socially acceptable, otherwise people start thinking thoughts, if you know what I mean, and trying to suggest terribly tactfully that you might need some sort of sympathetic counselling— '

We were interrupted at this point by the arrival of Loz, who came in with the scent of the cold evening invigoratingly about him, so obviously full of secrets that Randy and I exchanged lifted-browed and interrogative glances. He was vibrating almost visibly with the force of barely concealed excitement.

'Something up?' Randy asked casually as he sat down in the club chair across from hers, leaning back and stretching out his long legs. He shrugged elaborately.

'No, why?'

'Come on, tell Momma,' she commanded. 'They might call on me to bail you out so the least you can do is to tell me what the crime is.'

'There is no crime,' Loz stated, frowning and very much on the defensive. 'It's just that I—ah—well, I shall be going out later tonight and I don't know when I'll be back. Maybe,' he threw at us defiantly, 'not until the morning.'

We were taken aback, more by the way he had spoken than at what he had said. After a moment's stunned silence, Randy returned her attention with exaggerated deliberation to her needlework and her voice when she spoke was cool.

'It's perfectly all right Loz, you don't need to give me any explanations about anything. I am only your landlady, not your jailer. If you want to throw yourself into some mad affair, nights of passion and all that, feel quite free to do so by all means. It's nothing to do with me. Just so long as it isn't conducted under my roof!' she finished smartly. Sometimes, when she is on her moral high horse she can sound just like the worst of my elderly aunts.

Loz relented immediately and came out with his secret, which actually turned out to have been worth waiting for. He had not abandoned his original plan to join a coven, it appeared. Contact had been made and he had delicately expressed his interest in becoming a witch (or warlock). Alas, he had missed the Lammas festival but since tonight was Halloween the coven was meeting to celebrate Samhain (their name for it) and within a matter of hours, Loz told us breathlessly, he was going to be introduced to witchcraft.

Randy and I just sat with our mouths open, gaping at him.

'I'd never have credited you with the guts to actually go through with it. How on earth did you manage to find this coven?' Randy asked at length with what appeared to be reluctant admiration. Loz set his jaw defiantly.

'Through an advertisement. I put one in the paper.'

'Oh, Loz, was that wise? You know what happened the last time you messed about with adverts,' I warned but he waved my words aside.

'That was quite different. I've been very careful this time not to commit myself in any way. I'm not going to actually join tonight, sign up or whatever you have to do,' he said. 'I'm going entirely to observe, as a guest. A visitor, that's all.'

'But where is it? How will you get there?'

Randy frowned, searching her mind, it was obvious, for any information she had absorbed on the subject of witchcraft (*Wicca, the practise, beliefs and history of*) during her years of reading informative works. 'Don't witches hold their meetings in the woods, or on the tops of mountains—?'

Loz gave her his smuggest 'That's all you know' kind of look.

'I'm being given a lift, and in any case it's not far,' he revealed. 'It's in somebody's house actually, in the basement. Opal says they have it all done up so that they can hold their ceremonies there.'

'Ah!' said Randy, looking up from her *petit-point*, eyes gleaming. 'Do we come to the nub of the matter? Who, or what, is Opal?'

'High Priestess? Chief Witch?' I guessed, breathlessly melodramatic, and Loz's face darkened at our splutters of amusement. The blood rose in his finely sculptured cheekbones.

'Really, you surprise me, Miranda,' he said in his prickliest tone. 'Tania is still only young so I suppose her attitude is excusable, but I would have expected you to know better. Wicca is very serious, it's a religion. Would you have been so irreverent if I'd said I was going to turn Muslim or Jew? But there we are—I suppose I must be fair, I might have been guilty of the same sort of behaviour myself—I realise now I was just as hopelessly ignorant until Opal explained all about it to me.'

Randy was staring at him worriedly. She had stopped laughing.

'Loz, you're not really going to go ahead with this, are you?' she asked. 'It's a crazy idea, I didn't believe you were taking it seriously. Okay, so talking about visiting a coven or even enquiring and getting an answer to an ad does no harm but—well, you're not really going to go, just like that? I admit I have only the vaguest idea of the kind of thing that goes on in witches' meetings but you could be stepping onto very dangerous ground here. I feel morally responsible. You live under my roof and I think you've rushed into this whole thing on a rebound, you've let those con merchants with their academy fantasies get under your skin. You can rise above that sort of thing without going to such extremes, Loz—you don't seriously want to be a witch—'

Loz was glaring back at her, two spots of red in his cheeks. It wasn't often I had seen him so ruffled.

'I don't recall asking for your opinion, Miranda,' he snapped in his loftiest manner. 'And I've certainly never given you any permission to act as a moral watchdog on *my* behalf. I am merely your lodger, a free agent thank you very much—'

'Oh, do excuse me. There's no need to say another word,' Randy interrupted in a brittle tone. I found I was watching their verbal fencing bout like the umpire at a tennis match, head snapping from one side to the other.

'You don't have to take offence. I'm simply making my position clear,' Loz said, switching to irritating mildness.

'I haven't taken offence. But right, if that's how you see the position, I get the message. I know *exactly* where I stand,' Randy countered and I could tell she was hurt. She hates anybody to guess how soft-hearted she is under her sophistication, but this time she was obviously too concerned to worry about her image.

Rising with an air of long-suffering reasonableness that she was very good at, pushing Turpin off her lap (he never even opened an eye), she stalked into the kitchen where she began to clatter the crockery about quite unnecessarily. After a few moments, though, the fit of pique passed and her sense of irony came to her rescue. I heard her warbling to the tune of the country western song *From a Jack to a King*:

'From a Dom/Fem to a witch—
What's the betting Opal's a bitch—
He's deluded, he's dropped a stitch
And he'll wake up with a start—'

Sharply amused, I turned a bit shamefacedly to Loz, who was still tense and had now gone rather white (he hated scenes). I spoke loudly so that he wouldn't become aware of Randy's extempore rendering in the kitchen, but it was with real concern of my own. I was fond of Loz too.

'Have you really thought it through? I mean, I can't help admiring you in a way, Loz, deciding to go ahead. But—into something like witchcraft? You know what Randy was trying to say. She didn't mean to upset you. She's just so fond of you and it does seem—well, a bit scary, to me anyway. A kind of extreme step to take.'

Looking gratefully at me, Loz relaxed into confidential mode. He took a deep breath and clasped the hand I was holding out to him encouragingly.

'Oh, Tania, I know exactly what you mean. And Randy—well, she's used to me by now. She'll understand I was a bit defensive because I'd been worried mindless myself about whether I was doing the right thing, I have to confess it. But when I actually took the plunge, when I met Opal, then it was all—She was—well, she—.' He flushed again, so overcome he couldn't find words. His eyes glowed golden amber.

I was more than impressed. I had never seen the normally self-contained Loz in the throes of such emotion. I waited respectfully.

'She is the most wonderful person I have ever encountered,' he announced after a reverent pause. 'She explained everything to me and I can see that there's absolutely nothing to be afraid of. She makes everything seem—sort of exactly right, as though it was meant to happen. This is what I've been looking for all my life, I'm sure it is. I know I've only known her a relatively short time but—.' He pressed my hand suddenly between his own and lowered his voice. I leaned closer.

'It has actually happened, Tania, what I've always dreamed about. I think I have fallen in love. At last. She is—.' He drew a breath, then confided: 'If things works out the way I hope they will, I'm planning to ask Opal to marry me!'

Wicked! I thought, bowed over. Overwhelmed, I returned the pressure of his hand with appropriate solemnity, maintaining my reverential silence. At that moment Loz looked more like a blond fallen angel than ever, and I considered privately that if Opal had any sense, whoever she was, she'd realise that she could do a lot worse than Loz if he did actually get round to proposing.

'What is she like?' I couldn't help asking. 'Can we meet her?'

'She's going to call to pick me up later. I'll invite her in just to say hello,' he promised. 'I've told her about you two and I'm sure that when you see her you'll both love her straight away. Just as I do.'

As I nodded absently, the actress in me was noting the corny clichés he was most uncharacteristically using. In spite of his professed arty image, it appeared that Loz could be stuck just as dumb as anyone else when he was in the grip of reckless passion.

'I suppose Randy and I aren't really being fair to you—or to Opal or the coven, if it comes to that,' I said, leaning back and letting go of his hand. Randy had calmed down in the kitchen and Loz too was looking less fraught. 'I mean,' I went on, warming to my theme, 'neither of us knows anything about witchcraft. It's just that—um—you know, the idea of holding black masses and worshipping the devil and—.'

'Worshipping the devil?' Loz had gone white again, this time with hurt and distress. 'Tania, how could you imagine for a moment—for one single instant—that I would ever even consider involving myself with anything of that kind! But there, that's exactly the point I was making,' he went on in such an earnestly forceful manner that Dick turned his head and Turpin actually looked up from his chair in sleepy surprise. 'Though witchcraft— or Wicca, as it's more accurately called—is an anciently-established religion, it upholds the worship of the Earth Goddess. It's got nothing whatsoever to do with the devil or black masses.'

As I blinked, a little taken aback by his onslaught, he reassured me kindly: 'I don't blame you, of course, Tania. Opal told me that's exactly what causes the trouble, people have become so conditioned to this kind of bad press—through sheer ignorance and fear of the unknown, really—that as soon as they hear the word 'witch' they get entirely the wrong impression and overreact completely. I think it's pathetic actually, to condemn people's beliefs and way of living without knowing the first thing about them—.'

'All the intolerant enthusiasm of a convert, I see,' said Randy's voice brightly from the door and Loz glared at her, then smiled.

'Wait until you meet Opal,' he said pacifically. 'She's coming to pick me up at eleven.'

Well, naturally, after the revelations we had just heard neither Randy nor I would have missed seeing the incredible Opal for anything and as the fateful hour approached we hovered attentively one each side of Loz like a couple of prison warders.

He was ready early, and we all sat alertly on the chesterfield waiting for the buzz of the entry-phone from the big vestibule at the main door where all visitors to the block of flats had to enter the building. When it sounded—just before eleven—Loz leaped up to answer it and we trooped hard on his heels into the hall. Randy and I were breathing heavily into his ears as he spoke into the phone, pressing the door release that would admit Opal. We followed him like a couple of beagles to our own front door and peered over his shoulders

61

into the corridor in breathless anticipation.

There was the sound of the vestibule door closing in the distance. Light, sharp footsteps were coming along the corridor past the doors of Flat 1 and Flat 2. Then she turned the corner and came into our view in silhouette. The light was behind her and I couldn't see her face. Only a dark outline. A dark shape. Dark.

I screwed my eyes up, trying to see—

Loki was the child of the giant Farbauti. He was in appearance pleasing, handsome and witty but in his character evil, and capricious in his behaviour. He was cunning beyond all the gods, a liar, a scandal-monger, a trickster and an accomplished thief.

Mischief and chaos were his delight and he could change his shape so that he might appear variously in any form: as an animal—a mare, a flea, a fly, a falcon or a seal—or else as an old crone or whatever would best suit his purpose and work his sinister designs.

Sometimes he has saved the gods with his humour and by his mischief provoked them to laughter. Yet for all of that he is still the child of a giant and so of their monstrous race. His own children by the giantess are the three most terrible of beings. They are Jorgmungand the great Serpent, who will come upon the gods spurting poison in the last battle, and Hel, hideous Mistress of the Underworld, and the wolf Fenrir, which slavers with waiting jaws to devour the sun when the time of Ragnarok shall come.

It is he, Loki, who will steer the ship of the giants at that time of terror and doom, the time of Ragnarok. All will be lost and the great Yggdrasil will shake and the forests tremble. The Midgard Serpent will rage and twilight will descend upon the gods.

4

She was wearing what looked like a riding outfit—black tailored jacket with a touch of crisp white at her throat, beige-coloured trousers and high boots that shone like a mirror. She looked fabulous. As we stared, goggle-eyed with admiration, I knew that Randy and I had the same thought: if Loz was trying to get away from powerful women, he'd run in the wrong direction. Lithe, taut, slender yet rounded this creature glowed with personality and confidence so that you could almost feel yourself shrivel by comparison. Talk about star quality! It was like standing with a pocket torch in the full blaze of the sun.

Before Loz, who was bursting with a kind of awkward pride, could make any introductions Opal smiled at us—though grinned would be a better word. The mischief in her smoky eyes was irresistible.

'You're Miranda, of course,' she said to Randy. 'I've heard how you look after Loz better than a mother—far and away beyond the call of duty.' (Needless to say her voice was as stunning as the rest of her, low, husky and beautiful.) She turned to me.

'And this is Tatiana, the actress. I shall certainly want to see your Player Queen, after meeting you. I'm sure she will be strange and unforgettable. You have a striking presence, don't you?' As I tried to think what to say in reply she went on: 'It's such a coincidence—if you believe in such things—that we should all meet like this. You see, my name is really Ophelia, but I altered it to Opal because I think I look anything *but* an Ophelia, if you know what I mean.'

Again I was lost for words and merely nodded dazedly. She swept Randy and me with a gracious glance before effortlessly taking control and ushering Loz down the corridor towards the vestibule.

'Don't worry,' she said, with a conspiratorial twinkle. 'I'll take care of him. He'll be quite safe with me.'

And then the corridor was empty, the slam of the vestibule door echoing in the distance. Randy and I were left alone beneath the stony gaze of her Pompeian marble and the merry eyes of the Bacchanalians frolicking amid their bunches of grapes on the wall.

We stood staring at each other in a silence

64

that crackled with lifted-browed portent, until Randy recovered herself enough to close the door of the flat and lead the way back into the living-room.

'Hmm,' she said after a few moments. 'If I didn't believe before in fate, or destiny or whatever you call it, I'd have to after this. There is only one explanation, so far as I can see. This woman is a hallucination and we simply imagined her. She just cannot be real— I mean, so far as Loz's yearning for a powerful dominant woman goes she's nothing more nor less than his dream come true. And not only that but so stunning it isn't humanly possible.'

'I can see why he says he wants to marry her,' I acknowledged, expecting Randy to shriek at this revelation. But instead she went very still.

'Seriously though Tania, what is going on here? After years of mooching around as one of the sweetest but most ineffectual people I have ever met Loz has suddenly conjured up his dream woman—*overnight*, out of thin air, because he *advertised* for her? Come on! And he's actually talking about *marrying* her? Somebody too perfect it's just got to be untrue, that he's known what, less than a week?' She added with significant irrelevance: '—*and* who's apparently a witch as well!'

If I had been paying attention I might have picked up on the fact that Randy was more deeply shaken than I had ever seen her before.

My response was extremely vague though, because I wasn't really listening to her words. There was something bothering me, niggling away at the back of my mind. Something I was trying to remember and could not. A word—a name—?

'Maybe things really are working out for Loz at last, and we're just prejudiced about it because Opal *is* a witch,' I said lightly. 'He was telling me earlier on about the wrong impression people get whenever witchcraft is mentioned. Apparently it's because it has such a bad press, all due to ignorance and superstition and fear of the unknown.'

'That's as maybe,' said Randy. She was sitting up very straight. 'But I'm more concerned about the most mammoth and unbelievable set of coincidences of all time that just seem to be taking place here, even down to her name being Ophelia, when you happen to be rehearsing *Hamlet* for heaven's sake! Is it possible, I ask myself? Or else—and this is what I'm really beginning to think, Tania—there's something very fishy going on in the state of Denmark!'

I was still grappling with that elusive thought, trying to pin it down. 'I can't see what, really. Loz seems quite happy—'

'Blackmail!' Randy said with conviction. She snapped her fingers crisply. 'That's it. That's got to be it.'

It was past eleven by now, and she was

normally early to bed and early to rise but any thought of sleep had been forgotten. Wide awake and alertly dealing with the problem, she frowned analytically.

'I mean, just who is this Opal if she isn't something to do with the scam Loz got himself involved in? I'll bet anything on it. He doesn't realise it of course, but he's been marked out as a potential victim. They're setting him up for blackmail.'

'They'll be disappointed then. He's got no money,' I pointed out, heading in the direction of the kitchen to make our usual night-cap. Coffee, decaf, so it didn't affect our slumbers. Randy followed me and leaned again the small pine breakfast counter with her arms folded, a gleam in her eye.

'No, but I have money—some, anyway. And so do you. It's looking very peculiar, Tania, positively sinister. And I'll tell you something else I find odd. She called you Tatiana, your full name. How does she know that much about you? Loz might have told her our names but why on earth would he want to provide a complete stranger with that sort of detail? That you were actually christened Tatiana because your mother had got hooked on Russian history after seeing the film of *Dr Zhivago* and reading about the assassination of the Tsar and his family, only you're always called Tania, the shortened version?'

I looked back at her, the coffee jar and

spoon arrested in my hands. I had been too preoccupied with trying to remember the thought that was eluding me, to take Randy's comments about blackmail seriously. But she was not joking. The woman called Opal had really upset her and I was surprised to see that she seemed more than uneasy. Almost frightened.

For a mind-jarring instant, I was back in the surreal world I had glimpsed before, on a wild, sea-strand with the waves crashing and booming somewhere in the distance, and lost voices keening in the wind. Even when I was jerked back again to awareness of the brightness and warmth of Randy's cheerful kitchen, something followed me, an almost palpable presence that gathered in on itself as densely as smoke, as though it would blot out the light.

The shadow of doom, the chill of the knife before it plunged home, the gathering of the wave before it broke in thunderous force? The images that flickered through my mind in that fraction of a moment made my skin tighten and go cold. I felt hairs rise on my scalp and the back of my neck and some of Hamlet's lines from our play came rushing into my consciousness.

Angels and ministers of grace defend us!
Be thou a spirit of health or goblin damn'd,
Bring with thee airs from heaven or blasts

68

from hell,
Be thy intents wicked or charitable,
Thou com'st in such a questionable shape
That I will speak to thee.

I must have quoted the speech aloud, and so convincingly that I found Randy was gaping at me looking as shaken as though I had suddenly gone off my head.

'Good heavens, Tania,' she said, managing to speak coolly after a breathless moment when I was sure she had actually had a mad impulse to just scream and run for it. 'You've made me go quite goose-bumpy. What was all that about?'

'Sorry,' I said, meaning it. I couldn't have explained what had happened, even if I had understood it myself. It was late and we were both tired. I shrugged. 'Put it down to stress and overwork at today's rehearsal. I was just following up a thought—maybe Opal really does not exist, like you said—.'

'So what are you suggesting?' Randy asked, the note of asperity in her voice revealing she had probably had enough of this sort of talk. 'That she's some kind of cyber-babe? A hologram? Are we into virtual reality now?'

'I don't think Loz even knows my name is Tatiana,' I persisted. 'My letters are always addressed to Tania Forrester or Miss T. *Nobody* knows my name is Tatiana, it's only ever dragged out on life and death occasions, official documents, nothing Loz is likely to have seen. Perhaps Opal has got these supernatural powers because she's actually nothing but a thought-form, a creation of Loz's subconscious born out of sheer wishful imagination—'

Thankfully, my spoofing about had the right effect. Randy lost her look of troubled vulnerability and, forbearing to comment on the dubious possibilities of the supernatural, resumed her original line of thought. She frowned.

'There's obviously something that could do with investigation going on here though. Nobody in their right mind would swallow a story that when Loz tried to find a dominant woman he simply got himself involved in some kind of scam, but actually managed to turn up his dream lover immediately afterwards when he was *advertising* for a *witch!*'

'You think there's a connection?' I queried. 'I can't see what, Randy. I mean, even supposing this Academy really exists—and do you honestly believe that?—what has it got to do with the coven and witchcraft? I suppose Opal really must be the real thing—she has to be genuine if they're going to a coven meeting—so perhaps that's how she knew about the sort of person Loz was looking for, and about the scam. Spells, or whatever. But what would be the point of all the cloak and dagger stuff? Why would anyone want to go to

70

such a lot of trouble just to get close to Loz? It doesn't make sense.'

She didn't answer, and after a moment I added something that when you came to consider it was perhaps the most disturbing thought of all.

'Even if somebody did have it in for Loz—for one of those crazy reason like a vendetta, or because his family swindled them out of a fortune or something equally ridiculous—what's that got to do with me and the fact that my name is Tatiana not Tania?'

There was a silence except for the milk hissing to the boil for our coffee. I lifted the pan and poured it into our mugs. Randy swizzled hers thoughtfully with a brown sugar stick.

'Witches do have powers of some sort I suppose. Maybe they—I don't know—did something and found out about your name,' she allowed at last in a low voice. 'You're right though, I honestly can't see why or for what either, Tania. But I'm beginning to feel—well, disturbed about this whole thing. Very uneasy altogether. We're all the most ordinary sort of people. Loz is so harmless he's unbelievable and none of us is important or famous enough to blackmail—not even you, though you might be later when you're a successful actress. We've got no connections with drugs or the underworld —gang warfare—organised crime—.'

'And none of us has accidentally been a

witness to something so dire that we have to be bumped off in order to keep it secret, I simply refuse to believe *that*,' I said, speaking with deliberately loud bravado. When Randy got this concerned, things had to be bad. I wondered briefly whether to suggest calling in the police and I could see she was toying with the same idea but after a moment she shrugged.

'Let's face it, there's nothing we could report to the law. There's been no crime committed and I'm inclined to think it would be Loz's behaviour they would regard as suspicious rather than Opal happening to know what your name was. Those adverts! For Dominant Women—and witches!'

At the picture conjured up by her words— the idea of trying to explain to some upholder of the law with a notebook about Loz's efforts to Find Himself—it was impossible to keep a straight face and we both started to laugh.

'We shouldn't, I know,' Randy gurgled. 'I wouldn't hurt Loz's feelings for the world, and I do regard that Academy scam as scandalous but—you know what I mean.'

We went back to the security of the living-room, the warmth of the fire and the reassurance of Dick and Turpin's obvious conviction that life was never intended to contain worries, expressed by throaty and contented purring that sounded like a couple of small electric saws.

After a few moments silence Randy appeared to recover her equilibrium. She said in almost her usual brisk tone: 'Maybe Loz will be able to tell us more when he comes back though I've certainly no intention of waiting up for him. I suppose it will be quite interesting to hear at first hand what goes on in a coven.'

'Mmm,' I agreed absently. The hot milk in my coffee was warming me through, and the unsettling effects of my vision and Opal's potential weirdness were fading fast. That elusive, lost thought was preoccupying me again, fretting at the edges of my mind, increasingly irritating my consciousness with a conviction that it might be important. If only I could remember what it was. Something I'd heard recently? Or maybe read somewhere? A word? A name—?

'*Ragnarok—!*' I blurted out suddenly. 'That's it. Ragnarok.'

Randy stared blankly.

'You're being very fey tonight, Tania. What about Ragnarok?' she queried after a moment.

'I don't know,' I admitted. 'What is it? Ragnarok?'

Not being a very IT kind of person, I'd found Randy more useful than the Internet if you wanted to clarify the odd snippet of information nobody else had ever heard of. She seemed heartened by the very irrelevance of my sudden change of subject and informed me energetically:

'Talking about coincidence, there's a coincidence if you like. I happened to come across an article that mentioned Ragnarok only the other day. It's the same thing as Doomsday, apparently. Like the Book of Revelations, the End of the World, you know, but this is the Scandinavian version. There are stories about it in Norse mythology. The magazine's on my bed, I'll get it.'

'Doomsday?' I repeated blankly and she nodded.

'Yes. Something very Wagnerian, I think. *Gotterdammerung* and all that. But naturally, Revelations wouldn't do—the Book with Seven Seals, and the Four Horsemen of the Apocalypse—though heaven knows, they're frightening enough I think. It always gave me nightmares as a child if anyone read from the Book of Revelations on Sunday in church. But of course, it would have to be the Scandinavian version you'd want for this, wouldn't it?'

It was my turn now to look blank. I had no idea what she was talking about.

'For your play,' she prompted helpfully. '*Hamlet*. It's Danish history, isn't it? Didn't you say you'd all been researching the background to the story in Danish myth and legend? I'm fascinated. You'll have to explain what it's all about to me. I never knew there were connections between *Hamlet* and the End of the World.'

Neither did I, I thought, though I didn't actually voice the words aloud. I was feeling very confused by now. It hadn't actually helped to remember that elusive reference, because so far as I was aware, I had never heard any mention about Doomsday or the Ending of the World with regard to our production, innovative though it undoubtedly was. Yet somebody must have said something about Ragnarok, or why else would the word—and the vague, shifting images that it conjured up—have lodged in my head and continued to nag so insistently?

*   *   *

And it is he, Loki, who will steer the ship of the giants at that time of terror and doom, the time of Ragnarok. All will be lost and the great tree Yggdrasil will shake and the forests tremble. The wolf Fenrir will swallow the sun, the World Serpent will be freed and twilight will descend upon the gods . . .

*   *   *

It made no sense at all that I could see. My head seemed to be heavy with a sort of fog that made it difficult to think straight and I reassured myself that I was probably more tired than I realised. Our adrenaline levels—or certainly mine—were falling rapidly after all the drama of Loz's departure for a night of witchery, and our speculations about Opal's possible role as a Master Criminal (Mistress, in her case).

I was yawning as Randy returned from her room with a glossy magazine in her hand.

'Here we are,' she said encouragingly. 'Page twenty-seven.'

A glance at the appropriate page revealed it as lavishly illustrated with somebody's imaginative interpretation of a full-scale battle between ancient warrior types and all kinds of peculiar monsters, including various fire-breathing dragons. Hardly the stuff of *Hamlet* as we know it. In spite of myself, I was curious about what the connection was—

*　　*　　*

THE TERRAN CHRONICLES: ENDTIME EXPLORED
by Sven A. DeWitte.

'It is significant that all the civilizations which have risen and fallen upon the Earth have been preoccupied, to a greater or lesser degree, with the importance of death and what comes after it. Some, such as the Ancient Egyptians, as well as the occupants of primitive burial mounds, were laid to rest with food and other necessaries to fortify them on their journey into the Afterworld.

Even cultures such as those of the Native American Indians burned or otherwise destroyed the precious possessions of the departed soul so that these could accompany their owners into the dark—or at least, cause no hindrance to the soul's journey by remaining in the physical realm. Often, servants or wives suffered death so that they could go with their lord into the beyond.

'Since death is the only certain fact of life, it is not surprising that it assumed such importance within the rituals of every culture. What is perhaps of more significance is that death was not always considered in the light of an end to life—many believers over the centuries have regarded life itself as nothing more than a preparation for death. Even the founders of the science of the mind, psychology, recognised the power and presence of 'Thanatos', the 'Death Wish' which alternates with the Life Instinct, 'Eros', within the human mind.

'Yet paradoxically, almost every religion offering hope and consolation to the living has had a dark side that promises death, doom and destruction. Nothing will last. Sooner or later, the eternal battle between Good and Evil that characterises the whole infrastructure of human existence will reach a climax and the end will come.

'How this will occur is variously interpreted according to differing belief systems. In the Revelations *of Saint John, horrific images portray the Armageddon, the coming of*

Doomsday to the Christian world. In Germanic legend is foretold the Gotterdammerung *(Twilight of the Gods), and in Scandinavian mythology the* Ragnarok *(Fall of the Gods), the ghastly downfall of the immortals who dwell in Asgard, led by Odin, their powerful All-Father (also called the Hanged God, the One-Eyed, God of Cargoes and Father of Battles).*

'*Prophesies of doom and cataclysmic upheaval when evil will overturn the rightful order of things seem to occur with remarkable frequency. But in compensation, from the mists of history and myth there always arises also a hero figure that takes upon itself the responsibility of confronting and doing battle with the powers of chaos and darkness. It is with the hero that all hopes for the future survival of the laws of ordered rightfulness must be placed.*

'*The destiny of the hero seems to be ordained and not necessarily of his own choosing. Sometimes (as with the Christ), the hero assumes god-like characteristics; but it is interesting to note that he is generally portrayed as flawed by human weakness. The legendary King Arthur, for instance, as well as many of his knights—heroes all—were brought down by their human failings.*

'*But however difficult the hero's task might seem, however doomed to failure, the hero fights on, pledged to sacrifice even his life if necessary, rather than abandon his allegiance to the right and to his honour or allow evil to prevail. In the words of the poet T. S. Eliot, worlds end 'not with a bang but a whimper'. Civilisations fall not against the backdrop of dramatic spectacle, but in a slow, helpless toppling into chaos or desolation. Sooner or later the inevitable will happen. The end will come.*

'Sooner or later the wheel turns full circle and the moment of doom is upon us. The hero figures of our cultures are armed and ready to take up the fight. Yet often we may not recognise the truly heroic. Even the everyday man or woman in the street may feel the call to contribute something to the general good, to try to stave off the dark for a little while longer, to seize a few more days—hours—moments—in the light.'

Blinking, I put down the magazine, turned out the light and burrowed deep under the warmth of my duvet, more than ready for sleep. I still had no idea what the connection might be between the End of the World and myself—or even, as Randy had suggested, Ragnarok and Hamlet. The plot, as they say, seemed to be thickening fast. But though mention of Ragnarok was obviously supposed to provide some sort of clue I couldn't for the life of me see what it was.

Sven A. DeWitte's prose was not my kind of thing at all. I thought it frankly awful and was inclined to take his melodramatics with a pinch of salt, but there was a good deal in what the article had said to ponder on and I mulled it over as I dozed off. That mention of Odin, for instance, the leader of 'the immortals who dwell in Asgard' seemed to ring a few bells. Hadn't he been referred to in the words I had heard when I had the vision about hanging from a tree, the evening Loz had first mentioned joining a coven? Obviously, I thought, the first step was to find out more about Odin, the leader of the Immortals who dwell in Asgard—

In the half-way stage between sleeping and wakening, fragments swam disjointedly through my mind. In a way, of course, the answers were all there. Hamlet had been a Prince of Denmark—so how fortunate that Daddy lived in Copenhagen—

> '—*powerful All-Father, (also called the Hanged God, the One-Eyed, God of Cargoes and Father of Battles)*—'
> Copenhagen and the Tivoli Gardens—
> '*I know that I hung on the windy tree*
> *For nine whole nights,*
> *Wounded with the spear, dedicated to Odin,*
> *Myself to myself*—'

I stirred, turning over on my side. Thankfully I was not in the Tivoli Gardens on my own even though I was hanging from one of the trees. Daddy was not there because he was away on an oilrig, I could see him waving

80

vigorously across a dark and choppy sea but Rowan had come to share my vigil and appropriately, had decided to wear his costume from the play. Instead of the furs and breastplate of Hamlet's father though, the Ghost was clanking towards me in glittering golden armour that made him look like Sir Lancelot in a second-rate production of *Camelot*. And the Tivoli Gardens had turned into the battlements of Elsinore Castle, which were filled with knights and ladies who were singing a rousing chorus that I identified as the Champagne Chorus from *Die Fledermaus*, and waving fake beer steins theatrically in the air—

Again I stirred. It wasn't very comfortable hanging from the tree and I was trying to hear what the voices were saying—

'—*the hero figures of our cultures—.*'

Lashing rain as the storm hit soaked through me, chilling me to the bone. I was lost on the wild sea-coast, lost in the tempest and the mournful, terrible keening in the wind—

'—*we may not recognise the truly heroic—.*'

It was all dark. Dark. Dark. Dark.

'—*dedicated to Odin, myself to myself.*'

*   *   *

Loz had arrived back at the flat at an unearthly hour while Randy and I were still asleep, and he appeared in the kitchen while we were having breakfast wearing his Noel Coward paisley silk dressing gown, the effect of interesting decadence spoiled only slightly by the white T-shirt and jeans underneath. We took this as a subtle indication that he hadn't managed to get much sleep and intended to catch up on it later.

He toyed rather delicately with the cup of black coffee Randy placed before him, but in answer to our questions about his night with the witches, was inclined to look blank. There was apparently not a lot he could tell us regarding the activities of covens.

Speaking personally, he said, he had found the whole experience rather a letdown. Even though he had been warned the witches would probably be 'sky-clad' (a euphemistic term for naked, one gathered), it had still come as quite a culture shock when they paraded in with nothing on to perform their rituals—which seemed to consist rather unexcitingly of invocations and chanting and holding hands in a circle.

Loz told us he had been so taken aback he hadn't managed to notice much about what they were actually doing and I could quite believe it, since he is one of nature's sensitives and starts to flap at even the prospect of topless sunbathing. As light relief for the sinister scenario Randy had been dreaming up the previous evening, the picture couldn't have been more effective.

'You should have let yourself go and enjoyed the view,' said Randy wickedly, while I couldn't help asking what I was dying to know.

'Was Opal sky-clad as well?'

'Naturally,' said Loz stiffly.

'I bet she was worth looking at,' I quipped exchanging a wink with Randy, but he did not respond.

'I found the whole thing quite distressing,' he admitted in a low, pained tone. 'I honestly didn't know where to put myself.'

'So you won't be joining them permanently, then? You've given up the idea of being a witch?' I asked and he considered for a moment before replying.

'I don't know, Tania. I admit it wasn't what I expected, but then the whole idea was to protect myself against those awful Dominant Women—!'

'Who don't exist,' Randy reminded him forcefully. He turned to her, frowning. 'If I could only believe that, Miranda. That the Academy and everything was a fake—.'

'The sooner the better you forget about them, Loz. Chalk it up to experience,' my cousin advised in her briskest manner, pouring out more coffee. 'Whoever or whatever they were, they can't do you any more harm. Nobody can. I mean, just think about it. Who could anyone blow the gaff to? Tania and I both know—'

'Know?' said Loz guiltily, worried all over again.

'About you answering the ad. About the beautiful mistress. About everything. Your secrets are all out Loz, and Tania and I are simply not bothered about them. You've got to believe me. Nobody can threaten you or blackmail you or do anything at all to you, I promise.'

Randy was at her most reassuring, though I could see her patience was beginning to wear a little thin. Randy does not, so to speak, suffer fools gladly and has no time for indulging histrionic souls who are perfectly capable of helping themselves. Though of course, even she would have agreed that you had to make an exception where Loz was concerned.

There was a pause. The sufferer took a piece of dry toast without noticing and crunched it thoughtfully. He was beginning to look more cheerful.

'So I don't really need to learn how to do spells?—that's even if they'd tell me and I don't know whether they would.'

'It is a bit drastic to decide to become a witch just because a few Fem/Doms try to con you,' I pointed out.

'Being absolutely, utterly realistic, it won't make a great deal of difference whether I join up or not,' he concluded at last.

Randy relaxed visibly.

'What will the coven have to say though?' she asked. 'Did you arrange anything with them about membership? And what about Opal?'

'Oh, I was only there as a guest, there was no question of membership,' Loz said. 'On the whole I think they'll be quite relieved. I couldn't help getting the impression they were not at all sure I was suitable. And Opal—well I have to admit, she told me to think very hard before I decided to commit myself, and to make absolutely sure I was doing it for the right reasons.'

'Sounds like they sussed you out all right, then. I reckon they got you all tied up, partner,' commented Randy in an unexpectedly realistic Way Out West accent, and Loz allowed himself a pale smile.

'Uuh,—perhaps I did go a bit over the top.'

* * *

None of which explained, though, how Opal had come to know my name nor what she/ the witches/ the Dominant Women wanted with Loz. But by the time I arrived home that evening Randy was very much back on form and inclined to dismiss the matter.

'Over-reaction,' was her crisp summing up and I was reassured to see she no longer had any doubts about spooky, or even criminal under-currents. 'I'm sorry Tania, but we really let things get out of proportion. What on earth did we sound like, for heaven's sake? I suppose we're simply not used to covens and witches and people like Opal. If you live that sort of life it must seem quite ordinary—and don't ask what sort of life I mean because I don't know myself.'

'My cousin, the philosopher! *There are more things in Heaven and Earth, Horatio,*' I grinned, donning an oven glove to lift out the meal she had left warming for me. Crisp roast potatoes and chicken, yum! We had had a late rehearsal and I had come home ravenous.

Randy was preparing tomorrow's vegetables at the kitchen table. She looked up and smiled.

'Thank goodness Shakespeare had a word— or rather a phrase—for everything. At least Loz seems to have got over his panic, and he's apparently sorted things out with Opal. They went out together earlier, she came to fetch him. I suppose he was right really, his private life is none of our business. I think we can leave it at that.'

'We're going to have to, unless I ask her outright how she happens to know my name.'

Randy made a dismissive gesture. 'Well, coincidences do happen,' she said vaguely. 'Pure chance probably or a lucky guess.'

'Truth being stranger than fiction?' I added a helpful cliché of my own and didn't pursue the matter further. I had more important things to concern myself with, I reminded myself austerely, than Loz's choice of friends.

5

Let's get this quite clear: it wasn't that I was particularly worried about the End of the World. I had dismissed Mr De Witte's gloomy speculations on the subject as sheer tabloid ranting—next thing, it would be Nostradamus and Old Mother Shipton! But those visions that had started to insinuate themselves into my consciousness were another matter, one that, I was increasingly certain, needed careful investigation.

So where exactly was the place to start? Well, for openers, the fact that although so far as I knew I was quite sane, I seemed to be undergoing some kind of unusual mental brain-washing involving large numbers of references to Scandinavia. It had to be more than mere coincidence—all those little mental jolts and memory flashes I kept getting— Daddy's connections with that part of the world—*Hamlet,* for heaven's sake, when the powers-that-be could just as easily have decided on a Shakespeare play that was far more jolly for their Elizabethan Festivities. *Twelfth Night,* for instance, would have been tailor-made, even down to the fact that it had actually been written to entertain Good Queen Bess and her court as a Christmas treat originally.

And then, what about all the other seemingly coincidental little items that had just happened to crop up? A convenient magazine article helpfully mentioning Odin and all the other characters I had never heard of? The fact that though the odds were probably millions to one against it, I had just met a woman who claimed to be called Ophelia, the unlikely name of Hamlet's ladylove?

Suddenly, references to Scandinavia—and more particularly to Scandinavian mythology —seemed to be confronting me everywhere. And it wasn't just Scandinavia and its myths in general, was it? One way and another—even, if you included it, the fact that our play was *Hamlet*—I seemed to be getting an awful lot of specific references to one country in particular.

Denmark.

*   *   *

I knew hardly anything about Denmark even though my father lived in Copenhagen. I suppose it sounds odd and as though he did not care, but Daddy had always lived a separate life to the one I shared with Gran in the Staffordshire Moorlands—in fact he seemed to inhabit a different planet. I saw him occasionally and we kept in touch, and that had always worked very well so far as I was concerned. I had never felt any desire to spend holidays with him or visit the place where he lived, and before we had started working on Hamlet I hadn't even been particularly interested in Denmark as a country at all.

I had no idea whether Daddy had adopted the lifestyle and traditions of his Danish girlfriend or whether he remained very much that peculiar species of world citizen, an 'Englishman abroad'. I had never really thought about it. Daddy was not into superficialities like postcards and chatty letters, text messages or e-mail. And so far as I was aware he found it convenient to have a base in Copenhagen, and Denmark a pleasant enough place to return to, but that was it.

I think it was Noel Coward who penned the witty immortal line about Norfolk: 'Very flat.' And you could say that pretty much summed up my view of Denmark. What I actually knew about the country so far had come from the odd guide book or tourist brochure and it had always appeared to me to be a rather boring sort of place that had never aroused much of my interest—not like Venice, say, or Russia, mention of which was immediately emotive. I had definite plans to travel on the Trans-

Siberian Railway some time.

When it came to the subject of Scandinavian myth and legend I was equally ignorant. Of course, we had been working for the last few weeks on *Hamlet* and exploring Danish history but I couldn't connect the play's artificiality, its theatrical form, with 'real life' myself. Though they seem more real than reality sometimes, Shakespeare's plays are essentially personal interpretations of history rather than serious fact-finding exercises.

Neither the glossy tourist picture nor the larger-than-life stage drama had brought the true Denmark close to me. They seemed to have little to do with my own sense of ordinariness, my personal reality. What I did find intriguing—and a lot more than intriguing, if I was honest—was the vision that persisted in hovering somewhere at the back of my mind, that vision of a desolate windswept shore with seas grey and wild beyond the mist, lit by the intermittent flashes of fire and smoking torches crimson in all the dark and doom.

Now this really did seem to mean something. I could not have explained how, but it appeared to be connected in some way with an aspect of Danish history or tradition that was intensely personal to me. The visions that I had been getting had stirred my blood and chilled my soul far more than any accounts of Viking pillage and plunder had ever done.

So right, we'd established that there was some kind of connection with Denmark. But even if there was, I had no real idea how it related to me. I had never been out of England, never got any closer to Denmark than our production's mocked-up set of the castle of Elsinore.

And yet almost, if I thought about those words I seemed to have heard about hanging on the tree, it was as though these were things I actually remembered, things I had experienced myself in some long ago and forgotten past.

What, I could not help asking myself slightly uneasily, did it all mean?

*   *   *

In spite of Randy's confident assumption that everything—everything she was aware of, anyway—revolved around *Hamlet*, I could not see any link between my visions and the work we had been doing on the play, although Ted was constantly encouraging us to delve into our psyches for inspiration. He urged the necessity to release and externalise whatever secrets we might be harbouring in our deepest depths; for this, he maintained, would give authenticity to the psychic subtext of his production. And he might well have been right, but so far as I was concerned all that had happened to the Player Queen was that she had started having disturbingly vivid visions about hanging from trees on some ancient seastrand! How this was going to help our production was not, to me at least, exactly clear.

But since I had realised that it was I, not Gran, who was the one who was different, that I had some special sort of psychic gift, I had kind of accepted that the only thing to do was to treat my visions as matter-of-factly as possible. That sense of awareness of a ghostly dimension around and beyond what I had previously assumed was reality, why deny it or try to fight it?

Actually, I had to admit it was a relief to be able to establish that my extra senses were not signs of serious mental imbalance, or plain craziness. Those glimpses of realities beyond the woods and hills of my childhood, presences in nature, in trees and in water, figures moving always just at the periphery of my vision—in my heart I knew that I had always been aware of them. Nothing had really changed, except my confidence in myself and in my own particular way of relating to the world.

Whatever was going on regarding Denmark and the Scandinavian myths though, this was something else, something I could not fathom intuitively. It was a mystery. As in all good mystery stories however, I was apparently being provided with clues—

I had to admit I was intrigued. After making

the brilliant deduction that the name of Odin, as well as all the other references that kept recurring, obviously meant something I was supposed to know—or if I did not know, find out—I concluded briskly that the first step was obviously a spot of background research. To satisfy my growing curiosity, if nothing else.

*   *   *

During the lunch break the next day I bought an up-to-date Guide to Denmark at the local bookshop, but they had nothing about Scandinavian legends so I went on to the public library. I like libraries. I enjoy the literary atmosphere you get when you're surrounded by books, particularly if they are old, and Gran had always encouraged me to treat reading like some sort of interesting journey of discovery. It was with a pleasurably child-like sense of anticipation that I plunged among the stacks of shelves, on stage one of my quest to investigate Scandinavian mythology, which was apparently situated in a distant, rather dim corner.

I bumped quite literally into a solid obstacle—another person who was bent over scanning the books at ground level—but as I backed off with a confused murmur of apology, realised I had actually headed (or been guided?) directly into ghostly realms once again. The figure now steadying me with a hand under my elbow was none other than the Ghost of Hamlet's father. It was Rowan, *my* Rowan, to use Randy's emotive phraseology.

'Sorry, did I tread on your foot? I was just looking for something about Scandinavian myths,' I said rather self-consciously, though why I should suddenly feel so self-conscious I could not have explained. I saw Rowan every day in class and at rehearsals, he was simply another of the students and I had always, even on the occasions when we went out for a quick drink together, felt perfectly at ease in his company before. Didn't I say the word that always sprang to mind with regard to Rowan was 'steady'?

But somehow, this afternoon things seemed different. My awareness was fine-honed, heightened without my realising it to a point where the everyday was filled with symbols and portents. In the unlikely setting of the public library, in the shadowed angle of the bookshelves, my head was filled with images of windy trees and stormy coasts and all the tempestuous cacophony of Wagnerian drama. I found that Rowan's tall, still figure loomed into my consciousness with curious fatefulness. It was as though this crossing of our paths held all the significance of destiny. I even wondered for a rather wild instant whether he had actually been waiting for me. When he spoke his words were casual and commonplace

94

enough though.

'I think most of the Scandinavian myths are out. Ted's seminars about the history of Denmark and the *Hamlet* sources are obviously proving inspirational. I've seen several of our lot with their noses in library books,' he told me.

'Oh, blow!' I felt unaccountably disappointed, and sensed he was amused.

'What were you looking for particularly?' he enquired after a moment.

'Mmm? I don't know. Just general information, sort of. About Odin, the Hanged God. And Ragnarok—the End of the World, the Scandinavian Doomsday. And—and—' Suddenly, as though water bubbled up unexpectedly from the earth, another thought forced itself into my mind. Scuttling quickly like a lizard. Trying to hide itself in a crack, a fissure in the rock—

Loki was the child of the giant Farbouti. He was in appearance pleasing, handsome and witty but in his character evil, and capricious in behaviour.

Definitely the sort of character you might have problems with—

'I need to know mainly about Loki,' I added, without realising what I was saying. 'Somebody called Loki.'

Rowan was regarding me quizzically, his brows lifted.

'No problem at all there, girl. I'll treat you to a coffee and I'll see if I can satisfy your curiosity. Come on, we've got time.'

'You—ah—know about the Scandinavian myths?' I asked, as I trotted after him out of the library and down the steps in the thin autumn sunlight. Somehow I had not expected this new development, and I turned it over thoughtfully in my mind as Rowan headed with a purposeful step across the paved forecourt towards Buzz's (much frequented by the drama students). He took his time before he offered in explanation:

'I had a particularly privileged upbringing, you might say. I was brought up, so to speak, on myths and legends and some of my best friends are heroes, the heroes of all those sagas and epics that were written by long-gone, dry-as-dust authors. I am going to share a secret with you now, girl, that will effectively rub out any ideas you might have been harbouring about my strong man macho image.'

He was teasing me and I found myself enjoying it. I think I have already mentioned that I liked listening to Rowan speak, he had one of the most interesting voices I had ever heard, unusual and compelling with the softness of a Lowland Scots accent shading its deep tones.

Naturally, as students of dramatic art we were very aware of vocal technique. Most actors and actresses have good voices but it is surprising how few really distinctive ones there are.

'I spent my childhood cooped up in a little book-room on the top floor of an ancient town house in Edinburgh, with my nose stuck in one dusty volume or another,' Rowan went on. 'In the best tradition of story-telling, I was a weak and sickly child who had to be forcibly dragged out to play any kind of sport—dance came later as a revelation, but a sportsman I most definitely am not.'

'Fencing?' I was compelled to interrupt, for Rowan was brilliant with a foil. He was far above the standard we students were expected to achieve, in a class of his own. I knew he worked with a private fencing master. He moved a dismissive hand.

'Fencing is not a sport so far as I am concerned, girl. It's a necessary part of my life. As are the sagas and the epics. My father is a professor of literature, you see, and I've never known a home that wasn't wall to wall in ancient volumes—hardly any furniture to bother about, we eat and practically sleep on piles of books. They're my father's passion as well as his work. He's collected them over many years.'

'Really?' I said, utterly fascinated. 'Really?'

Rowan's blue eyes darkened and crinkled as he smiled down at me. By this time we had reached Buzz's, and were standing waiting to order our drinks at the counter. The gold-panelled glass windows and mirrors were glinting points of light, and the warmth of the interior was fragrant with mysteriously spicy undertones to the smell of fresh coffee. Students were everywhere, but I suddenly saw two stools emptying and dashed across in time to grab them. Rowan followed a few minutes later with two wide cups steaming, mouth-wateringly dark and thick with cream—just as I liked it.

'Now, the main source of Norse myth and legend—the stories you wanted to look up about Odin and Ragnarok and so on—is a work referred to as the *Prose Edda*,' he informed me when we were both seated. 'It was written by a man called Snorri Sturluson. He was an Icelander, he lived in the early Thirteenth Century.'

I was only half listening. I had the strangest impression that I had never really looked clearly at Rowan before. His voice seemed to be subtly different, and I was suddenly tinglingly aware of small details about him, the way his dark hair curled close in to his head, the strange depth of his eyes, the unsuspected strength of his finely shaped hands.

'You look very far away from me, girl,' he said deliberately, when I made no response. He leaned across, smiling. 'What can I tell you about the gods?'

But I could not answer. One more weird experience was happening to me, but this one was glowing and ecstatic, at a point on the spectrum I had never known before. It was as I imagined the feeling might be if I had taken some wonderful drug or been hypnotised. The world seemed to expand and thrill, and I wanted to hold onto the moment, to let it last for all eternity. I did not know what was happening and I did not care. But I was aware somehow, with the keenest regret, that such delight was not possible, that I might have only a glimpse before the intensity of the vision faded.

'Tania? Is something the matter?'

Rowan was leaning forward frowning in concern, and the moment had passed. I blinked, lifting my coffee cup in both hands to sip the warm liquid. I felt spaced out, disorientated. Far too many things were occurring far too fast and I concentrated on just one, the simple act of curling my hands deliberately round my cup. The sensation of warmth, the feel of the thick stoneware gave me a focal point, something I badly needed to ground myself. You could have too much of joy, this sort of wild joy. You had to get used to it slowly.

'Sorry, Rowan,' I managed to say after a moment. I wondered whether he thought I was a fool, or mad, but was reassured when I looked into his eyes. They were steady and warm, and there was something in his gaze that I wanted to hold onto. Something that made me feel as though unseen hands were smoothing my skin with silken unguents, and little coloured lights were switching on everywhere inside me, and fountains were starting to play. It was crazy and wild and reckless, and yet somehow—most inexplicably —intensely calm too. And perhaps strangest of all, though not surprising really when you remembered it was Rowan who was sitting there with me, steady. Kind of safe. But most mysteriously, thrillingly, dangerously safe.

I wondered briefly whether I had fallen in love. Or what?

'Let me give you a brief outline. Odin was the supreme divinity of the main group of Norse gods called the Aesir,' Rowan went on in more or less his normal tone, but to me his voice was deep with unspoken meanings. 'He was terrifying, the god of war, the 'Allfather'. He was skilled in magic and wisdom, and called by more than forty-nine names. He granted victory in battle, yet for all that he was still treacherous and not to be trusted.'

I was not really listening. I found myself suddenly repeating the words that had come to me in the vision, the words I had been unable to recollect before, but which now, somehow, were fluent and familiar in my mouth.

'I know that I hung on the windy tree
For nine whole nights,
Wounded with the spear, dedicated to Odin,
Myself to myself.'

100

There was a pause. I looked at Rowan and he looked at me and the cheerful clatter of the coffee shop seemed to fade into a distant, far murmur. Time stopped. The few seconds it took me to draw my breath might have spanned years—centuries—aeons—'

'Can you tell me what it means?' I managed to ask at last, though I was not really sure what I was asking. 'Do you know?'

Then someone pushed past me, knocking my elbow slightly so that I was abruptly jolted back to reality. The noises of chatter and crockery, husky muzak and the spitting of the coffee machine zoomed into focus again, brash and loud.

'You're quoting from the *Havamal*—the Words of the High One,' Rowan said easily, once more the fellow-student I knew so well. The shadowy other I had glimpsed in the blue darkness behind his eyes had gone, and it was difficult to believe what I had seen when our gazes locked and held. He did not ask how I knew the words, but went on: 'Odin, it is said, bestowed the gift of inspiration and poetry and himself spoke only in verse. In the Words of the High One, he described the terror of sacrificing himself in order to win the runes, wherein which lay the secrets of all magic and wisdom.'

'He got the secrets of wisdom by hanging from a tree?' I echoed blankly, and Rowan smiled. All of a sudden I found that the fascination I had felt before was back. It was like being on a roller coaster, and it made me breathless.

'Ah, but the tree was the World Tree, Yggdrasil. A great ash whose roots linked all the three levels of existence. The god hung upon the tree without food or water for nine days and nights, wounded and screaming.'

All will be lost and the great Yggdrasil will shake and the forests tremble. The Midgard Serpent will rage and twilight will descend upon the gods . . .

These were keys that might unlock hidden and closed doors. The phrases passed through my head like the sound of horns in the mist, calls to arms, thrilling as some secret language. I shivered and thought I must have spoken aloud, but Rowan did not seem to have heard anything. In his gorgeous actor's voice, that seemed to thrill through to my very bones, he continued gravely:

'*Kinsmen die, riches depart, every man must himself die;*
'*I know one thing that never dies—the fame of a dead man.*'

The very phrases, the shapes of the words, seemed to hang in the air glittering as jewels. The sense of magic grew and I hastily drank some more coffee to save myself from becoming completely bemused and bewitched, both the words and by Rowan's voice.

'That's a comment on the hero,' he said matter-of-factly.

—the hero figures of our cultures—we may not recognise the truly heroic—

'—Now, as for your query about Loki. He was not an immortal, even though he was the companion of the gods. And yet perhaps Loki was there before the world began, since he represents chaos and mischief and the dark. He is the mirror reflection of Odin, his blood-brother, and he can take many forms, seldom appearing in honesty as himself. But Tania, whoever he seems or whatever form he takes, do not trust him.'

'No,' I found myself saying. 'No, right.'

Then, getting a firmer grip on myself, I added pointedly: 'Sounds as though they were a miserable lot though, your immortals. Nothing but loudmouths, petty gangster types if you ask me.'

'Not all of them. There are other gods.'

Rowan had spoken in a low voice, but it was so strangely penetrating it seemed to close round me like a cloak and reverberate in my ears. He looked straight into my eyes.

'There is Njord, the god of the wind and the sea.'

Well, if I had been bewitched before, this was sheer enchantment. The way he said the name seemed to conjure up a sense of shimmering power. I saw colours, the subtle shades of blue deepening to green, and had to make a conscious effort to concentrate.

'. . . Njord was of the group of gods known as the Vanir, and it is thought he was the consort of Nerthus, who was the great Earth Mother. Some authorities even believe they might have been far closer than that. Some think Nerthus and Njord were actually one being, the same divinity.'

. . . for this was anciently, before the time of the other gods . . .
I had a father then, and a mother, I had a name to which I answered. But I forgot them, forgot them all, forgot my name and my family and my tribe after Nerthus reached out to touch me . . .
. . . all was said. I was hers and I had always been hers, like the hound who knows his master but knows not the how of it . . .

No wonder Randy thought relationships were hell. By this time I had lost the plot altogether, and was feeling quite incapable of normal rational behaviour and thought. What I desperately needed was some time and space to myself. I had to get away from Rowan's suddenly magnetic presence, to absorb and try to make sense of what was happening to me—to us?

So somehow I must have finished my coffee, though I think I was probably grinning foolishly, lost in a kind of drunken daze as we walked back for afternoon class. Fortunately, it was a rather unconventional session of improvisation where we were role-playing the inmates of a Victorian lunatic asylum being visited by a party of gentry, and I was able to let off steam a bit without anybody—least of all Rowan himself—thinking I was behaving in any way oddly.

I had no idea whether what I was experiencing was the effect of falling in love, or whether I was being haunted. Possibly both. What I did know was that I was floating in the most sublime sensation of rightness—of recognition—that I had ever known. And it didn't even matter that for a while, I had been back in that increasingly familiar vision on the lost, wild shore, hearing those desperate voices cold in the wind, and seeing shadows that were beginning to grow, possibly, just a little too close for comfort. I knew I was on the right track. I was going the way I had to go, and there were answers in those ancient Scandinavian myths even though I had not as yet found out what they were.

For the moment, I simply did not care. I had had more than enough of the world of visions and gods and heroes; the joys of prosaic, boring old everyday reality were beckoning with all the sloppy comfort of an old pair of trainers when you just want to relax and chill out.

The Guide to Denmark in my bag, for instance. It was solid and reassuring. Full of information about things you could see and feel and touch, like *smorrebrod* and *kroner*, hotels and tourist attractions.

Helsingor (Elsinore in English) is twenty-five miles to the north of Copenhagen, noted for 'Hamlet's Castle', the setting of Shakespeare's great tragedy.

. . . Absorb the atmosphere while walking round Kronborg Castle, (actually built in the late Sixteenth Century in the Dutch Renaissance style) in its stunningly dramatic setting on the coast overlooking the Oresund, which separates Denmark from Sweden . . . Stand on the platform where the Ghost appeared to the terrified sentries and imparted to Hamlet the details of his murder at his brother's hands.

. . . Wonder at the brooding mediaeval ramparts and great bastions, the starkness of stone stairs and rooms that make up the royal apartments.

. . . Tread the floor of the oak-beamed Great Hall, echoing and empty and hear the boisterous carousing of the Court, the quaver of poor Ophelia's mad song before she passes to her watery grave, the clash of rapier blades as the final act of the tragedy reaches its terrible climax . . .

6

I had never seen Elsinore, of course, though probably Daddy might well have done and I had no idea what the Great Hall of Kronborg Castle looked like. But in my dreams that night, I found myself in some enormous ballroom where music was playing, and crowds of people thronged down the great stairs to join the dancers.

Though I hadn't actually been 'born in a trunk', you might say that it was no wonder I was studying Performing Arts, since a love of theatre ran in the blood of my family. My mother had been, so I was told, intended for the operatic stage. Because she had died so young she had never sung publicly and there were no recordings of her voice, but according to Gran, she had been immensely gifted.

Gran herself was more orientated towards ballet and dance—she had once briefly studied Greek dancing herself, as well as keenly supported all local amateur theatre—and there were shelves full of books on theatrical subjects at home. I used to curl up with them on the window seat at the top of the attic stairs on blustery afternoons in the holidays, in the early years when I was entertaining unrealistic hopes of becoming a ballerina.

Gran had been inspired, she told me, by

seeing touring productions of the Ballet Rambert as a young girl, and particularly by the richness and artistry of the classic film *The Red Shoes*. Over the years she had collected some beautiful volumes of photographs and memoirs and one of my favourite pictures had always been a dramatic shot of a ballet called *The Haunted Ballroom*.

It wasn't the characters in their romantic ball-gowns, drifting in and out of the light, which caught my imagination, but the unusual angle from which the photograph had been taken. The cameraman had been somewhere at the side of the stage in the darkness of the wings, looking into a bright pool of light with part of the scenery and stage machinery in the way. The effect was of looking through bars into some fabulous, but far distant chamber out of time and space, which you longed to enter but could not.

I used to stare at the picture and wonder with a delicious shudder, what might await the intruder into that shadowy ballroom. Passionate fulfilment or betrayal? Ecstasy or pain? Love or death?

All terribly Freudian, as we had discussed in class when we began to explore our psyches in depth. I had been fascinated as well as disconcerted to discover that there was practically no thought, action or word one might experience from babyhood, which was not deeply significant in some (probably sexual) connection. And as for *The Red Shoes*, well, even seemingly innocent fairy stories, along with all the other traditional tales and ancient legends that were generally regarded as kid's stuff, were actually darkly gruesome. *The Red Shoes* is an exploration of obsession and terror.

'I never realised how awful those old stories were before,' I could not help exclaiming impulsively after one startlingly revealing session. 'To think we take it for granted that fairy tales are suitable for young children. But when you examine them, they're absolutely crammed with loss and suffering and death, as well as all those—uh—well, sexual undercurrents kids shouldn't even know about.'

Perhaps I was over-reacting here, but I had just been informed that my preoccupation with the haunted ballroom probably had nothing to do with the sumptuousness of the theme, the romance of costume and design, the beauty of the dance itself. It almost certainly sprang, I was advised, from fear of my blossoming womanhood—a longing to become an adult clashing with reluctance to accept the responsibilities and burdens adulthood would inevitably bring. Mainly in a sexual connection, of course.

This had been near the beginning of the term when my psychiatric persona was just getting into its stride and I had not yet acquired the habit of looking for the sub-text in everything.

'It is there though, woman, terrifying,' Tyrone, the tall, lithe black student who had been cast as Horatio in our play, assured me mock-solemnly, with devilment at the back of his eyes. 'Soon as you open your mouth you give yourself away.'

But I was not listening. My thoughts had taken me a few steps further.

'When you think about it, you know, it's no wonder children get frightened sometimes at fairy tales,' I said slowly. 'They're dangerous, they teach young minds all sorts of— well, disillusioning concepts. They give the impression that it's not really safe in the world. Not really safe anywhere.'

'Perhaps that is why they are so necessary,' Rowan, who was fetching the drinks, had commented as he sat down. I had not really registered his throwaway remark then but now I remembered it clearly because in my dream, I had somehow been transported to the haunted ballroom. I had passed through the barriers and was standing on the great staircase in the centre of that dazzling throng.

Everyone was wearing elaborate costumes, fancy dress, I assumed, though I wasn't sure whether I might actually have wandered inadvertently into a performance of some ballet because many of the dancers from Gran's book were there. But surely, nobody would go to a ball with animal's heads—and I could see tall antlers—head-dresses with horns—faces masked into slits for eyes.

The music was being played on some kind of ancient instruments that sounded alien and strange. There were pipes, bells, and beneath the tinkling strains, a pulsing rhythm that caught me by the heart and began to increase its throbbing so that my own heart-beat increased, straining me forward down the stairs, into the centre of the throng.

Bodies pressed me all about, I felt the touch of velvet and lace and subtly, without realising it, the frightening roughness of fur—of hoof. The scents and lights swam. The perfume of roses was so sweet it made me feel faint, but beneath the sweetness I caught the acrid stench of something I could not name, something dark and animal, something I did not want to recognise.

My heart was pounding now, my breath coming in gasps. I was trapped, and closing ever nearer there were figures moving in the patterns of the dance. The lights were gone, only the flare of torches in the dark, circling round me, advancing and retreating, masked faces on every side, whichever way I turned—

And now horns sounded, the dancers in their filmy gowns had vanished and the shapes that stalked me were hard and sleek, shadows in the undergrowth. There was no escape. The fairy tales were right, there was no escape. It

111

was not safe in this world—not safe in any world—

I heard Rowan's voice.

'Perhaps that is why they are so necessary.'

There was a sudden stillness. The horns and the music had stopped. The dancers froze where they stood.

'Of course,' I thought with the most overwhelming surge of relief. 'It's really terribly Freudian, doesn't mean what it looks like at all.'

Preoccupation with the haunted ballroom—nothing to do with the theme. Sprang from fear of my blossoming womanhood—a longing to become an adult clashing with my reluctance to accept the responsibilities and burdens adulthood would inevitably bring. The responsibilities and burdens adulthood would inevitably bring—

I had a father then, and a mother. I had a name to which I answered. But I forgot them, forgot them all, forgot my name and my family and my tribe after Nerthus reached out to touch me . . .after Nerthus reached out to touch me . . .

*   *   *

The following afternoon, Opal the witch turned up uninvited and unannounced at my Theatre School. We were in one of the big studios working on *Hamlet,* and I was sitting on the floor near the long mirrored *barre* watching the scene on the battlements of Elsinore where Tyrone, who was playing Horatio, had his confrontation with the Ghost.

Normally the Ghost is portrayed as a doddering ancient—sometimes just as a voice or a shadow—but Ted, of course, had his own innovative ideas. He considered the Ghost was the sexiest character in the play, the presence that controlled all the complicated physical relationships—between Hamlet and Ophelia, Hamlet and his mother and Gertrude and her new husband, King Claudius. Rowan was therefore to be a dominating figure who looked anything but dead, and he was going to be stunningly attired in a long fake fur cloak thrown back from flattering body armour that made centrefold male model types look like also-rans, and showed off his lithe dancer's physique.

He had been instructed to visualise himself as the magnetic centre of the action, the point to which all the other components gravitated. So now he stood tall and fateful as some immoveable dark monolith, and the others weaved their way round about him in kaleidoscopic patterns.

'Stay, illusion,' Tyrone was intoning in a sing-song chant as though he was performing a magic ritual, while a teeming group of 'shadows, terrors and unquiet spirits' (Ted's

113

words) hovered and fluttered as eerily as they could.

'If thou hast any sound or use of voice,
'Speak to me.
'If there be any good thing to be done
'That may to thee do ease, and grace to me,
'Speak to me.
'If thou art privy to thy country's fate,
'Which happily foreknowing may avoid,
'O speak—'

The scene was unexpectedly gripping. Moments of theatre that work can take hold of you by the scruff of the neck and shake you into submission. I found I was making a similar (though unspoken) plea to my own ghosts, to the one that was being expressed in Horatio's passionate words I was sending out a prayer to whatever presences hovered beyond the boundaries of knowing and seeing, to the keepers of secrets to which I could not aspire, for wisdom. I asked humbly for guidance, for knowledge of what was to be done, for what action I must take, for what was necessary in order to achieve and maintain the peace—

O, tell me— Speak to me—

Then, suddenly aware that the back of my neck was prickling with the sort of uncomfortably cold feeling you get when you are being watched without knowing it, I turned my head sharply. A figure in elegant black casuals, gold chains glittering chunkily round her neck, was standing just inside the door staring in my direction. As I stared back she lifted an imperious hand and beckoned.

At first I couldn't make out who she was. Strangers were not allowed on the school premises so I assumed she must be one of the instructors: the fluidity of her pose and the chic dark clothes suggested visiting ballet mistress. I glanced towards Ted, but he was absorbed with Tyrone and Rowan and the unquiet spirits so I got to my feet and went across to the door.

It was not until she spoke that I recognised Loz's dream girl, the mysterious witch-woman, and when I did I could not repress the irreverent thought that went through my head. If she looked this good in trousers and a T-shirt, she must have been stunning 'sky-clad'.

'I'm disappointed,' she confided, for all the world as though we were old friends. 'I came especially to see you act.'

'I'm not in this scene,' I said rather shortly. I was feeling more than a bit embarrassed, because if Opal-Ophelia was here and looking so completely at her ease maybe there had been an easy answer to all our questions all along, no need for the drama—or rather, the melodrama—that Randy and I had been indulging in. If she belonged in the theatre, was actually attached to the Theatre School I

115

attended, then she was probably some sort of authority figure I was supposed to know. And that would explain, naturally, how she seemed to know so much about me.

'Oh, sorry, I didn't recognise you. Didn't expect to see you here. Are you—? Um—Are you a—? Do you act—or teach?' I managed awkwardly, and she flashed me a careless little shrug along with her conspiratorial smile.

'I'm entirely an amateur,' she demurred, though I didn't believe that for a minute. If I was certain of anything, it was that this woman would have been right out there with the front runners, whatever she decided to try her hand at. 'I had another reason for stopping by, actually. I wanted to invite you to have dinner with me tonight. Can you make it?'

'Excuse me?' My mind seemed to have seized up. For a minute I had thought Opal had said she was inviting me to dinner.

'I know rather a decent little place that's not too far away to make it a bore getting there,' she said, absently watching as Ted put the 'shadows, terrors and unquiet spirits' through a routine carefully choreographed by Zoe, our enterprising modern dance adviser, where they closed in on Horatio and tried to strangle him.

Then she turned her head and I all but reeled before the impact of her smoky eyes. They seemed to hit me, batter me. 'We have to talk. Just us two. Girls together. No Loz.'

It was all wrong. My first confused thought

was that this was some sort of come-on, but gut reaction told me it was far from that. I actually felt a kind of blow in my solar plexus that made me go nauseous and sick for one awful moment, before I was left gasping like a fish with my mouth open, struggling to breathe.

I had no idea who this woman was or where she had come from or what she wanted, but it was blazingly obvious there was something going on here that was far more dangerous than any fanciful visions I might have been trifling with about hanging from trees in some previous existence. Let's be honest, this was plain frightening. I was way out of my depth. My back had gone cold, but there were beads of sweat breaking out uncomfortably on my body. I was so tense I couldn't move. I tried to moisten my dry mouth, to say something that would break the spell, but Opal the witch was already leaning forward conspiratorially.

'I'll pick you up at seven thirty,' she said, and smiled so directly into my eyes that I could feel my legs and feet turn to paralysed lumps of ice. For one horrific instant my heart actually seemed to stop.

The effect lasted until I heard Ted's voice breaking up the class and was able to glance round. When I turned back, the woman had gone and there was only a faint scent lingering on the air. Something that reminded me of dark exotic orchids, blooms that were

117

overblown, already heavy with the presentiment of death, the cloyingly sweet rotten smell of decay clinging about them.

* * *

Randy arrived home that evening a little later than usual, and caught me getting ready to go out. Her fine brows lifted speculatively when I told her why I was wearing my black dress and putting my hair up.

I was actually feeling more than a bit speculative myself. The scene in the studio had shaken me so much I had needed a whole hour to recover over several cups of hot sweet tea in the cafeteria. Slowly the sickness and coldness retreated but during the time I sat there alone I had an opportunity to think the matter over, face up to the solid facts, such as we knew them, of this whole peculiar situation. Particularly in respect of the weird and unaccountable appearance in all our lives, like a geni popping up out of a lamp, of Opal-Ophelia—who let's face it, was hardly the sort of acquaintance you might normally expect to bump into in the course of your average everyday grind.

Not only did she seem to have some spooky kind of inside information about us—about Loz and me, anyway—but she had apparently been able to bewitch Loz on sight, and I could not account at all for the effect she had had on me. Eye of newt and toe of frog simply wasn't in it!

And fact: I was not just imagining things here—or even experiencing ghostly visions courtesy of my extra senses. Because, like, fact: the ghosts were different. I was used to ghosts, I had actually been used to them for years: I had realised this once it dawned on me that it was I, not Gran who actually possessed the gift of 'Sight', or clairvoyance or whatever it was.

That other dimension had always been there for me, something as natural as breathing, I could see it now. I had been aware of the ghosts ever since I could remember, taken them so much for granted I had never really thought of them as ghosts at all. They had been simply there in the background, rather like background music. And I had no problem with that, I could accept it quite happily.

What I could not accept was what had just hit me in the studio. Otherworldly though any visions I might have previously experienced had been, disorientating and mysterious, they had never shaken me up as badly as those few minutes eye-to-eye with Opal. The ghosts had never left me feeling weak and sick. They had never—in however subtle a way—made me feel personally threatened. And that, I told myself shakily, was exactly how I was feeling now.

While I drank my tea and tried to calm down I attempted to think the matter through logically. To be rational. Be sensible. In the end, having got over my first fright, I decided I was actually more annoyed and angry at having been manipulated by a woman I hardly knew than seriously worried. But all the same, I couldn't just follow my instinct to walk away and refuse to have any further dealings with Opal-Ophelia. That was perhaps the more mature, sensible attitude to take but there might well be more at stake here than my own gut reaction to a stranger I did not like.

For instance, Opal-Ophelia must have had some reason for slithering so determinedly into our lives. Even if she just happened to work in the theatre—even if she was actually connected with the Theatre School—you couldn't deny that there was something extremely odd about her behaviour. But maybe, I began to think now, it had nothing to do with the supernatural at all.

You can see how traumatised I was feeling because over my second cuppa, I even started to reconsider Randy's original suggestion that Opal was one of the Academy's Dominant Females, who were in the process of setting Loz up as some kind of victim. Or, now that she had apparently shifted her attention, was the victim to be me? Certainly I had more money than Loz and—as Randy had shrewdly pointed out—would be a better proposition for the criminally minded. Though I could not even begin to explain how some gang of potential feminist blackmailers operating in London, just happened to know that Tatiana Forrester, First Year drama student from Rudyard, Staffordshire, had been left money by her mother. Or—as my mind flapped uneasily along yet another possible train of thought—that this hapless unknown had a quite well-off father, who might perhaps be induced to respond favourably to kidnapping threats.

I even toyed for a wild moment with the possibility that Opal's invitation to have dinner with her indicated she had immediate action in mind. Did she—or possibly the whole gang—intend to kidnap me tonight? It didn't bear thinking of, but fortunately I was able to get a grip on myself before my thoughts got completely out of hand. Crazy conjectures about kidnapping and blackmail—or even dope rings and the white slave trade—would get us nowhere.

There had to be some reason for Opal's sudden interest in Loz and me though, and whatever it was I felt that the sooner the better we got it out into the open. Then at least we would know what we were trying to deal with. Maybe, I rationalised to myself, I was actually panicking about nothing, building up a *grand guignol* scenario simply because the woman had an unusually overpowering personality. She had, after all, said she had come to the rehearsal to see me act—I mustn't forget that. And if she was really connected with the theatre there were any number of reasons why she might want to take an interest in a promising student.

Even her initial interest in Loz could be explained away if she was keeping an eye open for talent. Loz happened to possess stunningly good looks, he had cheek-bones to die for and Opal might have been investigating his potential as a new face, a new profile. There was really only one way to discover her motive, and that was to go along with her invitation to dinner. Take it from there. Play it by ear. Though judging by the reaction I had had towards her that afternoon, I doubted whether I would actually be able to eat a thing.

But I'd go, I decided. And once having made my decision, I felt better. At least, I told myself, I was aware now, on my guard. And I could feel my fighting spirit perking up again. After the fright I had had, I needed to feel as though I was back in control, that I could stand up and beat Opal-Ophelia at her own game. I was an actress, wasn't I? This was just another part. I'd play the role of laid-back Dominant Female type myself, and play it to the hilt.

And though she had taken me by surprise in the studio, caught me undefended, as it were, it wasn't as though I had no resources of my own to draw on. I couldn't claim to be a witch of course, but I had my own shadowy world at my back, the ghostly powers of my childhood to give me strength.

Somehow, just thinking myself back into the familiar landscape I knew so well, the glimmers of lake and trees, even the scent of lavender and lilac in the rain—as well as Penhaligon's Violetta fragrance—conjuring them all up, Gran's inscrutable presence and the secretive sanctuary of home, I felt a charge that seemed to empower me so strongly I was reassured and comforted. The threat of whatever dark influence Opal-Ophelia might possess dwindled to nothing by comparison.

*   *   *

I made careful plans for the evening though. To bolster my confidence I opted for power dressing, but under-stated. Thatcher rather than Madonna. Instead of clumpy Doc Martens and the rainbow lace-and-brocade Vivienne Westwood basque I had managed to unearth in one of the charity shops in Muswell Hill, I got out my severest dress and black strappy shoes with wedges and heels that added inches to my height. I was trying out the additional effect of an old pair of huge tortoiseshell sun-specs, blinking behind them into the mirror when Randy looked into my room.

'Opal asked you to dinner?' she said unbelievingly. 'Opal asked *you* to dinner? How extraordinary.' Then after a moment, as though enquiring about the health of some delicate invalid, she lowered her voice. 'What about Loz? How did he take it?'

I shrugged. Trust Randy to go straight for the jugular.

'Loz is staying at home. It's just girls together,' I informed her a little uncomfortably. My disquiet over Opal's behaviour had turned into annoyance because Loz had been really hurt—he had in fact taken immediate offence when he found he was not included in the dinner invitation. I heard him muttering in a distinctly waspish tone:

'Uuh. Seems I was right. You can't trust anybody these days.'

'For heaven's sake, Loz, you don't seriously imagine I want to go, do you?' I said, horrified to hear myself snapping aggressively at the poor man. Randy and I generally took extra special care never to injure Loz's delicate sensibilities, which had all the susceptibility of hot-house plants. As Oscar Wilde might have expressed it warningly, one touch and the bloom was lost.

I drew a deep, calming breath, tried to speak reasonably as I assured him with complete truth: 'I can't think why I agreed to go, actually, because there's nothing I fancy less than an intimate evening with *your* girl-friend, thank you very much. She caught me off guard and conned me: but look, how else are we going to find out who she is and what she wants—what she was doing in the rehearsal and how she knows my name? You've got to admit it, some very peculiar things have been going on and it's time we had a few answers.'

He didn't seem convinced, and at the look on his face I said in some exasperation: 'Well, all right, I just won't go if it upsets you so much. It will be quite a relief if you want to know. So there you are, Loz, you can apologise, tell her I'm unfortunately not available—that I've been called away—got flu—*died*—. Anything.'

'Oh! Please!' Loz interrupted in his best Sidney Carton voice ('it is a far, far better thing I do'), 'I would hate to consider myself responsible for *anyone else* having to betray their word and break an implied promise. There's no need at all to worry about my feelings, Tania. By all means go, just go.'

He removed himself in a stiff and dignified manner to his room, where he was even now listening to Baroque Ensembles, that I assumed were assisting a sense of virtue to soothe his lacerated feelings.

'Well, all I can say is that it looks more than peculiar,' Randy was continuing, frowning at me in the mirror. I could see the tiny puckers along the fine skin of her forehead. She tilted her chin consideringly. 'What possible reason could Opal the witch have for asking *you* out Tania? I mean, you hardly know her.'

She was of course only putting into words what I had been thinking myself, so I did not bother to comment. I carried on doing my hair, twisting it as severely as I could on the top of my head and jabbing grips in with such force that I hurt my scalp. As I grimaced and yelped, Randy's brow cleared. Her lips started to twitch.

'Oh-oh. So that's it. We got it all wrong. Well, who would have thought?' She shook her head with pensive regret. 'And poor Loz has missed out again.'

'I don't know what you mean,' I said, though of course I could see only too clearly what she was implying. The most embarrassing feature of this whole episode was that everyone else would jump to the same conclusion: that having schemed her way into Loz's confidence by pretending to be a witch (or even by actually being a real one, who knew?) Opal had now callously cast him aside because she had deeper designs on me. And if we were to stretch credibility a bit further, people might even assume she had had her eye on me right from the start and had only been cultivating Loz as a means to an end!

I couldn't just laugh this one off, though. Because the truth was that I simply didn't believe it. I might have found the prospect of unwanted attentions from a strange woman more preferable actually, easier to handle than the crawling, though unformed apprehensions that had been tugging at my nervous system ever since my encounter with Opal in the studio. They were still there, churning in my stomach, making me feel light-headed and slightly nauseous, almost as though I was going to be ill again. And the fact that I had no real idea what I was apprehensive about was perhaps the worst thing of all.

7

Some sort of allergic reaction. Maybe to the scent Opal had apparently been wearing, with its underlying fragrance of dark orchids just past their bloom. That had been my first confused accounting for the strange paralysis, the sickness and chillness that had affected me in the studio. Even when Opal had gone and Ted dismissed the class, I found I could not move though the other students were pushing past me uncaringly. Typical actors, they were so wrapped up in their own destinies they simply didn't notice anybody else—in any case it was the lunch break, and drama students, like students everywhere, are single-minded when it comes to their food.

127

I was right in the centre of everything I knew to be safe, friendly and familiar yet I was icy cold, cold all through, cold to the very marrow of my bones. When the stiffness wore off, I knew I was going to start shaking uncontrollably.

I was afraid I would pass out. The palms of my hands were pressed stiffly, fingers spread, against the wall for support. I was barely able to stand.

I felt an utter fool, angry now as well as wretched. Hunched over, trying to take deep breaths, concentrating on my leg muscles, willing them to move so I could stagger to a chair, sit down and put my head between my knees.

My mind was spinning, and I blinked my eyes against a sense of vertigo. The moment seemed to go on for ever, though I suppose it really lasted no more than a few seconds.

—lost, naked and shivering—neither in space nor time—

And then, somewhere in the far, far distance I heard Rowan's voice. He was saying my name, and I felt his hand warm on my shoulder, surprisingly strong in spite of its gentleness, shaking me, gripping the bone hard. His touch released me from the icy paralysis. I jerked round, so intensely relieved to find him there that I just fell against him, and his arms closed reassuringly round me.

He held me, saying nothing, asking no questions, while I tried to steady myself. I gulped great lungfuls of air. My face was bruised against the hard muscle of his chest, I was clutching at his black sweatshirt with both hands. I still couldn't speak.

'All is well, girl. Take it easy.'

Or something like that, anyway. It was the tone of voice rather than the words that got through to me, and somewhere at the back of my mind I remember having the ridiculous notion that Rowan would have made a good vet. Terrified animals—rabid dogs, panic-stricken sheep and little furry creatures like rabbits and hamsters—they would all have calmed instantly at just the sound of that voice.

'Sorry,' I wheezed desperately. 'I'm—sorry.'

'No need to be sorry. All is well. Everything is well, girl, you are fine—be easy now, you are safe, you are fine now, it is all right, everything is all right—'

And somehow, the fear receded. The ground was steadying beneath my feet. I could breathe. My heart began to slow its frantic pounding, while Rowan's voice spoke on somewhere above my head, wonderfully deep and slow and reflective, as though nothing had happened.

'Strange eyes, that female had. I'd put it down to frustration myself. Whatever she said to upset you, credit it to her attitude problem and the chip she's carrying a mile high on her shoulder.'

'Rowan Luath, you are nothing but a chauvinist pig,' I mumbled accusingly into his pectorals, feeling better by the minute. He smiled. I could hear it in his voice although I was still leaning thankfully against him, and couldn't see his face.

'Oh, it had to be something the female said, girl, to make you turn so green. Don't try to tell me I have the wrong of it. But yet, stay a while—as those old writers of heroic poetry might have phrased it. Could the delicate cheesy tint that suffused your brow have been nothing but an artistic reaction to Zoe's choreography and Horatio's bit of voodoo with the unquiet spirits? It wouldn't surprise me, on reflection. Willy Shakespeare is probably spinning in his grave, at the prospect of his greatest Dane in the guise of Baron Samedi, summoning crowds of the Un-Dead to congregate at Elsinore.'

This was so ridiculous I couldn't help a spurt of laughter. And I found that laughing at—or with—Rowan brought my sense of independence back. I managed to lift my head, pulling away from him.

'That woman—her name's Opal Something. She actually came by to invite me to dinner,' I informed him, through lips that were still a little stiff.

'Oh, indeed?' And now I could see his eyes

smiling. 'An invitation that knocked you over, is that it? Well, girl, if it is so I see my fate is sealed. I cannot be competing with looks like hers.'

But I knew somehow that his words were only filling in the space between us, as it were. Beneath them, he was saying something quite different. A little awkwardly, I pulled myself away from his chest and smoothed my hair back, conscious that I was being affected now in the same way I had been affected when we talked about the Scandinavian myths the previous day.

It was all happening again—silken unguents, coloured lights, fountains, the lot, swirling in among the rainbows. And the thought that Rowan had just been holding me in his arms went through me like an electric shock, making me tingle. I was aware of my cheeks beginning to burn.

Rowan mattered, I was certain of that now, not a question or doubt about it. In the world of illusion in which I was increasingly finding myself, Rowan was the one thing that was solid. He was real. The word that came into my head was 'lodestone'—magnet—something that exerted irresistible force. Something you couldn't fight—something you didn't want to fight.

'Actually, she's a witch,' I found myself saying, but he didn't react to this provocative statement as I expected. He took my arm again, lightly but deliberately. When he spoke his voice was low, but it seemed to penetrate to my very soul.

'She has misled you, Tania, I am thinking.'

'How do you mean?' I asked. I was finding it difficult to think now, difficult to experience any sensation at all except the wild desire to let all control go, to surrender my will and abandon myself to the power of the force that was drawing me irresistibly towards—

Well, it might have been my destiny that was beckoning or it might have been simple lust, I had no way of knowing just then. Rowan was staring at me intently and I could not look away. I was very conscious of his hand on my arm and the touch of his fingers. I had lost any ability I might have had to concentrate or even to reason for myself.

How long the moment lasted, I had no idea. It seemed to gather itself like a wave, holding me suspended in time and space. Though I could see his lips move and knew that he was speaking, I heard nothing of what he said until the wave broke in silvery fragments when he took his hand away and my senses returned.

'Be yourself; only be yourself, and all will be well,' his voice was advising me gravely. Whatever that meant. All I knew was that I had to get away from him in order to think clearly. My knees had gone wobbly again, though this time it was not from fright but from some other, deliciously decadent emotion that was the last thing I wanted him to know about.

Fortunately it appeared that Rowan was still in the real world and didn't appear to have noticed my strange and quite uncharacteristic behaviour. He was suggesting tactfully that I should go and sit down in the cafeteria and have a cup of tea. He offered to come with me, but I assured him hastily that I would be quite all right without supervision and in fact really needed my space just then.

'Of course,' he said, in a suspiciously understanding tone. 'You have had a shock. But if there's anything at all I can do to help, girl—'

I looked up to see his eyes filled with such blatant amusement that I couldn't help myself.

'Beast!' I said helplessly. Of course, he knew exactly what he was doing, the effect he had on me. 'Go away, will you? Just go away and leave me alone.'

'Ah!' he responded. 'That's better. I'm glad to see the damage is not permanent. You are obviously on the mend.'

*   *   *

What with one thing and another I sincerely hoped Opal-Ophelia would forget all about picking me up, because then I could have indulged in the quiet evening I sorely needed to sort myself out. But it was not to be. She arrived on the dot of seven thirty, and when I went out of the vestibule door I saw some kind of sleek, low car of a make I didn't recognise standing in the courtyard outside the flats. Opal opened the passenger door and I slid into the leather seat beside her very much on my guard.

I had decided to adopt a dignified, aloof manner, reasoning that the best way to get through the potentially sticky evening was probably to try and stay out of it as much as I could—be polite but unforthcoming, wait for her to set the pace. Keep myself to myself, as it were. Consequently I said nothing as we slid down the short drive and she turned the car easily and smoothly out of the gateway, negotiating with quick expertise into the traffic. I kept determinedly silent as the car hummed on through the glittering streets—the lights were on and shining like watery jewels everywhere, the streets glistening black since it had been raining.

Opal was concentrating on her driving and did not appear to notice anything untoward in my attitude. But after a while, when I had begun to relax a little out of sheer anticlimax, she half-turned and flashed me an unexpected grin.

'So I've managed to get you to myself for a chat. Did Loz take offence, or didn't you tell him?' she asked. I wasn't sure I cared for the cosiness of her tone, the assumption of familiarity, the same suggestion she had put across in the studio that we were old friends. But I managed a perfunctory sort of half-smile in return and said noncommittally:

'He's listening to Baroque Ensembles. They are his refuge when he feels life has failed him.'

Opal wrinkled her nose and chuckled. She seemed completely at ease, no more harmful tonight than any other typically pushy female of the breed I had learned to recognise since I moved to London. High flying career women, business women, movers and shakers who liked to take men on at their own game just for devilment and the sheer sense of power. Rowan's words about her attitude problem came into my mind and I had to repress a stab of amusement.

I started to feel superior instead of wary. There was nothing threatening me here. Okay, so I'd let her get away with conning me into this trip, fallen for her bullying tactics. But when you got down to brass tacks, Opal-Ophelia was nothing but an ordinary—well, no, not quite ordinary, I had to admit it—but she was only a woman, wasn't she? I could see that now, she was just another woman, a woman like myself.

And if she was concerned with the Theatre School, a member of my own profession, that would account for a lot. There were any number of attitude problems in the theatre. It might even explain why she had dropped Loz for me. She couldn't stand the competition. Loz could have beaten her hands down where attitude was concerned any day.

'You are—uh—in the theatre, then? An agent?' I hazarded, becoming curious. I saw her mouth curve slightly and felt rather foolish—she had obviously been aware of exactly what was going through my mind. But she answered composedly enough.

'Oh, very much in the theatre, as you must have gathered. And I'm extremely interested in you and your potential. What made you decide to be an actress?'

I found this even more reassuring. I could deal with blatant nosiness, I thought, and I had met people who were interested in fostering talent before. There might even be something here for me career-wise—though I did not relish the thought of being represented by Opal and perhaps having to work closely with her.

I obediently sketched out something of my background and acting experience—the usual type of thing, lessons as a kid, amateur productions, school plays and so on.

As she listened, throwing in the occasional comment, I was able to deduce that she had a very shrewd knowledge of the theatrical scene. From the names she mentioned I gained the distinct impression she was on familiar terms with various luminaries of the stage and screen who were only words—names in lights—to me, a mere beginner in the business. In spite of myself I was impressed.

Somehow we got onto the subject of star quality—talent—whatever you call that magic spark.

'Yes, for all his little quirks Loz is very gifted,' Opal remarked unexpectedly, adding with a pointed sideways glance: 'And so are you.'

At my polite moue of acknowledgement she half-smiled.

'Oh, I think you are. During the course of my work I've conducted surveys—I've had to—exploring the possession and the possessors of this special gift, this ability. Genius. It's a subject that I find endlessly fascinating.'

'You think Loz is a genius?' I asked her blankly.

'I think you're more likely to be one. Don't you recognise yourself? Consider a few other geniuses for a minute. Byron for instance, was a very tortured being. He had it too, the self-doubt, the torment, the alienation from lesser souls that stalked him like a dark shadow, haunted him.'

'Did he?' I said rather dismissively. I wasn't interested in Byron's relationship problems—not just then, anyway—and the last thing I wanted to do was to start in-depth psychoanalysis of the less reputable aspects of my own persona in front of Opal-Ophelia. 'Strange, but I always got the impression from what little I know of Lord Byron that he was far from being alienated from lesser souls. Quite a lad, is more the picture I have in mind, a devil with the women.'

'But that was only the surface image,' Opal insisted. And I picked up something in her voice that made me sit up mentally though her tone was light, almost casual. 'There's a price to be paid for the gift. The black side, the one that stays hidden, that has to be taken and suffered too. Think of the devils and demons that ride you—your own moments of doubt and despair—your powerful self-destructive urge—'

Since death is the only certain fact of life . . . many believers have regarded life as nothing more than a preparation for death . . .—the power and presence of 'Thanatos', the 'Death Wish' which alternates with the Life Instinct, 'Eros' within the human mind—

I did not know whether she had spoken the words aloud, or whether they were simply surfacing from the depths of my subconscious in the apocalyptic tones of Sven A. DeWitte. But her voice had changed in the last few seconds so that I hardly recognised it. Harsher and deeper, it made the hairs rise on my scalp and I went momentarily cold. Try telling yourself she's just an ordinary woman now, I thought crazily.

I'd been a fool to come, to get into a car with her. But even as the thought passed through my head that we'd been right all along, she was a crank who might be dangerous and my smartest move would be to make an urgent excuse to get her to stop, whip the car door open and disappear into the nearest Underground, I knew that I would not. For wasn't this, whatever it was, the move I had been anticipating? Wasn't this what I had been waiting for?

Cards on the table, I had airily told Loz, was what we were after. Get Opal-Ophelia to show her hand. Oh, I'd known something would surface all right, though I had not known what. Even as I tried to convince myself Opal-Ophelia was just a pushy career type I had known all along, deep down, that she was something else.

Oh yes, I had been expecting this confrontation. Showdown. Pistols at eight. It was actually a relief to see action at last, since I'd been made more than enough of a fool of by this woman. I was ready for her.

*   *   *

I had hardly noticed where the car was heading except that it was into the city. Skirting carefully around Opal-Ophelia, trying to gauge what really lay behind the words of an apparently casual conversation with all my senses alert, I had been too absorbed to notice much else, so it came as quite a surprise—a shock, even—when suddenly we reached the 'little place' she apparently had in mind for dinner.

The car turned into a dim, narrow mews lit by a strategically placed lantern in an iron frame. The walls of the buildings on both sides were covered with creeper of some kind, and there was an alley that opened out into a different world—a paved and elegantly lighted courtyard. Obviously one of those establishments you hear about but never encounter unless you live a very different kind of life to the one I was used to as a drama student. There was no sign announcing the name of the place, patently this was unnecessary since access was restricted to a chosen few. You could tell this immediately by the atmosphere.

Understated refinement and elegance was the keynote, hinting subtly at all the delights good taste, gastronomic perfection and a choice of wines for the most discerning palate could offer. This promise of a secretive heaven seemed to emanate from the very building itself, with its tiny windows and unpretentious entrance door, and it absorbed us as we went in.

I was more than impressed to be there. This

was really out of my league. Some private dining club, I concluded, that was so discreet there was no suggestion at all it was a place of business. It might have been the home of intimate friends who were delighted you had decided to drop in.

*   *   *

We were conducted from the entrance hall into a room on the left, and guided to a table set for two beside a window. There were flowers, soft lights. I caught sight of my reflection—all eyes, very much on the alert—glittering reflected in the dark of the small panes. We sat down.

What now?

As a result of those few eerie moments in the car before we arrived, I have to admit to being keyed up. My pulse was racing. Randy's panicky suggestions about blackmail and organised crime started to twitch a little nervously at the corners of my mind as I glanced round. The place looked all right, positively luxurious even, ultra-respectable, discreet and exclusive but I told myself that meant nothing. Lull the victim, that was surely the first thing the bad guys would do before they showed their hand and put whatever plan they had into operation.

When you are in that sort of mental state, it is easy to understand how stories of your life flashing before your eyes if you are on the point of drowning, for instance, can occur. I am sure they really are true. My mind seemed to be working faster than my chaotic thoughts could crowd into it, but with the most amazing clarity. In a fraction of a second—or what seemed as brief as that—I had thought through whole complicated scenarios, reasoned every possibility out.

People always thought everything looked all right. They did it each time they walked into the spider's web—or the Gingerbread House—or Red Riding Hood's grandmother's cottage and the jaws of the wolf. Fairy tale images, yes, but hadn't we agreed only the other day in class that the fairy tales were necessary because they warned you life was not what it seemed, that you couldn't trust a book by its cover as the saying went, and all the other maxims that saved you from making a fool of yourself—

Or getting kidnapped by white slave traders—Or lured into some establishment that looked exactly like the one I was in but would turn out later to be some sort of Hell Fire Club where your drink was going to be spiked and you were going to be subjected to all kinds of unimaginable horrors—

But nothing had happened to me yet, had it? I forced myself to take a deep, steadying breath, admonishing myself for leaping into the realms of melodrama, panicking entirely unnecessarily. Another breath and I started to feel better. After the third, I had recovered my senses enough to gather my wits together and remember that I was supposed to be giving a performance of cool to match Opal-Ophelia's.

As a start, I looked round casually. (What they call casing the joint—well, just as a precaution in case I was now being too trusting.) The room we were in was low-ceilinged but spacious with an air of discreet opulence that was very much the real thing. There was Spanish leather, Venetian glass, hand-printed fabrics and genuine antique carved wood.

Other diners were present, I saw now, but they were hardly visible at carefully screened tables where small lamps twinkled like stars. The whole ambience was subtle and reassuring. I realised something else too. That even here in somewhere like this, a place obviously intended only for Beautiful People where all the other women I could see seemed to be drop-dead gorgeous, we were attracting notice. Or at least, Opal-Ophelia was. She stood out against the classiest competition as something especially stunning.

As she settled herself opposite me, I studied her across the table. From what she had been saying as we drove, I now assumed she held down some kind of high-powered job with a casting agency or similar organisation. I imagined she must be earning a fantastic

143

salary, but it was not money alone that accounted for her ability to be able to turn heads the way she did with no trouble at all.

Witchcraft?

Well, whoever or whatever she was, she most definitely had some sort of flair and the theatrical in me couldn't help but applaud wholeheartedly. Her appearance, for instance, was nothing short of inspired. She was wearing a red crushed velvet dress that clung without clinging, and her hair (which had seemed long and tied back out of sight on the previous occasions I had seen her) turned out to be hacked off close to her head. Tonight it was spiky and geometric, like the black petals of some shiny and exotic species of chrysanthemum. In the soft light, her eyes were darkened, her wide mouth glistening softly red in exactly the same colour as her dress. Glumly I admitted to myself that she looked exactly what I would have liked to look like if only I had had the flair, the poise, the figure—oh, and of course the spare cash as well.

Still nothing untoward had happened to me, and I was starting to feel much better. Quietly confident.

Menus were brought. I had learned from the times Daddy had taken me out for meals, not to try and pretend when confronted with lists of unintelligible dishes on a menu so I asked for soup and a green salad. I accepted a glass of wine, which turned out to be heady and fruity. And then, fortified as it were, I simply sat and waited.

I reminded myself again that this was no casual meeting. If I had over-reacted before, I mustn't let myself get lulled to the other extreme, mustn't make the mistake of trying to delude myself this was just a friendly, social affair. It was far from that. Opal-Ophelia had brought me here for some reason of her own— some very good reason, judging by the trouble she was going to and the amount this cosy *tête-à-tête* would set her bank balance back—

*　　　*　　　*

I came to with a jolt, and saw Opal's face very close to mine. She was leaning across the table, her eyes gleaming darkly, reflecting the red and gold of the brocade drapes at the window.

'Don't frown. It spoils your looks,' she said in a soft, hypnotic tone. The sibilants sounded like the hissing of snakes.

'Sorry?' I said, blinking, jerking myself away from her.

'Looks are an asset for any actress.' She seemed to be smiling, but I wasn't sure I was seeing her straight. I wasn't sure I was hearing her right, either. Her voice had changed again, and there was something else behind her words, something I couldn't quite make out sounding subliminally beneath that soft hissing. 'Oh, you are blessed with looks, of course and I love the dress too, you have a knack for creating your own style, don't you? But I notice that you're not wearing any jewellery.'

'So?' I got out with difficulty.

'Do you never wear your silver?' she queried, insinuating, soft as silk.

'Silver? Do I—? You mean instead of gold?' I was lost now, confused, imagining it must be the wine. She seemed to be talking some kind of other English that didn't make sense to me.

'Your fishes, I mean. Your silver fishes,' she pursued in that same hypnotic tone. 'The silver necklace that you wear sometimes? I wondered, that's all. I thought Loz mentioned it.'

*   *   *

With a great effort, I tried to focus my attention. I had obviously been drugged, I concluded, my mind starting to race madly, my mouth going dry, panic warnings sounding off in my head though another part of my brain pointed out reassuringly that this was highly unlikely. I had hardly taken more than a few sips from the glass and Opal's wine had been poured from the same bottle.

But what was she talking about?

'I've got no idea what you mean,' I said, and my voice must have been louder than I intended because the couple at the table nearest to us looked up in surprise. Opal raised her brows interrogatively, but said nothing.

'Look,' I went on awkwardly after a moment. 'I—um—well, yes, maybe we'd better get a few things straightened out here and now. I'm sorry if I am being rude when you've been kind enough to ask me out—show an interest in my work—'

I was fast losing the thread of what I had been trying to say. In fact, what exactly *had* I been trying to say?

'Let's face it, I don't know the slightest thing about you really, do I?' were the words that came out of my mouth next, again uttered so loudly that the people at the next table looked up. 'And to be honest, I'm not altogether happy with the fact that you seem to know so much about me—'

Talk about most embarrassing moments! The colour was mounting in my cheeks and I was getting very hot and disturbingly light-headed. I tried to speak again, make myself clear, but something had happened to my voice. It emerged in little spurts, slurred and indistinct.

'I can't see why you should be interested in my jewellery. Even if I had it. Which I don't. And Loz would never have mentioned it anyway. Even if he did. Because there isn't any. So he couldn't.'

I broke off, trying to keep a grip on my fast whirling senses. What was happening to me? This was frightening. Was I going mad? Really mad, this time?

The bubbles of real panic—far more frantic than any imaginative rambling about organised crime—were just about to burst all around me when suddenly, like a lifeline thrown to a drowning man, rescue came.

I stopped panicking, and did exactly what I had to do in order to save myself. I knew what it was because I could hear the instructions in Rowan's voice echoing in my head. Clear—calm—insistent instructions.

'Be yourself, Tania. Only be yourself, and all will be well. Be yourself. And all will be well. Will be well. Will be. Well.'

Summoning all my resources, I stared directly towards Opal-Ophelia, trying to focus on her blurred image against the candle flames. Strangely, the light cast a dark instead of a pale nimbus around her and her face was lost in deeper shadow.

I would be myself. I would say what must be said.

'Let's just stop all the polite small-talk, shall we? Why have you brought me here? And what is all this about? I'm not interested in any kind of friendship with you, I'm not interested in being a witch, if that's what you are. I didn't encourage you, you forced yourself on me and I've tried to be polite, but things have gone far enough. So I'd appreciate a few straight, simple answers. Who are you and what do you want?'

8

And now the sounds of the restaurant—room, club, whatever it was—seemed to fade far away. I was suspended in timelessness. I stared into the woman's eyes even though I could not see them, and she stared into mine. The moment might have been an instant or it might have been aeons of eternity.

'No matter if you have no silver fishes,' she said then and her voice sounded again that strange one I had heard in the car. The words grew deeper and coarser. 'They have surely been transmuted. It is you who are the One, with the fishes or without them, and I have found you. Yet what are you? Merely an infant, a child, you are no worthy adversary for me. I will flick you with my finger, I will crush you beneath my foot—'

I tried to speak but I seemed to be weighed down heavily, both in my body and my mind. There was only vast darkness and space around me, and the howling of a great wild wind. Then the gale caught me and threw me down so that I was frantically scrabbling against unfamiliar earth. I could feel wet coarse grass beneath my hands, and wet sand.

Somewhere very near sounded the boom and roar of the sea.

I was lost, naked and shivering. The levels of the world were turned upon each other so that I was neither in space or time . . . I had the freedom of the whole air and yet I could not move . . . held immobile in a living death, suspended helpless between earth and sky and knowing neither of them for comfort.

There were voices keening in the wind that blew cold from the sea, the voices of souls lost and beseeching their way. The first heavy drops of the storm that gathered itself together out there in the darkness stung my flesh like knives . . .

Light flickered erratically, piercing the dark. Still huddled over, clutching at the sand, I managed to lift my head and saw that there was the cavernous black of deep sea-caves all around me, their entrances vaguely outlined in a red glow. The figure of Opal-Ophelia loomed tall and menacing before me, standing on a huge sweeping staircase made of rock. She was like a flame in her red dress, which had now become an elaborately Gothic ball-gown with a long train, and her eyes were glittering in the light of a many-branched candelabrum that she held high in one hand. The candle flames were smoking and guttering in the draught and cold wind. They caught the

150

movement of the waters that lay just out of reach of their light, just beyond the streaming wet sea-strand where I was crouching, terrified.

I was lost, naked and shivering. I was neither in space or time, held immobile in a living death, suspended helpless between the earth and the sky, knowing neither of them for comfort—

'You are quoting from the Havamal—the Words of the High One—Odin describing the terror of sacrificing himself in order to win the runes, wherein lay the secrets of all magic and wisdom—'

It was Rowan's voice again but faint and far away, echoing somewhere out in the darkness, borne on the wind. I felt sick, very ill, my head was swimming and there was nausea rising in my throat. I clung desperately to consciousness as I strained to catch the broken phrases. Rowan would tell me what to do.

'Loki—perhaps Loki was there before the world began since he represents chaos and mischief and the dark. He is the mirror-reflection of Odin, his blood-brother.—Whoever he seems or whatever form he takes, do not trust him.'

*　　　*　　　*

But it was too late, too late now. I was alone on this terrible shore where the great stair snaked up to heaven and the waters ran like blood. I was alone with my enemy. I screamed aloud, though I did not know what I was screaming.

'Rowan! Help me! Help me!'

Then as clearly though he was beside me, the words that had closed round me like a cloak when we had spoken in the Coffee Shop were there again, powerful as any amulet of gold shot with precious gems. They shattered the dark like the sound of trumpets, ringing so that the very ground shook. I heard them and I had my shield, my defence against the dark. I clutched it close, hugging it to me, straining it against my heart.

'There are other gods. There is Njord, god of the wind and the sea . . . the consort of Nerthus, who was the great Earth Mother . . .

'Some think Nerthus and Njord were actually one being, the same divinity.'

'There is also Njord,' I cried, the words swept from my lips and tossed into the chaotic night. 'There is Njord, Njord, the god of the wind and the sea—!'

And new light was visible now, breaking in points of rainbow fire through the gloom. I found I was no longer alone. Three other people were standing in a little group some distance away, a man holding up a lantern that

152

sparked reassuringly as a twinkling star, with two women beside him.

My heart smashed smotheringly against my ribs, and I cried out involuntarily when I saw them. For how could this be?

One of the women was Gran, my grandmother—I recognised her though she was somehow wavering in and out of focus, at one moment herself and in the next instant the elderly crone I had seen before. I recognised the others too, they were just as I had always known them over the years of my growing-up when they had been frozen in time, clasped within each other's arms in the eternal sunlit garden by the lake at home. My great-grandmother, the girl in the lilac crepe dress, and her laughing lover, my great-grandfather, now they too were here with me on this nightmare dark seastrand.

Even as I turned to look at them, the girl in the lilac dress moved, coming forward. Her hair lifted round her shoulders in the draught from the sea-caves, and I could see that she was trembling. The skin on her bare arms was crawling, her jaw clenched tight against the tremors of fear. She took the old woman's hand, and then the two of them advanced protectively towards me, towards the place where I crouched low on the wet sand. Together, they deliberately placed themselves between me and the blazing figure of Opal-Ophelia.

It was a gesture that touched me to the heart, for they were far gone in fear. I could feel their terror, sense that for all their courage they were desperate, far beyond the limits of their strength. But with new strength now, I managed to scramble to my feet, staggering on the clammy ooze. I plunged unsteadily forward, shouting words wrenched from somewhere deep within me that burst painfully from my mouth. I flung them in defiance towards the enemy like a weapon, knowing that my own voice too was changed. It was not mine, or at least I did not recognise it. It sounded thunderous, powerful, as though it would echo to the hidden stars, it was challenging, clear, commanding, alive.

'No! No Ragnarok! No Ragnarok! No Ragnarok!'

A sort of puzzled, thwarted fury crossed Opal's face and blazed from her eyes. Wax gutted in frantic drops from the candles, making tiny spitting sounds as they landed on the wet steps. She seemed to surge down the rocky staircase almost to the bottom, the long train of her gown slithering sinuously behind her like some menacing crimson snake.

'You puny fool,' she hissed at me, venomous as any serpent now. 'Will you dare to defy me? Have you no vision of the extent of my power?'

Her rage was searing. It drove the girl in the lilac crepe dress and the old crone back, whimpering blindly. I could feel their terror quiver almost like a tangible thing, though they still tried to shield me from the fire of Opal's blazing fury, and my own fear dissolved into nothing in the wake of the pity and the love that flared through me.

I went to them, deliberately putting my arms round the girl and taking her gently by the slim, shaking shoulders. With reassuring words I placed her behind me, and then I did the same with the old woman. She was almost spent, her bones delicate, her heart fluttering like that of a terrified bird beneath my hands. They would have fought—perhaps died—for me, these two but it was I who was stronger, I knew that now, and that it was I who must fight for them. I could do it. I knew myself at last, I knew my own strength in those terrible moments as I turned to face Opal directly, adversary to adversary.

For another of those endless fractions of time we looked at one another. I did not flinch.

'Whoever you are,' I said quietly, 'I do not recognise your power.'

Then she shrieked so that the light trembled and the flames bloomed huge and red, all-engulfing. Her words seemed to boom like thunder, filling the caves, and her shadow leaped gigantically against the darkness of the dripping rock.

'It shall be so! I say it shall be so! I shall steer the ship of the giants at the time of

155

Ragnarok when the tree Yggdrasil shall shake and the forests shall tremble. I tell you the sun shall be devoured in the jaws of the wolf. The Midgard Serpent shall be freed. And twilight shall come upon the gods.'

I shut my eyes against the things that beat at me like swooping, circling birds with black beaks that would pluck out my eyes and tear strips from my flesh. I let the answer come from wherever it would, the words forming of their own accord in my mouth.

'And in the name of great Nerthus and in the name and power of Njord, I tell you there will be no Ragnarok. For I will take the silver fishes and safely steer the far distant seas as it was always decreed. And as for you—you will return from whence you have come.'

With another shriek of fury that seemed to shake the very ground on which we stood, she leaped forward and thrust the candelabrum into my face and for a few moments all I was aware of was the pain. Flames and burning wax seared my skin and I felt hands seize me and voices scream in my ears. I sank into a darkness where the sea moaned and throbbed, an eternal pulse in the far, far distance. Then coolness soothed and possessed me, and even the restless sea was stilled

*   *   *

I surfaced groggily at about seven-thirty in the

156

morning when Randy, frowning with anxiety, roused me to ask whether I wanted a cup of tea and to let me know she would be going off to work shortly. Her journey involved both bus and Tube and she always gave herself plenty of time.

'How do you feel?' she asked. 'Want to give your classes a miss today and rest?'

'No way, I'm fine,' I told her, feeling definite improvement as I gulped the fragrant cuppa. I could tell she was overly concerned because she had made me her extra special Lady Grey, and in one of her Minton cups instead of my usual mug.

'Hmm,' she said, eyeing me dubiously, but she took my word and did not bother to argue. As she stood in the doorway of my room on the verge of departure however, she promised meaningfully: 'We'll talk about it tonight.'

Fortified, I threw on my clothes and went off to class. My brain was a bit foggy but I managed to cope creditably with the day though I had to avoid any kind of thinking. What I really wanted and needed was to speak to Rowan, but I discovered to my surprise that he was not going to be present. He had been called away it appeared, unexpectedly summoned to audition at Sheffield for something so momentous he would have been a fool to turn it down, and he had left London the night before in a hurry. Even though, the gossip in class warned ominously, his defection

157

might mean he would not be allowed to complete his course at the school.

In the wake of what had happened to me the previous evening, it was not surprising I suppose that I felt strangely bereft. I needed desperately to see Rowan, speak to him. For it had been his voice—his words—that had guided me through something I had no explanation for and might well, when I allowed myself to think about it, consider to have been so terrifying the average person would have been sent into gibbering lunacy.

But Rowan had known somehow that it was going to happen. He had known that I would find myself in the sea-caves. It was Rowan who had told me the name of Njord, god of the wind and the sea, which had proved my only defence, Rowan whose eyes had shimmered a shifting green-blue while we had spoken, evoked those rainbow mists of azure and lilac and mauve. Rowan was the one who had given me a glimpse of something that I now knew I needed like air to breathe and food to eat, life to refresh my very soul.

I did not dare to let myself dwell on the full extent of my disappointment when Louise, who played Queen Gertrude, informed me rather smugly where Rowan had gone. He was not there, that had to be enough. Just empty space where his presence should have been. And I would see him again of course, he would have to come back for *Hamlet*, if nothing else, even if he landed this amazing job in Sheffield or wherever.

But I was too strung up emotionally to feel much relief at the thought that he would be back some time. It was easier to encourage myself to feed my sense of grievance at having been abandoned in my hour of need, remind myself that Randy had once again been proved right. Relationships simply weren't worth the aggro. Rowan was a man, after all, wasn't he? And—well, men! They were never there when you wanted them.

Somehow my sense of injury at Rowan's defection—and the fact that I knew he would have been extremely amused by it—actually did me more good than any unloading of my emotional baggage onto him would probably have done.

*   *   *

We had a rehearsal, so it was after seven and Randy was already home, busy in the kitchen with Loz in attendance when I turned my key to let myself into the flat. The savoury odour of something *au gratin* wafted to my nostrils, exactly what I needed after a hard few hours as the Player Queen—who now, thanks to Zoe, had some strenuous acrobatic mime to cope with. After I had dashed into the shower and perked myself up with spritzes of cologne water (the original 4711, favoured by Randy above and beyond all perfume except Paloma Picasso, which she said was simply chic) I was beginning to feel as though I belonged to the human race again. And by the time we sat down to eat, the soothing atmosphere of the flat and the rituals of full-scale dining at home were working their usual miracles.

Nevertheless there were of course, things that needed to be said about what had happened the previous evening. Randy had the determined air of an anxious parent who insists on knowing the worst as she sat us down to our meal. She was obviously intent on getting to grips with whatever she had to, however much it was going to pain her.

The story seemed to be that I had inexplicably fainted in the restaurant and been brought home by an appropriately concerned Opal in a confused and groggy state. By the time I'd been put to bed by Randy (an event I had little recollection of) I had apparently been protesting that I was quite all right and there was no need at all to call a doctor and would everybody please stop fussing for heaven's sake. So, reassured that I seemed so normal, Randy had decided to let me sleep it off, and I told her now as we ate that I'd been fine all day, except that I was tired. However, I added, you could explain that away by the physical work I had been doing in class and the intensive routine Zoe had just been putting the Player Queen through.

'There's nothing wrong,' I insisted, adding significantly, 'with *me*. But there is something very wrong about what happened. Because I did not faint in that restaurant. Opal did it deliberately. She shoved the candelabrum in my face.'

Before I could elaborate on what I had said both Randy and Loz froze into horrified immobility, heads jerked up, hands poised holding their cutlery over their plates.

'I knew we should have got that doctor last night,' Randy declared worriedly. 'You've had another twenty-four hours without treatment. It must be some kind of bug, first fainting and now hallucinating. Loz, you'd better call—'

'Will you shut up and just let me explain,' I interrupted in exasperation. 'I don't mean the real candelabrum—if there was one, which I can't remember. It happened in a—a sort of vision or something, but it was Opal who induced it. She started talking to me across the table and—well, she kind of put me into a trance. I can't explain it any other way. Except that I know I did not faint.'

Randy and Loz looked at each other cautiously. Then Loz said with some reluctance.

'I can accept that, Miranda. Sometimes she has had that effect on me too—sort of.'

As Randy seemed confused about to what to say next, I turned abruptly to Loz.

'Let me ask you a few personal questions.

About this woman. For a start, where does she live?'

He considered.

'Well, actually I don't really know. A flat in Pimlico, I think. She contacted me the first time, you see, replying to my ad in the paper and then when we arranged to meet, she picked me up—'

'Just like she did with me last night,' I said, nodding significantly. 'So we can't trace her that way, can we? No address, only the name—if that's her real one, and I'm beginning to wonder. What's her last name, Loz?'

As Randy and I stared at him, Loz looked very embarrassed.

'Ah—it seemed sort of meant to be,' he got out at last, his high cheek bones going pink beneath his thatch of blond hair so that he looked like a wayward cherub. 'We agreed that—ah—well, it didn't seem at all like meeting a stranger, and *she* said we weren't strangers because we had known each other in a previous existence. In fact, I thought exactly the same thing myself, and it just didn't somehow seem to arise—'

'Right, get the picture,' I nodded, sparing him such tender and meaningful cosmic revelations.

Naturally, Loz's Byronic nature would have thrilled to romantic fantasies from a beautiful woman who was also a witch and who

162

presumably knew about destiny. I went on: 'So she never told you her name. Opal—Ophelia Something then, though like I said, I don't think I believe it. Well, what did you do, Loz, apart from go to the meeting of the coven? When you went out with her, I mean? Did she ever take you anywhere else—the place where she works, for instance? Or tell you about it?'

'Ah—no,' he said, apologetically. 'She never mentioned much about work, though I did get the impression she was connected with Fine Arts. A kind of consultant—at Christies or Sothebys or somewhere like that. We just went to pubs for a meal, walked by the river. We talked about art, mainly. Music. Literature.'

'Just what I expected,' I said to Randy. 'She simply came and went out of nowhere. Have you got her phone number, Loz?'

'Oh, yes,' he said, eager to please, and pushed back his chair. 'It's in my Filofax. It's Pimlico, like I said.'

We'd all finished now and I pushed back my own chair. Randy, automatically efficient, stacked and removed our plates to the dishwasher in the kitchen as Loz displayed a page, his finger pointing to the number, which I punched out on my phone.

'Only one way to check.'

I tried twice but could only get unobtainable.

'Her mobile? Work number? E-mail?'

Loz bit his lip, looking sheepish.

163

'Did you ever ring her?' I asked, knowing the answer even before he shook his head.

'Well, no. Sometimes I'd think of it but she always seemed to ring first. It was as if she knew—'

He broke off and we looked at each other.

'My point exactly,' I said softly. By this time we were all sitting round the fire. Dick was leaning heavily against my legs and Turpin was purring lustily on Randy's lap.

There was a long pause.

'I asked about a bit today at the Theatre School,' I said at last. 'You know, how she happened to be roaming about in the building, free to walk into the studio while we were rehearsing. Nobody had any idea who she was, they'd never heard of her in the office. And none of the students—apart from Rowan, and he's not here so I can't check with him—none of them had noticed her coming in or speaking to me. Nobody's got any information about her at all.'

In the silence while Randy and Loz absorbed this I went on: 'Strange, to say the least, I'd say. And another thing, why should she have given Loz the impression she works in Fine Arts when she told me she worked in the theatre?—and not only that but I could have sworn she was genuine. She spoke like a real insider, she seemed to know all about everything and everybody in the business.'

Loz leaned forward.

'But she does work in the art world Tania, she must do. She was far better informed than any amateur. She's professionally involved, I'm sure, it wasn't just pretence. I do know a little about these things,' he added rather injuredly.

'Well, I don't know who or what this woman is or what she wants,' I told them, though I did not mention the surreal possibilities that were beginning to take shape in my head since they would almost certainly have convinced Randy it was time to call a doctor. 'But there is one thing I think we can definitely assume about her now.'

'And?' prompted Randy.

'She's dangerous,' I said.

*   *   *

London plunged into its crazy December whirligig, which I had never experienced before and which I enjoyed tremendously. I rode on the glittering crest of the wave feeling worldly and cosmopolitan and very much at the centre of things. We put up festive decorations in the flat, assisted by the pawing and pouncing of our feline duo, who queued to stand expectantly before the gift-wrapped tins of cat food Loz tied on to our tree with red ribbon. Garlands thickly silvered with tinsel—Harrods' best, provided by Randy—were looped elegantly across the green velvet curtains and Victorian choristers, cherubs and angels sang silently on all sides.

Even the candles that graced our evening mealtimes were festive. Randy's expert eye blended blue, green and gold with mauve and rose, and she created an incredible arrangement of dried flowers and leaves in glowing Renaissance colours as a centrepiece for the table. It stood glistening in a sort of hushed anticipation, as though it held its breath, beneath a dusting of fake snow that looked just like the real thing. The room was transformed, touched by magic.

And naturally, as you might expect, the atmosphere was building up at my Theatre School too. I was passing through the most wonderful, exciting time I had ever experienced, aware of living life with all its highs and lows to the full in an increasing richness of sensation. You never realise when you are storing up the milestones of your life, though I knew what we were doing with *Hamlet* was something very special, something I would probably never experience again.

There were all the usual drama student thrills, the moments of pure art, spills and temperament as well as those gorgeously corny plot-lines that everybody can indulge themselves up to the ears in when they are in the throes of 'putting on a show'. Wildfire backstage gossip. Enter Rumour painted full of tongues. Someone had seen the doyen of British film being escorted into the Principal's office with Ted. Was there some classic, overnight starring role in the offing for one or more of us?

Various theatrical Knights and Dames made their appearance—some of them were relatives of students—flitting tantalisingly round corners. Talent cracked under the strain to reveal the shimmering gold nuggets of possibility that might lift any one of us to the pinnacle of immortality. And of course, the first performance of my first London season as an actress came and went.

The occasion involved much entering into the community spirit, much mingling for me in the guise of Player Queen with the teeming hordes who made up our audience. I was gracious to wide-eyed tots, to the languid teens clustered in school parties, to laid-back sophisticates amused by the whole thing and to dazzled shoppers who probably thought we were taking part in some sort of wacky TV challenge programme. I hobnobbed, talking serious 'art for the masses' with counsellors and people in mayoral chains. In the event our production of *Hamlet* notched up triumph after triumph, both in the frosty courtyard outside the Civic Hall and later, post-performance, at the champagne bash laid on for us in the chambers behind its imposing façade.

The whole show was very long, and started in the afternoon. All credit to the local worthies, for the Elizabethan Christmas Fest was actually quite an undertaking.

A procession of Elizabethan revellers had been assembled to escort us—the 'Players'—through the streets, a practically impossible task if it had not been for the intervention of some appropriately attired 'Queen's men' who sorted out the teeming crowds with official expertise using ancient-looking batons of office and (possibly more relevantly) twittering two-way radios. Perched on decorated wagons, we wended our way past the High Street shops to the strains of appropriately festive music and jollity, the procession coming to a halt before the imposing façade of the Civic Hall where we proceeded to set up our 'stage'.

Meanwhile, in order to distract the crowds, our attendant revellers plunged enthusiastically into various renderings of Morris dancing, Mumming and 'guising' and other such traditional treats that brought forth 'ooh's and 'ahh's from the assembled citizenry. And then at last as the audience settled itself expectantly, the sound of a kettledrum rattled hollowly across the courtyard. We were transported to the battlements of Elsinore Castle, in the night watches where ' 'Tis now struck twelve'.

A brazier gleamed red. The guard, at his post, was a dim shadow swathed in furs. Enter to him his relief, Bernardo, calling sharply into the empty air 'Who's there?' and we were into the play.

*   *   *

Winter dusk in London is always thrilling, bright with lights and colours and sounds that haven't changed a great deal since the bustling scenes on Dickensian Christmas cards. It was utterly magical, and I loved it all: the triumphal progress of our Elizabethan players' cart through the crowds, the sweet sound of lutes and madrigals and the more raucous cavorting of clowns; the subtly pervasive fragrances of frankincense and myrrh that wafted, mingling with more prosaic scents like beer and burgers, from the enormous gilded church candles that Ted had insisted upon (and a public-spirited local shopkeeper had supplied) as Gothic atmosphere to light the scenes within the castle of Elsinore.

Purists might have thought church candles a little obtrusive in sexy Queen Gertrude's bedchamber and Ted had set them on suggestively tall phallic sconces—but why split hairs? They smelled divine and looked immensely impressive when the king was kneeling at his prayers.

It was a very physical experience altogether. Hot chestnuts that burned my tongue, spiced mulled wine as well as champagne at the banquet afterwards, which was served hilariously in what we understood to be a normally staid and respectable Council Chamber. Transformed for the Elizabethan Fest, this was laid out with things like syllabub and frumenty, and the merry throng was served by buxom wenches in mobcaps.

Randy and Loz had both attended the performance in person to cheer for me, and I had a First Night telegram and flowers from Gran as well as various 'Good Luck' cards and bouquets from the scattered Aunties and Uncles in the Midlands. Randy and Loz presented me with one single red rose in an antique silver holder that I could have as a keepsake when all the excitement was over. And even Daddy had sent something to mark the occasion.

He was actually in the Middle East, Dubai or somewhere, but he had made sure I received a very special and personal lucky piece that had been mailed from Copenhagen, a real fragment of theatre history, an original photograph carefully preserved in a now faded and flimsy folder. It was of those star-crossed lovers of British drama, Laurence Olivier and Vivien Leigh, in the famous production of *Hamlet* at Elsinore Castle when they were both young and beautiful and the world lay before them. There was a scribbled signature on it but I couldn't make out whose it was—I didn't think it was either of theirs, but that didn't matter. The gift was drenched with magic and stardust, and I felt, as I had often done in the past, that whatever people might insinuate about Daddy abandoning me or neglecting his duty to his motherless little girl, he probably understood and cherished me with a far surer touch than anyone was aware of.

*   *   *

There's a proverb about not wishing for something because you will probably get it. I had never understood what this meant before, but became completely enlightened when in the course of the after-show celebrations, the formerly unattainable Ted emerged from his ranks of massed admirers, screaming fans and worthies eagerly discussing further innovative community productions, to back me purposefully into a dim corner of one of the corridors.

There was no doubt at all what was on his mind. In fact I had actually noticed him eyeing me with a sharpening of interest as we were going through the full dress rehearsal, in just the way Randy had prophesied. I did look rather stunning I suppose (well, different, anyway), decked out in my Gothic blue and gold velvet with my hair in a waterfall of crimped waves down my back, dusted with glittering gold powder—and without my glasses on, of course.

But whatever had stimulated his interest, the upshot was that Ted got me on my own after the performance and deliberately put his arm in a more than congratulatory manner round my shoulders. He stared into my eyes in the way that made his fans swoon when he was playing Bad Boy Skaffy on the box most nights a week, and bent his head slowly down to my face. I think it was meant to be one of his notorious mean, possessive kisses but it actually missed my lips, landing somewhere on my ear, his mouth sliding on my long hair. You will be surprised to hear that this was because I had deliberately turned my head away.

'God, you are going to be a big star!' he murmured hungrily, and invented a few more lines that would have fitted perfectly into some future script. 'You're a fascinating bitch, Tania, irresistible when you want to be. Don't ever forget that I'm the one who found you first.'

Well as you know, there would have been a time—and not so long before, either—when I would cheerfully have rolled over, waved all four paws in the air and died for such a moment. It would have been the fulfilment of all my wildest dreams and evoked quivering abandonment, soaring ecstasy and a jelly-like melting into a blob at the very least. But by the time the moment actually happened, my idol had toppled from his pedestal. Painlessly and quite, quite irrevocably.

It was not Ted's fault. He was still just as good-looking, talented and charismatic. But unfortunately for him I wasn't interested in looks and charisma now. I had been given a glimpse beyond the clouds to realms of glory where the true and living immortals dwelt, and so my former idol's rapt attentions and the gleam in his eye hardly registered with me except to provoke a sweet smile and a deliberately ingenuous 'Thanks a million Ted, but it was really all down to your wonderful direction, we beginners have found it so inspiring working with you.' Then I brushed past him without another thought and went back into the clanging decibels of the chatter and the cheer.

Just a few feet away from me, talking to his ex-Queen Gertrude (and now that they were off-stage, ogling her cleavage with a shameless eye), was the Ghost of her first husband in his body-armour and fake fur cloak. He did not look at me, but I was content just with the awareness of his presence in the room. I could feel the pull that drew me to him as powerfully as though it was the magnetic pole, so that everyone else shrivelled by comparison. I knew that neither Ted nor any other man would ever stand a chance with me again.

Along with the rest of the cast, Rowan had given me a luvvying, congratulatory after-show kiss a few minutes earlier. It was the first time his lips had touched mine, and the conflagration I had briefly experienced was something far beyond the enchantment I had previously been aware of. It had consumed me, shrivelled me to ashes and then lifted me so that I rose, phoenix-like on the far reaches of some glorious and distant star.

I had no idea of quite what had occurred. But I wasn't going to start asking questions— mainly because I knew instinctively that Rowan wouldn't have answered them. And in any case, in the deepest recesses of my mind where the ghosts walked, I was already beginning to become aware of the answers.

9

The confrontation with Opal-Ophelia in the restaurant had happened exactly as I had experienced it. I was certain of that even though Randy had been inclined to feel my forehead and mutter about possible concussion or viral fever the following evening, when we were discussing the implications of my fainting fit. Having stuck to her guns once when she decided Loz was being set up to be blackmailed, and lived to regret such foolishness, she was not going to be drawn into the realms of fantasy again. So the kind of X-Files scariness my suspicions of Opal-Ophelia were hinting at only made her tut-tut more than ever and suggest an early night.

I did not try to argue with her. There was nothing to be said really, it was a waste of time trying to speculate since the only individuals who could have shed any light on what had actually happened on that dark and thundering sea-strand were the ones who had been there with me. Events were sweeping me far beyond my own depth, let alone the depth of people like Randy who had not actually passed through the experience.

I could not begin to guess how Gran and the two lovers from almost a century ago had been there, what part they played in the scenario that was unfolding. Neither did I know how Rowan was involved. But it was obvious that he was, and that he knew far more than I did about what was going on.

He had known what was going to happen when I went off to have dinner with Opal, I could see now that he must have known. Hadn't every word he had spoken to me about the Scandinavian myths and the gods been loaded with significance I had not been able to appreciate at the time? He had gone out of his way to try and warn me, prepare me, make sure that however naïve, however ignorant I might be, I was at least armed and able to defend myself against the enemy.

How could anyone ever prepare you for this kind of awareness until you actually experienced it? Oh yes, I too was aware of the enemy now, even though our paths had only crossed for the briefest instant. I too had stood and looked into those indescribable eyes and recognised the enemy for what it was. With the heightened awareness that came from the inner certainty of my Sight—the Sight that marked me and set me apart—I too had been able to perceive the looming dark presence that concealed itself behind the glamorous face and figure masquerading as Opal-Ophelia.

I had confronted the enemy and accepted its existence, even though I did not yet know what the battle was about—let alone the war. But instinct warned me that the scene on the seastrand had been only the beginning, a first clashing of weapons, as it were. And that whether I wanted it or not, this was my battle, my war.

The situation was mind-blowing it its awfulness, but in one way I could only feel a great sense of exultation, as though I had at last reached the end of a journey I had been making blindfolded without being aware that there was a journey at all. Everything in my life that had happened before this point had been in preparation, to bring me here, where I was meant to be, and to make sure I was ready for what was to come.

*　　　*　　　*

As I lay drifting off to sleep after drinking the hot milk Randy had insisted on (flavoured deliciously with cinnamon), I experienced another of those visions that I was beginning to realise now were actually flashes of visionary insight. Somehow, it seemed to embody all the visions that I had had previously, and bring them together into a sharp point of focus—if only I could have remembered what it was when I woke, for I had not been lying in my warm bed but on cold stone—

—lost, naked and shivering, neither in space or time—.

I was waiting, waiting. For the shadow of doom, the chill of the knife before it plunged home, the gathering of the wave before it broke in thunderous force. I knew this place, I had been here before. I had always been here. Waiting. Waiting. Waiting.

Odin describing the terror of sacrificing himself in order to win the runes, wherein lay the secrets of all magic and wisdom.

The terror of sacrifice. The terror of sacrificing himself—

*   *   *

So this was the dark core that lay at the source of my vision, the hidden mystery that provided the fount of my strength. I could see it all so clearly now, I understood at last. That somewhere, on some bleak and bitter seastrand, in some lost and forgotten time, I too had made the sacrifice. I too had submitted my will and my self in accordance with the decrees of fate.

When great Nerthus touched me and named me as her daughter all was said. I was hers and I had always been hers, like the hound who knows his master but knows not the how of it . . .

It was as simple as that. I was myself and yet I was more than myself, far greater than myself. I had a part to play in an unfolding story I was as yet hardly aware of. I had a destiny to fulfil. Only I could carry this role, and when the time came I would do it. It had all been long since decided, long since ordained. And yet, I had also been given the freedom to refuse the burden if I would.

But I had not refused, and with that awareness came also the reassurance that there was nothing to fear. For when I submitted my will, I had submitted myself also to guidance in the way I was to go, and I would continue to be guided.

As I turned sleepily, pulling the warmth of the duvet around me, I felt a strange and inexplicable peace settle within my mind. Somehow I knew the enemy had retreated for the moment. But even if—when—I had to face it again, there was no need to fear. I was aware dimly of presences in the room with me. Angels round my bed I thought wonderingly, vaguely recollecting an old childhood prayer, an invocation really—and yet surely I had heard it before. Somewhere—at some other time—when I had needed protection in the past as I needed it now—

Matthew, Mark, Luke and John
The bed be blessed that I lie on
Four angels round my bed
Four angels round my head
One to watch and one to pray
And two to bear my soul away

A child in a dark place, I crouched into myself, hugged myself into a ball, made myself small. The world was a domain of terrors too awful to contemplate. Night and silence. Loss and suffering and death. The fairy tales were right, there was no escape. Nowhere was safe—nowhere was safe—

And then I could smell violets, feel a gentle presence. The terrors receded. The darkness was filled with light that rocked me, comforted me, lulled me.

It would all come right. Intuitively I knew that whatever I needed, I would be given. I was not alone. Help was at hand. And as I slid into sleep at last, my final waking realisation was that the immediate answers lay in my other life, in the wooded secrecy of my home in Rudyard. That was where they were, the women who had been in the dream with me, Gran and the girl in the lilac crepe dress—

Yet what were a few more weeks in the

immensity of cosmic destiny unfolding? I would speak to Gran when I went home at Christmas, ask her to explain the things I did not know. We would have a long, long talk, Gran and I—

*　　*　　*

Rowan, however, was a different matter. In the two days before he came back from Sheffield and I saw him walking into class, I had had plenty of time to reflect on what had happened during the scene in the restaurant with Opal-Ophelia, and more particularly on the part he had played in it.

So somehow, I expected that when I next encountered him he would look different. Yet he was exactly the same, tall, lithe, with his dancer's and fencer's body taut and controlled, economical of movement and as real and physical as the rest of the students. There was no sense that he was a ghost, part of something that lay in another dimension—

Because that was what it really amounted to, wasn't it?

The dim seastrand didn't really exist, or if it did it was in some time long gone and far away. Opal-Ophelia, as I had tried to tell Randy and Loz, had no physical reality. I was becoming more sure of that than ever. She had come into our lives like something created from smoke, conjured up only to disappear again like a wraith. I might have pursued more detailed investigations about her than the casual asking around I had done at the Theatre School, but I knew in my heart that there was no point. I would never find any sign of the flat in Pimlico or the high-flying executive who worked for Christies or Sothebys, or was well known as a theatrical agent.

She simply didn't exist, I could see it now and even accept it without a qualm, as I had accepted all the rest that my Sight had revealed to me. Or at least, she would only appear again if and when she wanted to. I didn't kid myself that I had seen the last of her, but whatever future action was going to be played out between myself and the enemy that she embodied, remained to be seen. I needed to know more about what Gran had to tell me before I could even begin to try and make guesses.

All these thoughts were tumbled rather incoherently at the back of my head as I stood waiting for Rowan to walk into the studio on the morning he came back. I don't know what I expected him to say or do. But he just looked across at me and smiled slowly, and the same sequence of effects I was getting used to chugged into gear once again. Coloured lights, silken unguents, fountains—the lot. And then he came to me.

'Got over your nasty experience, girl?'

Did he mean the scene in the restaurant? Somehow all the things I had intended to ask, the questions I had meant to put about how he had known about what was going to happen to me, how I could have heard his voice sounding there on that terrible sea-shore carried on the wind from the pounding and heaving sea, remained unspoken.

I just couldn't do it. Well, put yourself in my place for a minute. How could I confront him outright and enquire whether he was actually a ghost when we were standing in such close and disturbingly intimate proximity? I could feel the heat from his skin and smell the faint tang of aftershave, or whatever it was that wiped away all sensation of other-worldliness and induced thoughts in me that were the very opposite of phantom-like.

As I hesitated, once more paralysed by his glance and the feeling that I was drowning in the look in his eyes—even though he was laughing at my discomfiture—he leaned forward deliberately and took my hand, holding it between both his own. And suddenly, at his touch, everything steadied. I knew without knowing how I knew, that whatever was going on, it was all right. I drew a long deep breath. There was no need to ask. I would be told all I needed to know when the time was right.

'That is it, girl,' he said quietly, as though I had spoken my thoughts aloud. And he added—though I was not sure whether this came from my own mind too, or even from his, whether he actually said it or whether once again I was reading things that were unspoken—a clear message.

'Trust me.'

Holding his lean fingers, feeling something pass from them into my own, I never hesitated.

'With my life, with my soul.'

Whether I had said the words or whether he read them in my own eyes, the statement had been made and lay between us. In that moment in the studio before we joined the rest—in just a fraction of a moment in time— something timeless and eternal had been created. A pact had been sealed in fire and blood, in love and death.

Or so I tried to tell myself afterwards. Though it was difficult to believe it, because after Rowan let my hand go everything changed once again. Normality returned, to such an extent that the last thing I could possibly have done was to make any mention at all about ghostly experiences and women with candelabra who stood on staircases on some dark seashore and shoved them in your face. It would have been as bizarre as asking Ted whether he intended to use the music of the spheres as background for our production.

Yet somehow I did not need to say any more, ask any questions. I did not need to know anything. The intensity of all that had been happening ebbed away like a kind of tide, time slowed down to the tick-tocking of clocks I recognised, and I caught up with myself where I had left off, as it were. About to plunge into the last few hectic weeks of term, behaving and thinking as I had always done, just an ordinary girl again, absorbed into the human dramas of everyday living in exactly the same way as everyone else. Ghostly dimensions simply faded into the background, I had difficulty relating to them. And I found that Rowan, who had recently been at my elbow quite a lot, on hand almost every time I turned round, suddenly faded into the wallpaper as well and became rather distant.

We hardly spoke privately, and he did not seek me out. In fact he always seemed to be some way away from me, across the studio or the room when we were working, leaving Buzz's just as my group was going in, or talking to someone else on the other side of the canteen. Strangely though, I did not mind. I knew he was there and that was enough. And when I did look at him or feel his eyes on me, there was unspoken communication between us, though exactly what was being communicated I wasn't sure.

I found myself content to let things be, remembering some words from the Book of Ecclesiastes that had always seemed overwhelmingly meaningful whenever I had heard them or read them—and as students of the theatre, we were well aware of the dramatic possibilities of the Old Testament. *To every thing there is a season, and a time to every purpose under the heaven.* There was a time to accept what you were handed out without question, not to start poking about for explanations. A time to keep your mouth shut and not query the *status quo*. A time to go with the flow, to let everything just happen and wait and see. Meanwhile, there were other things to think about.

*   *   *

One of them seemed to have taken care of itself because my intuition had been right about Opal-Ophelia. She had indeed apparently disappeared into thin air, or at least we were given no further sign of her. Loz actually took this quite badly, offended at such cavalier treatment of sensitive souls—mine as well as his own—but I pointed out that whether we had been victims of a designing woman or not, life was surely far less complicated for all of us without her. He soon saw the sense in this and cheered up.

It was difficult not to, as a distinctly hectic and festive atmosphere was frenetically building itself up everywhere. There's a lot of cheery yo-ho-ho and seasonal goodwill to enjoy in London, whatever kind of Christmas you are planning, and I was happy just to absorb it and indulge myself in the general sense of celebration, while also making the most of my magical first term at a Theatre School. On the social front there were innumerable parties and fun-times of all kinds—you know what students are like—and of course, I was going home to Staffordshire for Christmas.

Randy had a long-standing invitation to spend the holidays skiing in Austria with some cousins so she was also going to be away, but Loz had made no plans, and we began to worry about whether his gregarious soul might suffer if he was forced to spend a lonesome Yule. He had no near relations, his only connection was apparently a rather crusty and ancient Trustee with whom he had nothing in common, and though he enjoyed crowds, Loz took a long time before he would permit himself to get close to acquaintances.

He had spent the last Christmas as the guest of Randy's parents, when she carted him off for the festive season to their lovely Jacobean farmhouse in the depths of Norfolk. It hadn't, I gathered, been a great success. Loz had charmed Randy's people with his good looks and genuine eccentricity, but he himself had found life in the country something of a trial.

'You know Loz,' Randy shrugged when she was telling me about it. 'A brisk walk—especially in the rain—is his idea of Purgatory.'

'Having to wear ancient streaming

Barbours, green wellies and hiking boots Tania dear, struggling across miles of mud and manure,' Loz shuddered, wrinkling his nose at the memory and Randy smiled.

'You didn't take to the dogs either, as I recall. He spent a panic-stricken few hours having barricaded himself in the potting shed when Em and Rusty were trying to make friends.'

Loz went pink.

'I didn't know at that point that they were elderly and affectionate,' he said with dignity. 'They had very large teeth and I thought they were guard dogs. I am actually more of a cat person, as you know, Miranda.'

You can see why Randy and I were concerned about the prospect of Loz having to spend Christmas Day on his own. It would, we thought, simply not be fair on him. But one evening when we were discussing the problem, he revealed rather unwillingly that he had been invited to stay over Christmas with friends himself. He seemed particularly secretive and rather embarrassed about it and refused to give us any details—actually going so far as to accuse Randy in his prickliest manner of trying to interfere in his private life—so we backed off hastily and said no more.

'A lady, do you think?' Randy speculated afterwards, eyes gleaming. 'Honestly, Tania, Loz constantly surprises me.'

'I expect we'll hear all about it soon enough,' I said vaguely. I wasn't concentrating on Loz's holiday plans but my own, running my finger down the train timetable in preparation for booking my ticket to the Midlands.

'Well, at any rate we don't have to worry about him moping round the flat making heavy weather of it because he's been left on his own,' Randy said and went off to finalise arrangements with Sally, who lived on the floor above and had two cats of her own, for her to 'cat-sit' Dick and Turpin over the holiday period.

Rowan had actually disappeared without saying anything to me before the term officially ended. Louise (aka Queen-Gertrude-of-the-cleavage) told me—again rather smugly at having been let into his confidence—that he had gone back to Sheffield in a tearing hurry, summoned for further consultation about the fantastic job offer. I should have felt injured and disappointed—after all, I didn't even have a phone number where I could contact him— but strangely enough none of it seemed to matter. I had a distinct sense that things were being taken care of in ways I was not expected to comprehend. Though Rowan was not physically near me, I was very aware of his presence around.

And I was going home. It was in a mood of elated expectancy that I said goodbye to

Randy (who dropped me off at Euston) on a chilly December afternoon, and joined the crowds on the concourse to catch my train to the Midlands.

*   *   *

The very air was alive, keen as knives, the frost silvering the stars in the black sky. Hours later, I got out of the car that had met me at the station, lifting my head to look round and sniff the familiar smells of the countryside, lake and woods while Uncle Jack watched me, smiling. He had always driven me home whenever I had been away, and just the sight of his weather-beaten face could transform me into an excited child again even though I was grown up, actually qualified to drive myself now.

Uncle Jack was my great-uncle, Gran's elder brother, a large, quiet countryman with a presence that was immensely reassuring and strong. He rarely spoke at all, being more used to dealing with animals who didn't need socialising and polite chit-chat. He was in his seventies, his hair white but his eyes as bright and challenging as ever. He—and his silences —had been as much a part of my childhood as Gran, and in a way he had filled the role of grandfather for me (or even father to some extent, in place of my absent Dad) though he did not live with us.

There was a light in the porch, the familiar

mountain ash trees behind the house were black silhouettes limned against the dark, and all around was the hushed stillness of the deep winter countryside. Gran was there, framed in the brightly-lit doorway, her hands reaching out to me in welcome. Now I knew I was home. I left my bag for Uncle Jack to bring in and ran up the stone flags of the path, straight into her arms.

Confused impressions were tumbling through my mind. I was very tired, numbed by the hours on the train. The all-ways-challenged Rail Service had transported me safely to my destination, it was true, but in the end I had had to stand. So it had been in a crowded space that allowed just the width of my shoulders, leaning against the side of the train with eight or so of my fellow passengers, our luggage taking up all the available floor space, that I had passed the journey. And it had been very cold—the heating was playing up—and I had begun to feel light-headed long before I had arrived at the station to be rescued by Uncle Jack.

Once settled in the warmth of the 4x4 and on the road to Rudyard, my head grew even lighter. It seemed I was being whirled as though on a Russian sleigh, with bells tinkling ever so faintly, through the green depth of an eternal forest, evergreen on evergreen, to where Gran waited for me somewhere in this bitter starry darkness. And now, as we hugged each other and I felt her warm cheek against the cold skin of my face while the lights beckoned behind her, the refrain that ran insistently through my head was something I remembered fleetingly from my other life in London. Some of the students had sung it as part of the Elizabethan extravaganza, accompanied by viols.

Trip no further, pretty sweeting,
Journeys end in lovers' meeting.

But was I at the end of my journey? Somehow I seemed to sense, in the hush of the vaulted black sky that burned above me with stars from void to void gathered, waiting, that I had hardly even begun.

*   *   *

Staffordshire is a hospitable county. Relatives and friends came and went as though on some kind of conveyor belt of goodwill during the days leading up to Christmas, parcels and cards overflowing their tweed coated and sheepskin-gloved arms. Amid the glitter of golden bows and vivid holographic red and green wrapping paper, goodies and tissue-wrapped bottles, we seemed to be waving one carload away as the next arrived.

I made a shopping trip to Leek, our little market town set snugly in the folds of the high moorlands, where Christmas lights blazed and the Salvation Army band was energetically proclaiming Joy to the World. Feeling the breathless thrill of childhood again, I had lunch with Gran at the Swan, a black and white timbered Sixteenth Century hostelry that has a particularly interesting piece of history so far as I am concerned. Its yard was once the site of a theatre, the sort of inn-yard theatre where the carts of travelling players might well have rumbled in over the cobbles and drawn up in all their gaudiness and festivity, just as our own 'Players' carts' had recently drawn up in front of the Civic Hall. A real link with my pal Will Shakespeare, I feel, an ancient echo of the 'wooden O' at his famous Globe.

After our meal, I slipped across the street leaving Gran finishing her coffee and went into the grey-stone church of St Edward, whose battlemented tower was brightly gleaming in the sunlight against a vivid blue sky. This, one of the most joyous and accessible churches I know, was buzzing with activity, carols sweetly sounding like the voices of angels, ringing out and up to the wooden panels of the roof above the nave.

Some of the windows in all their glorious Pre-Raphaelite richness of colour are by William Morris—one a Burne-Jones—and the building houses priceless tapestry work that was patiently stitched by earlier ladies of the town. Like the woods and waters of Rudyard, I had always found something here that spoke to my soul, and though I couldn't of course reveal details to anyone else, I felt intuitively that after my encounter with Opal-Ophelia I very much needed this sort of communication.

Christmas Eve and Christmas Day were very traditional. Gran and I went to the midnight service and sang carols by candlelight. We shared our turkey and stuffing, pudding and mince pies with Uncle Jack and Auntie Bee (the widow of Gran's brother Theo) after making the rounds of all the other Aunties and Uncles to pay our usual Christmas calls. We drank sherry in a merrily festive atmosphere, pulled crackers, laughed and kissed under the mistletoe. We gathered round the piano and left the TV to stand silent while Uncle Rob gave a passionate—if rather off-key—rendering of 'Tit-willow' from *The Mikado*. He was as always accompanied by Auntie Pam, resplendently yellow-haired and bolster-bosomed (a positive Valkyrie from an earlier era), who plunged straightaway afterwards into something very complicated that crashed up and down the keyboard and was, needless to say, received with thunderous applause by her audience.

I was prevailed on to 'do a bit of your acting for us, duck'. So, knowing they expected something histrionic, I hammed up Ophelia's mad scene, at which everyone nodded sagely to each other and said it stood out a mile, there was no doubt about it, I was a natural for the stage, they'd said so all along and hadn't they been right?

It was all as familiar as it had ever been, the ghosts of Christmas Past and Christmas Present brightly reassuring amid the cheerfulness of long-established family tradition. But I could not kid myself and just sink back into it unthinkingly after the revelations I had had during the last few months in London and my encounter with Opal-Ophelia—not to mention what had happened between myself and Rowan (though exactly what *had* happened, I fell to wondering bemusedly whenever I thought about him).

Things would never be the same again. I was no longer the child who could be protected by the elders of my family, no longer the uncomplicated little girl who knew that what she experienced was real in the same way that it was real to everyone else. My realities were very different now, but it was not until I had come back home that I was able to appreciate just how vastly different both they and I myself had become. I found myself a stranger in a strange land even as I sat surrounded by the familiar faces I had known since babyhood.

Then my moment was presented to me. Gran and I were alone at last on Christmas Night. All the others had left, and everything was quiet except for the ponderous tick of the grandfather clock in the hall. Cheery celebratory clamour was for the moment stilled. My father's ritual phone call (from Houston, actually, he was currently working in Texas) had come and gone.

I knew this was the time when I must honour the task I had somehow been assigned, ask Gran for whatever help she could give me. I must enter that other dimension again, talk to her about the ghosts who had made themselves known to me: the phantom of my mother, the ghost of Gran herself and the young shade of her own mother, the slender girl in the lilac crepe dress. Those unexpected ghosts who had been with me on the dark and streaming seastrand and who were a part of what had happened to me there.

10

In fact it was easier to broach the subject than I had expected. Auntie Bee and Uncle Jack, who had spent the day with us, got to talking nostalgically about the 'old days' and Gran got out the big box of family photos I have mentioned before, the treasure chest that had helped to enliven many a rainy afternoon when I was a child. While Uncle Jack allowed himself the luxury of a nap, oblivious, Auntie

Bee and Gran reminisced about ancient wedding groups—from swing-time to Flower Power—and beamed mistily over wide-eyed tots in short trousers and unlikely bonnets and frills. (There was even one changeling in a long christening robe that was me!)

As they were absorbed in recalling long since 'hatches, matches and despatches', I rooted through the box for the picture of the lovers who had come to be so important to me and when I found it, put it carefully to one side until a more suitable moment should present itself. Now the moment had come. Gran and I were alone. I was free to pick up the photograph and study it more closely.

There she was, the girl in the lilac crepe dress, standing within the embrace of the young man with the laughing eyes. The postcard-sized picture was clumsily hand-tinted and I could see now that the girl's lips were too red, her hair too heavily darkened, this was an artificial image that held little of the vivid, quicksilver reality.

Thinking back to the evening when I had confronted Opal-Ophelia across the table in the restaurant, I could remember the girl clearly, remember what she had really looked like as she came towards me, spreading her hands wide in an effort to protect me. Flushed cheeks, soft skin, hair like gilt flower filaments as they caught the sun. I remembered her quick indrawn breaths, how she had been trembling when I took hold of her to push her to safety.

I found my grandmother was regarding me gravely, questioningly and I spoke at random, not knowing what prompted my choice of words.

'Gran, do you know anything about silver fishes? Have I ever had any? On jewellery, a brooch or something when I was a girl?'

There was silence for a moment, a long-drawn-out stillness.

Then Gran nodded very slightly as though resigned.

'You had better tell me what has happened,' she said quietly. 'Something has happened, hasn't it?—happened at last? I could tell as soon as I saw you, when Jack brought you home from the station.'

'So you do know about them then, these fishes or whatever they are?' I queried and she nodded again, looking down at her clasped hands. She gave a deep sigh before she spoke.

'I have wondered often when—if—it would happen to you, Tania. Your mother saw nothing, you see. It never touched her, though of course, perhaps later—she died so young—'

Well, I had it now from Gran's own lips. The truth. I suppose I had still had some kind of last-ditch hope that it might all turn out to be just a figment of my fevered imagination. Those visions and images of Scandinavian mythology—the wild seastrand, Odin and the terror of hanging from the tree, the shrieking and keening of lost souls in the wind—let's face it, the whole story was really insane. But here was Gran calmly confirming apparent impossibilities, and she was exactly the same solid, familiar person she had always been.

Or was she? As I looked at her now, I saw that it was not only I who had changed. There was a stranger looking back at me from behind my grandmother's eyes.

'*What is it?*' I could not help myself asking in a low, fierce whisper. I had gone ice cold and my skin was crawling. Not just because Gran knew exactly what I was talking about, but because in spite of her surface cool, this was something that frightened her, frightened her very badly.

'What is it? Gran, for heaven's sake, what?' I said again, and seeing my face she leaned forward and took my hands, holding them tightly.

'It's all right, Tania, I will explain in a moment. But first, what has happened to you that you wanted to tell me about?'

She was herself again, the brisk, no-nonsense Gran I had always known. So I told her the story, leaving nothing out except (for some reason I could not identify) my involvement with Rowan, which I would not have been able to explain anyway. It was quite a relief actually and I felt better—more in control, as it were—trying to put the whole thing into some sort of coherent narrative form.

I made it sound as brisk and matter-of-fact as I could. Loz's quest to discover himself, the letter from the Dominant Women that had edged him in the direction of witchcraft. How Opal-Ophelia had appeared on the scene. How she had come to the studio to find me and given me her invitation to dinner. Then I started to describe what had happened in the restaurant.

'We were just talking to each other—at first, anyway—though I can't remember what she said. I've tried Gran, but all I can recall is that she mentioned something about fishes—silver fishes.'

'Ah! Yes.' Gran drew a breath, her eyes distant. I was thinking back, concentrating.

'She said she knew I had these silver fishes because Loz had told her about them. Well, that was a lie of course. I've never had or worn anything that remotely resembled silver fishes, and even though Loz does take an interest in what Randy and I wear, I can't see any reason why he would want to discuss our jewellery with complete strangers.'

Gran's gaze sharpened again. Her hand tightened on mine. 'Go on.'

I took a deep breath, shaking my head.

'What can I say, Gran? It doesn't make any kind of sense. The story was that I fainted but I did not. I went to some place—was kind of transported—'

'Yes,' she said unexpectedly. 'I know. Tell me about the place.'

'Well, it was near the sea, I think. I could hear the waves. There were sea-caves. And Opal was standing on a great staircase carved out of the rock. Her dress—the one she had been wearing in the restaurant—was red, but somehow it had turned into a fantastic gown with a long train trailing and she was holding a candelabra. There might have been a candelabra in the restaurant, I can't remember, but the one she was holding was huge, with lots of lights flaring—I don't know where it had come from—'

'Yes,' Gran said again, quietly. I was beginning to speak less defensively now. I knew the story was ridiculous, that it couldn't possibly have happened and that any responsible doctor would probably insist I needed to be certified. But Gran was not laughing at me. She knew, she understood.

'Anyway, you were there too,' I told her. 'I don't know how, but you were there and so was Great-Gran—the girl in this picture. I've always thought she was with me somehow—kind of haunting me—but it was weird to see her there—see both of you. She was young, just like she is here but you were—well, you looked like a sort of ancient crone. Gran, have you known all along about this place, the cave?'

'Not the cave. No,' she said, choosing her words with care. 'I have not been there consciously. We were with you in spirit, I suppose. Something like that. I understand that magic is concerned with the will and the intent rather than actuality, and we would never have left you to face her—it—the woman—on your own.'

I stared. Gran talking about magic—will and intent—as though she was discussing the ingredients for a cake? And I'd thought I was the one she would think was crazy.

'You tried to protect me, both of you,' I said, reckless now. 'You and the girl in the lilac crepe dress—and that's how I'll always think of her, not as an ancestor, just as someone like myself. Young and lovely—because she *was*, Gran—'

There was a glimmer in my grandmother's eyes that might have been laughter or tears— or a mingling of both.

'I know, I know,' she breathed and suddenly I recollected that of course Gran had known her so well, this girl-woman. She had known her as her own young mother, toddled to her on baby legs, listened to her singing lullabies in the room in this very house that we called the 'old nursery'. I swallowed my emotion fiercely down.

'And she was brave, so brave,' I told her. 'She ran to stand in front of me, tried to shield me. But when I caught hold of her to pull her

201

to safety, I could feel her trembling and I knew she was terribly afraid.'

'Yes,' Gran said once again, quietly. I gave a little shrug.

'Well, the rest of what actually happened while we were in the restaurant or whatever it was, I can't remember. We said things, though I don't recollect what, but I know this woman Opal seemed to be speaking in some other voice, rough and kind of raspy. I was doing the same if it comes to that, screaming out words I didn't have any control over.' I stopped as one of those words swam suddenly into my consciousness. 'Ragnarok. We were talking about Ragnarok—'

Gran looked puzzled.

'It's the End of the World, apparently, the Scandinavian version. Like Doomsday,' I told her. 'And don't ask me what that's got to do with the price of fish Gran, because I don't have a clue. I've only just remembered that bit.' I made a gesture of exasperation. 'Anyway at the end, just before I really did black out— faint or whatever—she got furiously angry and she—pushed the candelabra into my face.'

I found it was still frightening to relive that moment, and I dug my fingers deep round my folded arms, hurting the muscles, glad of the momentary pain. It grounded me here in the quiet room with our familiar old chairs and the faded richness of the Turkey carpet I used to think was magic when I was a child. I

202

looked round at the polished little upright piano standing gleaming against the wall and the dark beams full of shadows overhead. Outside in the hall, the steady, reassuring ticking of the clock was like a heart beating, and I could hear tiny sounds beneath my conscious mind that told me the minute hand was coming up to the twelve. In a little while the clock would strike and chime the hour.

'The flames were very hot, I could feel the heat and smell my hair singeing,' I said, then gave a little shaky shrug. 'And after that I don't know what happened. That was it, Gran. Everything went black, as they say.'

I was trying to speak lightly but she must have heard the undertones in my voice.

'Tania,' she said, leaning forward. She took my hands and looked straight into my eyes. 'Tania, I think I am prouder of you at this moment than I have ever been. And I have something to show you.'

I tried to collect myself as she rose and went up the stairs, slowly because of her arthritis. I heard her moving about in her bedroom, and after a few minutes she came back with a small package in her hand. She handed to me, and as she did so the grandfather clock in the hall whirred and began to chime. Twelve times. It was twelve o'clock and Christmas Day was over.

Gran said 'Wait' as she turned to where the crystal glasses were set out by the door, and while the clock was still chiming she poured a drink for each of us. It was actually Auntie Rosalie's dandelion wine, which was far more potent than anything I had ever come across in the wicked metropolis, and was like swallowing liquid sunlight.

'There,' she said as she touched the edge of my glass with her own, and to my amazement her voice was low and fierce as I had never heard it before. 'They will not have it their way. We have our own strength, we will continue to defy them.'

When I looked questioningly at her she smiled a little wryly. 'All this is new to you Tania, yet it will not be for long. Now that, in the words of those who hunt, you have been blooded.'

I was even more surprised at this than at anything else that had been said in this fantastic conversation. Surprised to hear her use such a phrase, for Gran was an outspoken opponent of blood sports even though she came from a long line of country people who accepted and upheld the traditional ways of life.

'They must do as they see fit,' she used to say to me sometimes, when she had been admonished about her views. 'And I will do as I see fit. But I am no militant Tania, I believe all finds its own level in the end.'

Now she looked at me over her glass.

'Open the package,' she said quietly. 'They

are for you. This is the moment for you to have them.'

When I unwrapped the soft layers of old, worn tissue paper I saw she had given me what looked like a little pouch or bag. It was made of some kind of skin, very soft and supple to touch but obviously not new. In fact I was surprised to see when I held it out towards the light that it was actually worn quite dark with age and use, shabby and dirty.

I glanced at Gran questioningly and she nodded, so I upended the bag and tipped the contents out. Something hard and cold fell into my hand, spilling over onto my lap in a slithering heap.

*   *   *

The necklace was made from silver links intertwined with leaping creatures that looked vaguely like dolphins. The workmanship was crude yet there was something fine about it, something that set my heart pumping and stirred my blood.

'The fishes—the silver fishes?' I breathed, though I knew the answer. Even as I touched the links gently with the tip of my fingers, I could feel their power humming through to me like an electric charge, an ancient energy that only slept through the centuries and could never die.

Unless it was allowed to do so, murdered by

the crass stupidity of man, that would not recognise it or value it and sought only to use it for his own ends—

—and she who must hold the fishes and follow them across the vast worlds of water, the kingdom of Njord, and guide the lost mariners safely to land, must surrender herself to them as a servant of Njord and lose all sense of self, she must be no more and nothing save what they will make of her and do with her.

*   *   *

It was as though while I held the silver necklace I was in touch with voices that called across huge spaces of time, like picking up a radio signal. And I had my answers—or some of them, at any rate—about why I had been getting visions of the wild seacoast. For I was there again, and the voices were the ones I had heard keening in the wind, and I could feel the mist cold and clammy from the sea and see the ship on which I must disembark. The shadowy shapes of the men passed me as they went on board, their footsteps muffled on the sand, even the splashing of the water hardly there, merely a ripple in my consciousness like the ripples of a pebble thrown and spreading silently as I stood waiting, my cloak pulled tight about my shoulders and the silver fishes heavy on my breast—

206

With a great effort, I pulled myself back from the vision and opened my eyes to look across at Gran, as she sat in the warm, familiar room. She was watching me with a trace of anxiety.

'Gran, what is this necklace? It's—wonderful but terrifying,' I said dazedly. 'Where did it come from? It's more than just antique. It must be ancient, priceless—'

She nodded, settling herself more comfortably in her chair as though reassured.

'Now I will tell you what I know,' she said. 'The silver fishes are mine, by right and because they were given to me. Now they are yours. Keep them safely and if it is necessary, you too must pass them on to your successor.'

'My successor? You mean my grand-daughter—or daughter if I have one?' I asked, and she inclined her head.

'It has been with our family over many years, that necklace, though possibly not always. There must have been times of war—for instance—when it was passed on to successors who were not linked in blood but only in spirit.' She paused, as though once again choosing her words carefully.

'As to where it came from originally, I have no idea. I knew nothing about it until one day, when I was about your age—'

Eighteen—a significant age—the age of initiations and rites of passage—

'—I too found myself in conflict with this woman you have described, the one you call Opal. It was unexpected, frightening, the most frightening thing I have ever encountered and I was so terrified I thought I would die of it. Even now, I do not really understand what happened but somehow—without knowing what I was doing or why I was doing it—I stood up to her, stood in her way and barred her path to stop her. I had to, so that she could not achieve whatever it was she wanted to do. I knew in my heart that she must be stopped. No,' she interrupted, breaking off. 'Don't ask me why Tania, because I do not know the answers any more than you do. Only that some sense of the rightness of things told me she was ancient and evil and that I had to try with what strength I had to fight back.'

Whatever else I might have expected, it was not this. I stared at her incredulously.

'Gran, that's not possible. I mean, there's no way it could have been the same person. If you met some woman when you were eighteen she would be at least your age now, and the woman I'm talking about—Opal, the one Loz introduced us to—she can't be more than thirty at the most.'

Gran was nodding in agreement but the bright intelligence in her eyes was disagreeing too.

'It doesn't seem possible I know, but as soon

as you described her I knew it was the same person. I recognised her—and you have to understand that not only I but my mother also encountered her. I didn't understand it then and I don't understand it now, but—' She indicated the box of photographs. '—your great-grandmother, the girl in the picture, yes, she had a similar experience. It happened when she was about eighteen too, she said, so that takes us right back to what, somewhere like the Nineteen Forties. I told her, just as you are telling me, that it couldn't possibly have been the same woman. And just as I am doing with you, she recognised her and swore it was, even though the description was slightly different. So I have come to the conclusion that she—this woman—is probably not a woman at all.'

I found laughter suddenly bubbling up inside me like a wellspring, healing, cleansing laughter that swept the last remnants of my fear of Opal-Ophelia away. How was I ever going to be able to take her seriously after this?

'Sorry, Gran. I'm not laughing at you, but this whole business has got to be a joke. I saw practically all of Opal in the most clingy dress you can imagine—and Loz apparently saw her 'sky-clad' as well, a sight that all but sent him into orbit. I think I'd have been able to tell— and I'm sure Loz would have—if she was actually a man in drag!'

209

Gran was smiling too, but her eyes were vague and unfocussed as she stared back into the past.

'An interesting thought, in many ways. But it is not her physical presence I mean.'

'No, of course,' I apologised quickly again. 'Sorry.'

'Because after all,' Gran added, 'she must be able to change her physical appearance. It's not your description of her hair and face I recognise—and it wasn't the physical description my mother recognised either. It's something else—her essence—her being—not who she is but what she is— Or he—or it—'

Loki was the child of the giant Farbauti. He was in appearance pleasing, handsome and witty but in his character evil, and capricious in his behaviour . . . Mischief and chaos were his delight and he could change his shape so that he might appear variously in any form: as an animal—a mare, a flea, a fly, a falcon or a seal—or else as an old crone or whatever would best suit his purpose and work his sinister designs . . .

'A shapeshifter,' I said involuntarily, the word coming as it had done before from some hidden store of knowledge deep within my mind. I added randomly: 'She's supposed to be a witch, though, you know. Opal I mean. Would witchcraft account for it? Could she change her appearance with spells or whatever they do?'

Gran did not answer straight away, but as she got up and refilled our glasses she told me with a little mischievous smile that surprised me: 'Possibly Tania, but I don't think it would work in the way you mean. You have never been aware of it but I know something of witchcraft, for there have always been the witches and the wise women in country places. The people needed their skill and reassurance, times when life was hard, when plague and pestilence stalked the land and their lords and far-off politicians fought among themselves and cared nothing for the poor and the suffering.'

'Oh, right,' I said, beyond surprise now. It seemed as though on this most magical of nights, in the magical hour behind the chimes of midnight, with the ancient silver fishes held tightly in my hands and Gran revealing things about herself that I had never dreamed or imagined, anything was possible.

Mentally I was reeling with sheer amazement at the nature of the secrets that were coming out, and I could feel the ghosts all around, crowding close. Holding me up, I thought practically. I was glad of their company. They were on my side, I knew that now more than ever. They were wishing me well, lending me their strength.

'Witchcraft is a celebration of life,' Gran's

voice said quietly. 'And there is no way this woman, whoever she is, can claim to play a positive part in that.'

'She took Loz to the coven meeting, though,' I reminded her dubiously and she gave a little shrug.

'Ah, but did she? You say he advertised for a witch, a coven or something of the sort and she responded. She could have claimed to be anything, but the only thing we seem to have really established about her is that she must be very proficient in delusion. With hypnotic ability she could convince her victims that anything she wanted them to believe was real or had happened.'

'That's true,' I said thoughtfully. I had never considered that as a possibility before and it opened up all sorts of new potentialities. 'So maybe Loz only thought he'd been to the meeting and she conned him. He actually never went anywhere with her at all.'

'I know there are covens in London, but no genuine worshippers of the Goddess would welcome the rottenness and evil that this woman embodies,' Gran said with quiet authority. 'In spite of her undoubted power.'

'What are you suggesting then, Gran?' I asked after a moment. 'If Loz never went anywhere and it was all in his mind, is that what you think happened to me as well? She just put me into a trance—or whatever—and I simply imagined the sea-caves and—all

212

the rest?'

Like the Haunted Ballroom, perhaps, in my dream? I had a sudden vivid recollection of the stifling heat and terror I had experienced as I stood on the great staircase in the ballroom and the masked dancers with their bestial bodies, their towering antlers and acrid panting breaths closed in on me. I had been on the point of collapse before Rowan's voice had saved me.

Perhaps that is why they are so necessary, he'd said.

Yes, I had forgotten that the grim secrets of myth had to be there to remind us to step carefully through the world. To enable us to face up to what we thought we could not take. Of course, everything could be explained away symbolically if you just sat down and thought about it enough. The sense of relief and release was such a physical thing I found myself laughing as my psychiatric persona, which had taken a bit of a back seat since I had started concentrating on the ghostly aspect of things, clicked efficiently into action.

'I've got it, Gran. This whole thing must have been created in our subconscious, Loz's and mine—and maybe even Randy's as well, since she actually claimed to see Opal-Ophelia. Because Opal isn't really a woman, you're right. She's nothing but a projection (that's the psychological term)—a projection of our deepest hidden fears about the problems of living and relating to other people. It all makes sense if you look at it like that. Loz is afraid of women dominating him— I'm afraid of growing up, taking on responsibility—I had a dream about it a few weeks ago. And maybe,' I added, inspired. 'Maybe that was what happened to you too, and to my Great-Gran. You each projected your fears so maybe that's why you saw her. If she doesn't actually exist.'

There was a long pause. I looked hopefully at Gran and she looked back at me. She said nothing and after a while I took a deep breath, bending my head to the links of the silver fishes gleaming dull in my hands.

'No,' Gran agreed, as though I had spoken. 'It is not as simple or as easy as that, Tania. This woman—or whatever she is—is unfortunately very real.'

'Like a sort of ghost, you mean?' I hazarded. 'Are we clairvoyants in our family then? Is that what it is? Are we psychics? Do we see things?'

Gran sat for a few moments gathering her thoughts. It was late and I was beginning to feel weary—particularly at the revelations of the past hour, which were far more staggering than I could have invented in my wildest dreams. Even the enterprising Ted and the fertile mental processes that had allowed him to practically reconstruct every aspect of *Hamlet* would, I thought, have been hard put

214

to beat the tale emerging from my previously eminently sane Gran.

I looked at her with new eyes. I had always loved Gran, respected her for the steadiness and security she seemed to represent in a world that was filled with those difficult 'other people'; the ones who seemed to lack the tolerance she so abundantly granted towards me. Her particular qualities as the person who had brought me up, were what had made it possible for me to grow and be the person I was intended to be, without being either pressured or stifled through outside interference.

But tonight I realised that as well as hardly knowing myself before, I had never really known her either, never appreciated the true worth of my grandmother. I had never been as aware as I was at this moment how blessed I had been to have her as my mentor and friend.

She must have been as tired as I was but somehow I didn't even consider mentioning it. I felt as though she was relieved, glad to be able at last to share what must have been the awesome weight of knowledge that she had carried in silence over nearly half a century. And with this realisation came the awareness too that there was no time to spare. I needed to know everything she could tell me for she was looking to me now, trusting me to take the burdens from her. Trusting me to resolve the dark mysteries she had been unable to resolve for herself.

11

'I don't think our family is clairvoyant as such,' Gran said slowly. 'I am not, and your mother was certainly never affected by this strange woman. She never 'saw' anything of the sort you have described. But you—well, you are different, Tania, and I think perhaps you realise that and know more about it than I do.'

I bowed my head, accepting the wisdom of her words.

'Yes, I know what you are saying. I understand,' I admitted quietly. She did not press for details but carried on, trying to find the right words.

'These are not ghosts in the conventional sense, what we have seen. Opal—or whatever this woman's true name is—and whoever she—or he—is in reality must I think be some kind of spirit that takes on a human form when it has a particular purpose in mind. There was a poem, by Keats I think called *Lamia*, I remember it from my schooldays. That was about such a woman—or such a creature—and it made a great impression on me as a young girl.'

'A bit like *La Belle Dame Sans Merci*?' I queried, and quoted the first lines in a suitably hollow tone.

'Oh what can ail thee, Knight at Arms,
Alone and palely loitering?
The sedge is withered from the lake
And no birds sing—'

'Ah, yes. *"La Belle Dame sans Merci has me in thrall",'* Gran repeated with quick understanding. 'Very much like that, I suppose. For we're talking about magic here, Tania. Enchantment.'

As I looked at her face in the warm light, shadows gathering softly behind her head, I saw them again, the phantoms: the girl in the lilac crepe dress with her fair hair and rose-petal skin, the ancient crone with wisdom shining jewel-bright in her piercing eyes. Just a glimpse and they were gone. I did not think Gran was aware of them but once more I was reassured. I was not alone.

'After my own experience I tried to find out more,' she continued. 'There are many creatures of that kind, spirits that can materialise in different forms from time to time. Some of them are extremely destructive. They are mentioned in folk lore and myth.'

'Like—the Amazons?' I hazarded seriously, picking up my glass. Maybe Loz's fear of Dominant Women and even Randy's teasing might still be very relevant. 'The Valkyries?'

Even as I spoke, a flicker of some thrilling shiver like a mild electric shock went through me. My mind made a series of leaps. The

Valkyries. They figured in operas about the *Gotterdammerung*, didn't they?—the Twilight of the Gods. And the *Gotterdammerung* was the same as Doomsday, the End of the World, I had it on the authority of Sven A. DeWitte and he ought to know. And Doomsday, the End of the World, was Ragnarok in Scandinavian myth.

Inescapable conclusion: there had to be a significant connection here.

'Well,' Gran said energetically 'something like the Valkyries I suppose, though I'm not an expert on destructive entities or beings. The one thing I did find out is that there are far more of these unseen spirits around than most people think. Although I understand psychiatrists are inclined to account for their activities by explaining everything away as proceeding from our own psyches. As you so rightly pointed out.'

She smiled and a little ruefully, I smiled back.

'I think the truest wisdom is to be able to accept truth when you encounter it, Tania. If nothing else, you will have learned this tonight.'

'What happened to you, when you met Opal?' I queried. My glass was empty. I was holding the necklace of silver fishes in my hands again. It seemed passive, still now, as though the power was held in check. Already I knew I would not part with it for the world, that somehow I had always been meant to hold the links in my hands. They belonged there, they fitted. And when the time came I would know what to do with them.

'I never actually met her,' said Gran, thinking back. 'She just—one day—it was in the woods, not actually on my eighteenth birthday but a few days after, and high summer—'

'Yes?' I prompted.

'She was just there, walking. It all seems so far away now. I was ill afterwards, you see, or the family thought I was ill, for days. Raving, delirious.'

'Heavens!' I said, the hair on the back of my neck standing up uncomfortably as a shiver went down my spine. I knew what it had felt like to stand in Opal-Ophelia's path.

'I don't remember what she said or what I answered.' Gran was frowning with the effort of recollection. ' Except that, like you, I knew I had to stand up to her. And in the same way you say you saw me in the caves, trying to protect you—'

'Yes?' I breathed.

'I saw my mother in the vision with me, and it was she who was trying to save me from—from—Them—' Her voice trailed off. It had started to shake.

'From who, Gran?' I did not like this, but I had to know.

She shook her head apologetically.

'I'm sorry, Tania. I am not as brave as you think. Even now I find it difficult. The terror was too great. There were hordes of wild creatures with her in the woods—creatures with animal faces—and she was leading them down through the rides and the avenues—' She swallowed, making a great effort. 'Not real rides and avenues, of course. The woods had changed to a great expanse of forest with no end and no escape— I tried to run and I could not. And she—this woman—she was at their head, leading them. She had great antlers— and there were giants stalking me through the trees, and the howling of the beasts for blood was something I shall never forget—'

'Gran!' My mouth had gone dry and I was cold, the chills rising uncomfortably up the back of my legs and spine, lifting the hairs on my scalp. I had seen those wild creatures too, the beasts with their antlers. I had heard them howling for blood as I stood on the stairs of the Haunted Ballroom.

I went across to kneel beside her, letting the silver fishes fall to form a dully mercurial pool on the carpet. Her fingers were trembling, and I rubbed them comfortingly. 'It's all right, it's over now,' I told her. 'It's all over. She can't hurt you.'

'But it isn't over, that is the trouble,' she said in a low, strained voice. The way she was gripping my hands frightened me. Gran had always been the strong one, the independent

220

one. I had always been the child who tried not to cling. 'It is not finished yet Tania, not resolved. Oh, she left me alone in the end, and I recovered from the fever and the delirium. But when I asked Mother what I had seen— where I had been—she told me what I am going to tell you now. It was what her mother had told her, the explanation given to her, when she had seen the evil woman herself as a young girl—'

'Yes, Gran?' Well, here it came. I might as well know the worst, I thought.

'It is the fishes you see, the silver fishes,' Gran said, still a little shakily but I was glad to hear the strength coming back to her voice. I picked up her glass and gave it to her, made her take a few sips. She continued after a moment in a much steadier tone: 'The fishes have been passed down over the centuries— Mother could not tell me how many centuries—nor where they originally came from—but they are passed on Tania, they are the mark of the one who has been chosen.'

'Ah—chosen?'

'One is chosen in each generation to carry the gift. Sometimes the gift is weak—it was weak in me and it was weak in Mother, so all that we could do was to block this woman, block her path—'

'Gran,' I said carefully. 'I don't quite follow you, darling. Can you be a little more specific?'

She drew a deep breath.

'Someone has to do it, someone has to carry the responsibility and the power,' she said.

And suddenly I did not need to hear another word. I could see, as though a light had been switched on, the explanation for many of the things I had known without being told, the things I had been only half-aware of consciously but had taken for granted in the hidden depths of my mind. Oh, I had joked with Randy about how I had been instilled with the conviction I was set apart in some way, marked by destiny, but Gran had known all along it was a deadly serious matter. She had known I might be needed. And in the best way she could, she had prepared me, made sure that if—when—the time came, I would be ready.

'Let's get this straight. You mean the power as in being able to see things?' I queried. 'See ghosts, Gran?'

'No. This is the power embodied in the fishes. For the fishes—the silver fishes—are the symbol of office Tania, the mark of the one who has been called—'

I had a father then, and a mother. I had a name to which I answered. But I forgot them, forgot them all, forgot my name and my family and my tribe after Nerthus reached out to touch me . . .
When great Nerthus touched me and named me as her daughter all was said. I was hers and I had always been hers, like the hound who known

222

his master but knows not the how of it . . .

'Gran,' I said, letting the images come from my inward knowledge in the voices of the ghosts. 'Do you know the name of Nerthus? Of Loki? Of Njord and Odin? Do you remember the seashore with the hanging tree, and the sounds of the lost souls? And the ship about to sail, and the men with their furs passing like wraiths in the mist, and standing on the wet sand holding the silver fishes in your hands and feeling them leap and pulse, alive?'

Gran turned and stared for a long moment into my eyes. She had suddenly become very still.

'Oh, Tania,' she said breathlessly.

'Do you, Gran?'

'No. Nothing.'

We looked at each other.

'I think—I used to think it was you,' I said, feeling my way. 'But—it isn't you, is it Gran? It is me who has this power. Whether I want it or not.'

'Both Mother and I knew we were only the keepers, the guardians,' she said quietly. 'Mother had been given the fishes by a very old lady, a distant aunt she met only once, who told her she recognised her as a successor. But neither of us was strong enough, Tania. We knew that. I wondered whether my daughter— But it was not to be, it was you, my daughter's

223

daughter, you who were the true Chosen One.'

I was too overwhelmed to speak.

'Mother had no more idea than I of what she had seen,' Gran went on. 'She told me that for her, the encounter had taken the form of a sea-battle. It had happened when she was on holiday with her parents—my great-grandparents—somewhere on the Welsh Coast, I think. The Opal woman—or whoever, whatever she is—had been standing in a sort of open boat filled with armed warriors. They had swords, axes and shields and wore helmets with horns. And she said the vessel had a striped sail and a high prow.'

As I listened to Gran's words, something that was both alien and yet familiar seemed to grip my consciousness. As though I looked into another world yet knew it, for I had been there before.

'Vikings?' I hazarded slowly.

'That was what I thought too,' said Gran. 'It may be a clue. You mentioned Odin—Loki— Aren't those the names of Viking gods?'

I thought for a moment. Ted's seminars about the history of Denmark were proving more useful than he had ever dreamed in all sorts of unexpected ways.

'The Viking era didn't start until about the Eighth Century,' I told her. 'Give or take a century either way. But I asked one of the students about the Scandinavian myths, and they date from much earlier—Odin and Loki and all that do, I mean. The myths about Ragnarok too. But like I said, I have no idea at all what Ragnarok has got to do with me—with us.'

Gran met my gaze, looking tired now. Very slowly, she shook her head.

*   *   *

I asked one of the students—

But it had not been just any one of the students, had it? It had been Rowan. I was still no nearer to really understanding what had happened between myself and Rowan than I had been the first time his presence and his voice bewitched me in Buzz's, but I knew as I struggled in my sleep that night with the echoes that haunted me from those other times and other existences, that I needed Rowan more than I had ever needed anyone before in my life.

For Rowan was my lodestone, my guiding star. He had come to my rescue in the sea-caves, he had laughed me out of the chill spell cast by Opal-Ophelia in the studio. He had the answers, the knowledge. He was wise, he would instruct me, he would advise me. More than anything else though, I was aware as I lay there alone in the darkness that all these were only excuses for what was really tormenting me.

I hardly knew Rowan, when you came to

think about it. I had no idea of whether I was in love with him or not. But my whole being—mind, body and soul—simply ached for him now. Rowan himself. His physical presence. The feel of his arms, the touch of his lips. Without him there was a rent in the fabric of existence, a great gaping void, a hole in reality and no-one else would ever be able to fill it.

With the silver fishes beneath my pillow and the phantom voices drifting uneasily across limitless time and space, I sent out a call from my heart. A prayer, I suppose you would say it was.

'Whoever you are, wherever you are . . .'

. . . Njord, god of the wind and the sea . . . consort of Nerthus, who was the great Earth Mother . . .

*   *   *

And again I was standing on the wild seacoast . . . and the voices were the ones I had heard keening in the wind and I could feel the mist cold and clammy from the sea and see the ship on which I must disembark. The shadowy shapes of the men passed me as they went on board, their footsteps muffled on the sand, even the splashing of the water hardly there, merely a ripple in my consciousness . . . I stood waiting, my cloak pulled tight about my shoulders and the silver fishes heavy on my breast . . .

. . . she who must hold the fishes and follow them across the vast worlds of water, the kingdom of Njord, and guide the lost mariners safely to land, must surrender herself to them as a servant of Njord and lose all sense of self . . .

. . . For so it was, so it had always been. I was hers and I had always been hers, like the hound who knows his master but knows not the how of it . . .

. . . I had always been hers . . .

. . . I had always been theirs . . .

*   *   *

Strangely comforted and at peace, I slept dreamlessly at last and woke to pristine brightness of a winter morning, my mind clear of all hesitations and delusions. I had no more need to try to understand any of them. Those visions about a destiny of being hounded by strange women—or at least, a strange woman, who was not actually a woman at all. A creature seemingly ageless, who had been pursuing us down the years with her band of warriors, her herd of giants and monstrous beasts, her red gown and her lighted candelabra. Somebody who was probably actually one of the ancient gods of Scandinavian myth—

I didn't have to worry any further about making sense of any of it. Making sense that other people would understand. It was enough that I had found myself at last, found who I was and what I was. Even though I could not really make any sense other people would understand of any of that either.

I dressed warmly in jeans and a sweater, my hair (still in the Player Queen's Minoan crimps, actually, which I had rather taken a fancy to) providing a warm splash of colour against the pale light of the day. And then, quickly making my bed—which meant giving the duvet a shake and plumping the pillow—I picked up the ancient skin pouch that held the silver fishes. They were what validated it all, everything Gran had said, everything I had always known intuitively. They were the symbol, the mark of the Chosen One, the one who had been called.

The hard shape of the necklace in my hands reassured me that this was no dream, no tale to while away the ghosts of Christmas around the fire with mulled wine and sweetmeats. I could feel the energies stirring, the power passing into my fingers. It was awesome. Impelled by some sense of the rightness of the gesture, I took the necklace from the bag and put it slowly and deliberately round my own neck as I stood for a long moment by my window.

I looked out at the familiar landscape of lake and trees, hardly seeing them. Yes, I had been given the freedom to choose. I could have refused to accept the role I had to play in the drama that was unfolding, whatever it was to be. And I was aware that one part of me was shaking cravenly, wishing I had turned and run as far from it as I could. After what had happened in the restaurant and what Gran had told me, I did not relish the prospect of crossing swords with Opal-Ophelia—whoever or whatever she was—again.

I wasn't sure I could cope. I didn't want to know the secrets that bubbled in those deep realms below the surface of reality where the dark things and nameless creatures slithered and entwined in bubbling mud and slime. For a moment while I stood there tensely my heart failed the thought of what might lie ahead. I had tested the strength and power of my enemy, and even as I tried to summon strength from within myself I was cowering, cringing, covering my eyes.

Then I thought of the girl in the lilac crepe dress—and Gran—and of how they had tried to protect me. They had been trembling even as they had stood in Opal-Ophelia's path, and the thought of their fear and their gallantry shamed me. I lifted my hand to touch the silver fishes and bent my head as though I was swearing a solemn oath, making a vow.

I would carry this burden. I would do it. For it was mine, and I could not ask anyone else to carry it for me. Even if they were willing, they did not have the strength. I was the Chosen

One. It was I who had been called to tread the dark realms in order to bring light to them, I who must drive out the things and the creatures in order to make the way safe for those who trod fearfully behind me.

As I touched the silver, drawing on the fishes for courage, I prayed to whatever gods ruled them—and through them, ruled me now—for the strength I would need. I had been called, I was the Chosen One. Everything depended on me.

'I'm a poor example for you to follow, Tania,' Gran had sighed at last, as we rose to go to bed. 'I never took any action after the hallucination—the fever—left me and the woman went, I was too afraid. A little literary work in the safety of the library, investigating the stories of the Lamia and so on, but I never tried to stand up to her again or put the silver fishes to their proper use, whatever that may be.'

'Gran, you were heroic,' I told her, touched.

The hero figures of our culture—we may not recognise the truly heroic—

'You fought for me and I will always be grateful to you for that. And to Great-Gran—though like I say, I still can't think of her as anything else but a young girl.'

'She was afraid too, I know,' Gran said. 'She told me what she could, but then I suppose we

230

both just waited, glad to be left alone. I wondered when—if—your mother would tell me she had discovered she possessed the Sight, but she never did so I could not pass the fishes on until now, and to you.' Suddenly sounding old and tired, she touched my hair as though blessing me:

'The fishes hold the power, Tania. Use them well.'

*   *   *

And so here I was in the frosty red morning of a Christmas card Boxing Day walking alone by the lake, one of my favourite places always, but particularly blessed in this hushed silence of mid-winter.

In London, as winter advanced, the view through the long windows of the flat had looked startlingly stage-Gothic: the urns on the terrace outside were draped in mist like cobwebs, the stems of the flowers skeletal and bare, as though they belonged in some desolate, haunted landscape. But here the leafless trees were old friends I had always known, softening the slope of the hills on either side of the lake. The rimed fields curved reassuringly. And the air was filled with birdsong. I could hear robins calling bravely and the chattering of a magpie.

The summer boats had vanished. The café was closed, the new Visitors' Centre deserted.

There was ice on the surface of the water and the ducks were walking flat-footed on it, a large Muscovy duck colourful among a group of mallards. Seagulls wheeling around them, screaming thin and high, and in spite of myself I found stage-Gothic melancholy starting to creep in even here. Weren't the cries of seabirds supposed to be the voices of drowned sailors?

I could feel the mist cold and clammy from the sea and see the ship on which I must disembark. The shadowy shapes of the men passed me as they went on board, their footsteps muffled on the sand, even the splashing of the water hardly there, merely a ripple in my consciousness . . . I stood waiting, my cloak pulled tight about my shoulders and the silver fishes heavy on my breast . . .

I dug my fists deeper into the pockets of my coat, and strode out briskly along the dark, flat curve of the Dam that marks the end of the lake. It was all very well submitting myself to some antique destiny, being prepared to venture into dark realms and fight for the light, but you couldn't get a lot of change out of that sort of thing in the real world. I had to be practical, avoid flights of fantasy, make sure I kept my feet firmly on the ground. Proceed on the facts.

So, Scandinavian myths, right. Well, what

did I know of the story so far, as it had been revealed to me and from what Gran had told me? I ran through a mental list.

Not only was some kind of sacrifice involved here, but Odin, the 'supreme divinity of the main group of Norse gods called the Aesir', appeared to figure quite largely himself in a sacrificial connection. So, point one: Was the sacrifice something that was going to have to be made to Odin or (as Rowan had quoted to me) was this the same sacrifice Odin had made himself, hanging upside down from the Tree of Life in order to discover the secret of wisdom?

Query: Just because I kept having visions and memories about hanging upside down from a tree, and was conscious of having made some sort of sacrificial surrender myself, did that mean I was getting wiser?

Next question.

Yet it was peaceful there beside the lake. I watched the ducks, who had nothing more complicated to worry about than how to manipulate their beaks through the ice into the water below slithering busily round in circles, as I pushed the deductive process a little bit further.

For instance, we knew now that Opal-Ophelia, the embodiment of the enemy, wasn't really a woman at all. She didn't exist. She was, you might say, just a figment of our subjective imaginations. No flat in Pimlico, no theatrical agent or big wheel in Fine Arts. Just an illusion conjured up, to vanish like the Bad Fairy in pantomime in a crackle of flash powder.

Right. But there was definitely an enemy. So if it wasn't Opal-Ophelia—and you could forget the impressive coincidence of that name, she had simply invented a connection with *Hamlet* and Shakespeare's pathetic heroine as a way of ingratiating herself with us—but if it wasn't a woman called Opal-Ophelia, who or what were we really dealing with here?

. . . in appearance pleasing, handsome and witty but in his character evil . . . cunning beyond all the gods, a liar, a scandal-monger, a trickster . . .
. . . he could change his shape so that he might appear variously in any form: as an animal—a mare, a flea, a fly, a falcon or a seal—or else as an old crone . . .

. . . or as a fiendish and devastating woman? Dark spiky hair, voluptuous figure, glistening red lips . . . ?

As simply as that, I faced the enemy with the mask plucked away. The Shape-shifter. Loki, the 'companion of the gods' who represented chaos and mischief and the dark. Who could turn himself into whatever form would best suit his purpose and work his sinister designs.

And somehow Rowan had known. He had known enough to actually warn me. I could hear his voice now, just as I had heard it when we first talked about the Scandinavian myths and legends in Buzz's, low and intense, vibrant with entreaty. Except that in my bemused and dazzled state, lost in those coloured lights and silken sensations that were drowning me in enchantment, I had not realised he was talking about Loki.

Whatever form he takes, do not trust him. Do not trust him.

*   *   *

So now at last, Rowan. I held on to Rowan in my mind. Partly because I did not have the courage yet to look the shadowy form of the Shapeshifter in the eyes, but mainly because I was drawn irresistibly as fate, always now, to the image of Rowan as my rock, my safe place, the overwhelming source of my empowerment. He could warn, he could protect, he had been able to follow me to the sea-caves and bring me back from those lost realms of thundering darkness.

So who was Rowan, really? Rowan of the Edinburgh childhood in his book-strewn, eccentric family home? Rowan of the dancer's disciplined body and fencer's quick-silver agility of mind? Rowan whose silence and restraint had left me to discover my own

235

strength and laughed me through the terror of considering that I might fail?

I watched the circling seagulls as I considered. Throwing all mental caution to the winds, jumping in with both feet as it were, I faced it—he had to be one of the other characters in the drama, didn't he? There was some sort of connection both with the mysterious Nerthus and her consort Njord, who had kept kept appearing in my visions. Well, Rowan obviously wasn't Nerthus the great Earth Mother—no way, nothing was going to make me believe that—so we were left with Njord, god of the wind and the sea— who might or might not—unless I was very much mistaken—

*　　　*　　　*

Look at it like this Randy, I tried to imagine myself pointing out casually. If I'm the Chosen One, and Gran and my great-grandmother and I have all been given starring roles in some sort of cosmic drama involving gods and heroes (or heroines, in our case) then why not cast Rowan too? Let's go for it and give him the male lead, Njord, god of the wind and sea?

Because the one thing I'm certain about Randy, and I've always been certain about even though people would have thought I was completely crazy if I had mentioned it, is that Rowan is, as they say, no ordinary mortal.

Okay, right, Randy would reply without turning a hair. So you're all really incarnations from some ancient story in Scandinavian myth, fine by me. The point is though Tania, the big question is, now you've sorted all that out, where exactly do we go from here?

I walked slowly along the side of the lake, hands in my pockets, head down, hardly seeing the twinkling Christmas lights on the houses clustered down the opposite hillside. Beyond them, high against the sky and on the periphery of my vision, dark masses of cypress and yew sounded a funereal note that slowed my thoughts.

I suppose I had expected to encounter some intensified form of the images I had always associated with home. The elemental spirits of the lake and the woodlands. The ghostly dancers in their faded finery treading the measures of long-gone Assembly Balls, the shadowy villagers celebrating midsummer with their flutes and bells, the cold, strange harmonies echoing across shrouded tracery in the snow—but where were they? There was nothing here for me on this morning when more than ever I needed advice, assistance. All was still, frozen beneath a spell of deepest enchantment—

'*The sedge is withered from the lake, and no birds sing,*' I found myself quoting aloud, shivering in spite of myself. Even the robins were silent, but further down the lake I saw the shadow of a kestrel rise against the sky, turning into the low red sun. And then suddenly, startling me, breaking the spell, the mobile phone in the pocket of my coat rang.

12

Sally's voice brought London and the flat and my other life into sharp focus. The mysterious world of sable and light shadows and silence around me withdrew into itself. I was about to wish her the usual chirpy compliments of the season, but she wasn't listening and she cut me short, though it didn't sound like her usual brisk, sergeant-major tones. I thought at first the battery needed charging, then I realised her voice was less steady than usual. Or was it because it was so determinedly matter-of-fact, that I knew something had to be wrong?

'Tania? Is that you?'

'What is it, Sally? Has something happened?'

I could not imagine what might have upset her so much. Nothing ever upset Sally. I had never known her to be anything but stolid and laid-back.

'I don't know how to tell you. Rather painful news for the holiday, I'm afraid but you'll need to know.' She paused, then said: 'It's Loz.'

'Is he ill?' I asked.

I knew this had to be bad. Even if Loz had been dying it would not have accounted for the odd note in Sally's voice that was sending feathers of ice from my feet to my neck and making the very skin on my head prickle warningly. I tried to speak as normally, as casually as I could. I did not want whatever was coming. 'Is he home? I thought he was staying with some friends.'

'Well, he may have been but he certainly came home late last night—to the flat, I mean. And he must have had a kind of fit or something, I really can't begin to imagine what brought it on, but he sort of went berserk and tried to smash the place up—'

'Loz did?' This was beyond even my powers of imagination.

'Yes,' said Sally. 'He made such a noise that people heard him and called the police—'

'What?' Not only beyond imagination, this was beyond the bounds of all credibility.

'It's not as bad as it might have been. There's not a lot of damage,' she said in what should have sounded reassuring tones, but in fact only chilled me even more. 'A few cups and plates, really, were the only actual breakages but he'd thrown around some of the stuff in the fridge and it was all rather a mess. The police managed to stop him before he'd had time to do much real harm. But that— well—' Suddenly her voice cracked, and I heard naked emotion. 'That's not really what I wanted to tell you—'

'Oh, God, Sally. What? What?' I was really frightened now.

'The worst thing—the awful thing—and I've absolutely no idea at all what made him do it Tania, but—' Again her voice broke and this time I just waited, making no effort to prompt her. My mouth was so dry I did not think I could have spoken, and after a few painful seconds she made an effort.

'He killed the cats,' she told me, low and unforgiving. 'He killed them. Both of them. Dick and Turpin. With a knife.'

I went completely cold. I could not speak for a moment. This was something beyond horror. I could not accept it and I could tell from the shock and grief in Sally's voice that she felt the same.

'It's true,' she said, sounding very tired. 'I'm sorry, Tania.'

*   *   *

So I had asked where we were to go from here, thrown the question out like a challenge into the ether and I had been given my answer. In the fraction of a second before I could even draw breath to speak to Sally, I travelled endless journeys into uncharted worlds, spun through aeons of time. I saw all and knew all— and then the knowledge broke away like spinning balls in the hands of a juggler, leaving me empty.

In that instant I looked into the face of the Shapeshifter, I saw and knew the dark countenance that blazed back at me. In that moment I recognised and acknowledged the enemy even as I made my own statement of defiance.

Something momentous, something cataclysmic had happened even before I was aware of it. I had, as it were, raised my standard here beside the lake on this winter morning though there was none to see but the tiny glittering eyes of the birds and the curious, interested gaze of the ducks. No massed ranks at my back save the trees standing in still and silent ranks, crowding down to the edge of the water.

But this was war, and we were heavily engaged now. Even while I had been walking in the frozen peace of the lakeside, the enemy had mounted a new and deadly offensive, striking were we were most vulnerable. The innocent are always the earliest victims. Trusting and helpless, they make easy prey. Loz and the cats had been the first to be singled out, stalked and destroyed—and because animals are of their nature blessed, I knew the cats did not need my concern now for they were in the care of safer hands than mine.

But what about Loz, who had been drawn

all unwitting into the conflict—

Oh yes, it was Loz who needed pity and prayers and help, because whatever anybody else might claim he had done, it was not Loz who had been responsible for this cruel outrage. I knew that instinctively. Poor, lovable Loz, who would have died rather than harm a fly, was the first human casualty of this new campaign in the grim and deadly battle between the shadowy enemy and me—us— whatever Gran and I and the girl in the lilac crepe dress represented.

My throat was choked and I swallowed.

'Oh, God! Poor Loz!' I said involuntarily.

Sally did not understand of course. Her voice had turned several degrees colder when she spoke again. I could tell she was hurt beyond words by what she saw as my callousness, devastated because I did not appear to be sharing her very genuine grief over what had happened to the cats. She had loved Dick and Turpin, treated them as much her own pets as her beloved Misty and Moppet, and she was never going to forgive Loz or forget what he had done. I realised too that she would never forgive anyone who took Loz's side, either.

'I think the police wanted to contact Randy and I gave them the number I had, but she is somewhere travelling—skiing isn't she?—so I don't know whether they have told her yet,' she informed me in a brittle tone, and I hastened to reassure her.

'Yes, thanks Sally, it's okay. I'll get in touch. I'll make sure she's put in the picture.'

'And I felt I had to let you know, obviously,' she went on, thawing slightly. I think she had charitably concluded I was too deeply shocked to be able to appreciate the full horror of Loz's crime. And being a person who hid a motherly heart beneath her butch exterior, she was anticipating how badly it was going to hit me later.

'That was good of you. I appreciate it.' Then I hesitated before daring to ask: 'How—? I mean, how did—?'

'It was a knife, like I said. One of the kitchen knives. The police—he was still holding it—oh, Tania, you can't imagine the sheer ghastly awfulness of it all—and on Christmas Day, too!' But before I could think of anything to say that would ease the rawness of the pain in her choked words, Sally had taken a grip on herself.

'The only thing we can be thankful for is that I imagine it was quick and they—they didn't suffer much.' She sounded bravely determined now and I tried to match her tone.

'Right. Yes. So—well, what's the situation currently? Where is Loz?'

'They took him away—to hospital. Some kind of psychiatric unit,' she said briskly. 'I've got the details if you want them. And everything's under control in the flat—I mean, all the—the mess has been cleared up—' She paused and I heard her swallow. 'I saw to the cats myself. I've buried them in the garden. I hope that's in order. Josh from Flat 2 gave me a hand this morning. We—laid them to rest and—and—said a little prayer.'

Something like a white-hot knife twisted agonisingly in my heart. I was rather surprised to recognise that it was anger. More of your seething fury actually, and not just for myself, but for loyal, faithful Sally's pain and for whatever horrors had been inflicted on Loz. And for Randy of course, off somewhere in the mountains, unaware. The cats—of whom I dared not for the moment think because I could not allow myself the luxury of grief— well, at least they were safe now. Opal-Ophelia—or whatever form of the Shape-shifter had invaded the flat—had used them callously, dangling their lives as bait to force the battle on me, but whatever she—or it— really was or represented, I felt only the overwhelming and instinctive certainty, as Gran had done, that her powers were limited. She could not inflict any hurts beyond death.

'Thank you, Sally. For everything.' I found it difficult to say more and she rang off after passing on the relevant information about Loz and repeating once again that everything was under control and she did not think there was any need for Randy to come home.

'There's nothing she could do—now,' she

said, meaningfully and I thought, rather reproachfully. 'It's all cleaned, locked up safely and I have the keys as usual. No windows broken or damage inside, no need even to claim insurance. You wouldn't know anything had happened.'

The line cleared. Connection broken.

I stood for a long time after that, just staring at the lake before I could force myself to move. I was alone in the silent landscape with the trees motionless, etched against the sky. Even the seabirds were quiet, and the ducks had moved away. Everything was very cold and very still.

The sedge is withered from the lake
And no birds sing.

Oh, but it was so much worse than sedge withering and the silence of no bird-song, so very much worse. I shivered suddenly, looking round fearfully as though I would see it in the very air around me, that cold cloud I could sense reaching out to overshadow us all—me as I stood solitary and chilled by the lake waters in an English valley; Randy, laughing and drinking chocolate as she watched the skiers in the winter sun of Austria. And Loz, already a hostage, a prisoner of war, confined not only within the walls of a hospital unit but by chains of some awful madness I had yet to investigate.

Forces were gathering, presences looming ominously. La Belle Dame Sans Merci was working her dark spells and she would lay them upon us to bind us and break us and hold us all in thrall.

The light was fading. I could not see. Was this the end?

No, I thought, No! No! I wanted to whirl and scream the word into the face of fate or destiny or whatever—whoever—had allowed this day to dawn, this moment to come. But then suddenly, like a light piercing and wavering through the thickening gloom (though I knew at the same time it had always been with me in the depth of my consciousness, something that had always been there), I was aware of the greatest revelation of all.

Too terrible for me to face before, I had never dared to look on this, the final answer. But now I saw it: that Doomsday is not something that will happen arbitrarily, it is something we bring on ourselves. It is not imposed by some omnipotent god but formulated from our own choosing, allowed to gather force, permitted to create itself.

I saw that we fashion our own destiny. That the End of the World is not something that threatens from without, but is nurtured within. And I saw my own task, the role I had been assigned in this drama of war and fate lying before me as clearly spelled out as though it was written in ancient script in the Recording Angel's book.

I sat down shaking on the stone parapet of the Dam, hunching myself over into the earth, clutching my coat tightly round my throat, wrapping my arms around me for warmth and trying not to faint as I forced myself to read what was written—there, in the angel's book?—or was the message here? It seemed to be written everywhere I looked—in the quavering slatey light on the water, the dark etched fingers of the trees that scratched against the sky.

Someone has to do it.

Someone has to carry the responsibility, Gran had said: and now I could take the message further in the light of my blinding new awareness. Someone has to carry the responsibility for the ones who cannot carry it for themselves. The ones who are helpless, trusting and innocent. The weak, the frail, the spent. Someone has to do it. And I was that one, marked by the silver fishes that hung heavy round my throat.

She who must hold the fishes and follow them across the vast worlds of water, the kingdom of Njord, and guide the lost mariners safely to land, must surrender herself to them as a servant of Njord and lose all sense of self, she must be no more and nothing save what they will make of her and do with her.

Even if the sacrifice was total, it had to be made, it had to be made in order to achieve the victory. And I made it in that moment without my own volition as I crouched there close to the earth, between the ground and the air and the water.

I kindled the flame to light the sacrificial fire, and offered myself. In humility, in hopelessness at my own inadequacy and yet in hope that the god would take the offering—everything I had to give—and transfigure its dross in the purifying flames.

Bending low, my eyes tightly closed, I surrendered myself in full consciousness to the will of the Earth Mother and to the silver fishes and to Njord, god of the wind and the sea ...

*   *   *

It was far more terrible than I had realised, more impossible than I had dreamed in my wildest and most hag-ridden visions. It was not Opal-Ophelia, nor even Loki the Shapeshifter that I had to face now. No enemy I could see. There was no confrontation, no adrenalin rush to propel me forward, no battle yell and clash of arms into which I was thrown to spend my strength and perish as gloriously as I could.

The Doomsday dark which closed in on me was not the dark of some great cataclysm, some crash of tidal wave and volcanic rock, some splitting apart of continents and raging of fire and flood that would consume everything in a tragedy of heroic and spectacular dimensions that would reverberate through the cosmos.

Oh, no. All that was illusion. When I saw the truth, I understood what Sven A. DeWitte had meant when he quoted T.S. Eliot's line about worlds ending not with a bang but a whimper. He had been wiser than I thought, wiser than I, in my ignorance, had given him credit for.

For Doomsday had come upon me now, and it was very still, very subtle, slipping in unawares in its terror and awfulness like the darkest hour before the dawn. The darkest night of the soul when the dawn is nothing but a tale—

—a tale
Told by an idiot, full of sound and fury,
Signifying nothing—'

Will Shakespeare had been no fool either, of course. He had known what he was doing when he put those despairing words into the mouth of Macbeth, when news is brought to him that Lady Macbeth has just died. Demon-ridden, wailing because she cannot clean her hands of blood, sleep-walking with terrified, unseeing eyes into her grave.

249

Macbeth sees then, too late, and bitterly recognises that he himself has been the engineer of his own tragedy. And I saw too, before the last flicker of my questing mind was stilled and the dark ice covered all—

That it was all illusion. That the dawn—light-years away—would never come. Would never come. Would never. Come.

*   *   *

Tears were stinging my eyes but they would not fall. They were as frozen as everything in the scene around me. Every smallest bird had stopped singing. The ducks had gone, nothing moved.

I lifted my head and felt a great sob tear through my chest and try to escape, but it could not. It was as frozen as the ice that blurred my eyes. So this was it, the Ending of the World. An ending of the expectation of any new beginning. The slipping away of hope. The apathy of nothingness. The abandonment by every god.

As I looked at the familiar scene I had known so well I saw it shrivel and fade before my eyes.

There was no such terror I would face in death, for there was no terror in death, no terror in life's end. The Earth Mother would stir again in her womb, and in due time would come the shoots of spring and the green promise of rebirth. All would pass and yet all would be reborn.

No, I knew the terror now for what it was. The icy hand heavy upon us that stills all, stills heart and hope, longing and desire and expectation. When all, all has gone and there is no promise of any return.

*　　*　　*

I was still shivering, and my teeth were chattering in the aftermath of shock as eventually—how long after I did not know for I had no sense of time—I managed to trudge painfully up the road back home. I was glad there were few people around, little traffic, nobody close enough to see how awful I must have looked. Tear-streaked and dishevelled, eyes blank. A survivor staggering out of the rubble in a war zone, a displaced person, a refugee seeking shelter.

I went clumsily into the kitchen, plunging into the warmth, drawn irresistibly by the comforting fragrant smell of coffee. Gran was just making it, and at the sight of my face she gave a quick exclamation and moved to take control. I was beyond speech for the moment, paralysed into immobility now, so after she had reassured herself that I had not had an accident, was not ill, she asked no more questions. She sat me down firmly in the comfy chair and added a generous dollop of brandy to my mug before placing it in my hands. She draped her old crocheted shawl that was weightless as a cobweb, but comforting as a big hug, round my unprotesting shoulders, and then sat watchfully down beside me, giving me as much time as I needed to gather myself together.

The coffee warmed me and after a while the shivering subsided. I managed, in hardly coherent bursts of speech, to tell her about Sally's call and what had happened at the flat. Even, eventually, to start trying to make decisions as to what was to be done.

'I think I'd better contact the hospital—speak to Loz. Find out how he is—hear his side of the story.'

'And phone Miranda?' Gran suggested.

'Yes, but—well, if there's no real damage and the police have gone—I can't believe it, Gran—police? Well, but if they've got everything sorted out and Sally's in control and—the cats are safely taken care of, there's no immediate hurry. Randy can't do anything, can she? I'll speak to her later. Better to see about Loz first.'

Though I was not looking forward to whatever he had to tell me, I knew I had to do this. I could not help the cats now, but Loz would surely need whatever reassurance I could give him that I understood he was as much Opal-Ophelia's victim as our pets had been.

It was odd, but unexpectedly I felt Randy did not need this kind of support from me. She had resources of her own that I had never appreciated before. And of course she stood outside of our involvement with Opal-Opehlia, Loz's and mine. I was irrationally glad that she was in a country where there was sunlight and the clean purity of the mountains, ice in the high glaciers that was not the dark iciness which had just paralysed me, chilled me through every fibre of my flesh and bone, to sustain her. Randy would find her own strength, her own consolation there that would help her cope.

Gran and I had arranged to have Boxing Day lunch with a few more of the relatives, and I asked if she would give them my excuses and plead a sudden virus of the gastric sort. She wanted to stay with me, concerned, claiming that I was far too shaken to be left on my own, but I insisted she should go. I'd recover faster by myself, I told her, though the truth was that I wanted to get the call to Loz over with. I didn't know what horrors it would unleash, and I wanted time to recover from them before I had to face anyone else.

So in due course Gran departed. I sat down determinedly with the phone in my hand as soon as she had left, and punched in the number Sally had given me.

It wasn't—so far—as bad as I had thought. After speaking to various people at the hospital, I ascertained that Loz was only under observation and was likely to be discharged in a day or two. He wasn't considered to be really ill, simply to have had some sort of breakdown. He was up and about, though apparently in very low spirits. It had to be done, so I asked if I could speak to him and after some delay they put him on the line.

He spoke. Very tentatively.

'Tania?'

'Hello, Loz,' I said, trying to sound normal but stricken to pity by the pain in his voice. Even his hesitation, his silence sounded like that of an old man. 'How are you?'

There was a muffled sort of sound.

'It's all right,' I assured him. 'I know Loz, Sally told me.'

Another long pause, and I could hear his uneven breathing. Then he said:

'Tania? Are you still there? Don't go—'

'I'm here. And it's all right,' I repeated again. 'It'll all be okay now, Loz, I promise. Everything will be all right.'

'You—ah—you know—about—?' he faltered and I said:

'Dick and Turpin? Yes. I know. And I know it wasn't your fault. It was Opal, wasn't it? Can you tell me what happened?'

There was the sound of an indrawn sob.

'Oh Tania! Don't!'

'You've got to tell me, Loz, or I won't be able to help you,' I insisted doggedly.

254

'What happened?'

'I was—it was too awful Tania—sinful—vile—'

'Loz!' I hated to be so seemingly uncaring but I had to keep him focussed, grounded. I had to break the spell Opal-Ophelia had woven about him. 'I've told you, I know it wasn't your fault—'

And then the dam burst. His voice rose agonisedly.

'But it was! It was! You don't know, Tania. You weren't there. I did it. I gave way to the temptation and let it happen. I killed them—I killed them—'

I went rigid. 'No.'

'I killed them, I killed them,' he keened in a long wail of despair that sounded as though it would go on for ever.

'You mean you actually did kill the cats? You really did do that yourself?' I said weakly. I could not believe it was Loz who had wielded the knife, and in spite of myself I could feel the same chill of horror and revulsion I had sensed in Sally.

'You see?' he said and I could tell he was crying. 'I was to blame—I am the one who must be punished—' Then in panic: 'Tania, Tania, please don't ring off—'

'I won't,' I said, though I felt so sick I was tempted to.

'I'll tell you everything. I have to confess—atone,' he said in a low, ragged rush of despair.

255

I had never heard him speak in such terms before, and felt as though a door had opened into his past that I would have preferred not to know about. There were obviously ghosts that haunted Loz too, more terrifying perhaps than the ones I was aware of. I felt as though I had learned a great deal about Loz in just a few moments. Stern figures murmuring of sin and repentance might well have been responsible for all his little affectations—like his insistence on ostentatiously having black satin sheets and black heart-shaped pillows on his bed, even though to my knowledge he had never shared it with anyone else. And his prickliness, his determination to be himself at all costs.

I began to feel the stirring of pity again.

'She phoned one day when you and Randy were out. Just before Christmas, when you were worrying about leaving me on my own over the holiday,' he blurted wretchedly. 'She told me she realised I hadn't been—well, at ease—at the meeting of the coven, but there was something else that would suit me better. A different sort of magic—She said it would bring me money as well as power, give me great wealth—beyond my wildest dreams—'

I might have been listening to the young student Faust explaining how he had come to sell his soul to the devil. I could feel myself going cold again.

'I suppose she knew my weak spot,' he hurried on apologetically, beginning to sound

256

more like the Loz I knew. 'I couldn't resist it, the thought of having a lot of money, enough to be able to do just exactly what I liked—Tania, oh God, Tania, I'm sorry, you don't have to listen to all this you know—'

'Yes, I do,' I said steadily. 'Go on.'

'But you've done nothing. I can't involve you. It's too—well, it's too frightening, too dangerous. If anything should happen to you—No, I won't do it, I can't tell you anything. I can't tell anybody. It's bad enough being so afraid for myself, the last thing I want is to make it worse, bring their anger on you as well—'

I realised that deep down, this man was probably in mortal terror. In as calming a voice as I could, I tried to find the words to release him.

'Just a minute. Let me get things a bit clearer. Who are 'they', Loz?'

'Don't ask me, Tania. You mustn't know,' he gabbled. 'I—don't—I hardly know myself. But I swore an—an oath—an oath of silence—Oh, God, oh, God, Tania, I don't know what to do—'

'Listen,' I said with all the authority I was capable of. 'Listen to me, Loz. You've got to believe me. Opal—whoever she is—whoever 'they' are—None of them can harm you any more. What happened is over, it's finished. They can't touch you now.'

Before he could argue, I tried again, more

257

reasonably.

'Have you told anyone else about what happened? The police? The doctor?'

'How can I? How could I?' he implored, almost weeping again and yet he was almost shouting at me too. 'You've met her, you know what she's like. But nobody else would understand. They simply wouldn't understand what I was talking about.'

'I understand. I know you were just weak, Loz,' I assured him encouragingly. 'You let her con you, that's all.'

'But that's no bloody—I'm sorry, Tania—but that is no bloody excuse, is it? No bloody excuse at all,' he shouted. And I found this shocked me more than anything else, this was a measure of the man's agony. This was the cry of a soul in hell. Loz never, but never swore.

'Ssh! Ssh! They'll stop you talking to me if they think you're getting upset—'

'It's no excuse,' he repeated desperately, lowering his voice so that I could hardly hear him. 'The blame is all mine. Oh, mea culpa! Mea culpa!'

Oh, God! I thought, even as I was trying to calm him.

'It's okay, Loz. It's okay.'

'Tania,' he blurted as though poison was being pumped out of him. 'My soul is damned for eternity—I have made a blood sacrifice to the Evil One and been given a new name and sworn an oath of allegiance—'

'Loz! What are you talking about?'

'It's true,' he wept piteously. 'I swore to you—and to Miranda—that I would never involve myself with such disgusting practices, and I meant it. Black magic and black masses—'

'Loz?' I said sharply. I could hardly draw breath for the thumping of my heart. Involuntarily, I lifted my hand to my breast and felt the cool shapes of the silver fishes. I clutched them hard, pressing them against me without knowing what I was doing.

'But I did it. I did it and I have to take the responsibility. She took me there—and I met Them, the others—yes, I admit she took me, but I went of my own free will—and of my own free will I did everything they told me to do—'

'You made a sacrifice? Made a blood sacrifice?' I was suddenly so revolted I thought I was going to be sick but something gave me the strength to swallow the rising nausea, to manage to keep talking. 'You mean you killed the cats because—the cats were— Oh, Loz, no. Oh, no!'

'I told you, I am doomed, my soul is damned.' And he was crying in earnest now, great wrenching sobs coming from his very depths. I was aware of a terrible sense of helplessness. What could I say, how could I hope to reach him from the far distance of my own swirling fog of horror and disgust.

My fingers were gripped so tight round the

phone that it hurt, and with the other hand I was clinging to the silver fishes. They were digging into my flesh but I was glad of the pain. It gave me something to concentrate on to keep away the faintness that was making me sick and light-headed.

Loz was still pouring out his confession through his sobs, saying things I didn't want to hear because I knew I would never be able to erase them from my consciousness once they had been spoken. Horrific, unimaginable words.

'—must have given me drugs I think—some sort of incense, very strong—I felt ill even before it began, you know how sensitive I am, Tania—'

I tried to speak but could not and the low, choked phrases went on and on.

'—awful sort of excitement everywhere—I knew it was wrong, but when I tried to leave, they—altar with—black candles—the stink of them turned my stomach—and then, a huge creature with a face like a goat—chanting—'

'Oh, Loz,' I managed. I was shaking and crying too now.

'Blood—all over the girl, she was only young—and then, did I tell you about the drums?—don't think she knew, they'd given her stuff to drink mixed with it—could see her little hand, just dangling over the side—more of them—unconscious by then—beating faster and faster—pretty far gone—louder and louder—inside my head—'

I just couldn't do it. I couldn't be expected to cope with revelations like these. Loz needed skilled help, he needed expert advice from people who stronger than me, people who were used to dealing with black magic and black masses and the Evil One.

'Tania? Tania?' Loz's voice, shaking like that of a frightened child, was what roused me at last. 'Are you still there?'

It was no use. I could not leave Loz's tormented soul wounded, crumpled carelessly in Opal-Ophelia's fist. I could not hide from the enemy, whatever form the Shapeshifter chose to take. Loz lacked the strength to save himself. I was the one who must fight for him. This was my battle, my war.

*   *   *

Be yourself, Rowan had said. Be yourself and all will be well.

That was what had saved me before, when I had had to venture into the depths of the sea-caves. It was the wisdom that would save me now that I trod the heaving red corridors of Loz's terror and anguish

Be yourself.

 Be yourself.

And all will be well. All. Will. Be—

13

I clung with all my senses to myself. To Tatiana Forrester.

For Opal-Ophelia had recognised me as I had come to recognise her, and there was no mystery now about where her knowledge had come from. She had known I was the Chosen One in the same way I knew she was the embodiment of Loki, the trickster, who brought with him all the power of chaos and confusion.

I clung to all the familiar images around me that would help me to enforce my sense of being. To the lake, the woods, the room in which I was sitting. To the picture of my mother in its silver frame on the sideboard. To Daddy in Copenhagen. To *Hamlet* and William Shakespeare and the Player Queen— to the girl in the lilac crepe dress—to Uncle Jack and the Aunties and to Gran—

And then, as though she had come quietly into the room and was standing beside me, I felt Gran's presence. I remembered what she had said about the true nature of magic. That it was concerned with will and intent, not unknown mysteries. Gran was wise, far wiser than I. It was she who had pointed out that all we really knew about Opal-Ophelia, whoever she was, was that she was proficient at illusion.

'Tania?' Loz was almost whispering now. He sounded hoarse, hopeless, as though the effort of confessing had drained him so much he was on the point of giving up. 'Tania?'

'I'm here Loz. I've been here all the time,' I told him, and my voice had somehow become steady. Steady and strong. 'Now, listen. I want you to listen hard. You are not doomed. Do you hear? You are not doomed. You have done nothing.'

'I don't want preaching at, thank you,' he ground out with a bitterness born of desperation. 'Especially since you don't know what you are talking about. It doesn't help to tell me God will understand—'

'I'm not preaching, and this has got nothing to do with God understanding,' I snapped back. 'Loz, listen, just shut up and listen to me, will you?'

He was so surprised that he gave a sort of gasp and went quiet.

'Opal-Ophelia is a fraud and a cheat, we know that,' I told him. 'But she's also some kind of hypnotist. She made me think I was in the sea-caves, I told you, that night I went out to dinner with her—'

As he started to protest I went on: 'Shut up and let me finish. She conned me into thinking I was somewhere else, and that's exactly what she's done with you. Not only this time, but when you went to the coven meeting. There wasn't any coven meeting, Loz. It was all in your mind, everything was in your mind. You didn't go anywhere with her, not ever, she just made you believe you did.'

'No,' Loz said faintly, but I could hear that there was a trembling note of hope searing through him. 'I couldn't have imagined such—such vileness, Tania. There was—you know I would never—but they brought a black bird, a cockerel, and I saw—Tania, I saw them do things I could never, never—'

'Look,' I said roughly. 'Look, I'm not saying you made this up yourself. Though if you've got some kind of churchy background Loz, it's more than likely that these are deeply-buried images, forbidden threats that were instilled in you about damnation and evil when you were too young to know anything about it.'

Morris, our tame shrink at the Theatre School would have been proud of that, I thought.

'None of it happened. She hypnotised you and put it all in your head by suggestion, some sort of brainwashing,' I told Loz. 'The things you told me—the girl on the altar—she didn't exist. Nor the black cockerel. Nor the blood and—and everything else. And you didn't do any of the things you thought you did. None of them. You did not do anything, Loz. Nothing at all.'

There was a tense pause. Then Loz said tremulously: 'But Tania, look what was done to—to the cats. How could—? You really

264

think—?'

'I am certain. Well, practically,' I said. 'Loz, whatever you believe you did, I would be prepared to swear—'

'Oh, Tania,' he protested in a whisper.

'—to swear on my hope of salvation,' I went on grimly, meaning every word. The most solemn of solemn magic was called for here. 'I would be prepared to swear on my hope of salvation that you would never, for whatever reason in this world or out of it, have picked up a knife to the cats, Loz. I believe in you, whatever you say. You did not harm Dick and Turpin. You were deluded into believing that it was you, but it was not you. It was Opal-Ophelia, whoever or whatever she is, who really killed—most cruelly and criminally, and in cold blood—murdered our pets.'

There was another long, long silence and I had a momentary panic that Loz had fainted— had died, even—but then he gave a deep sigh.

'Tania,' he said with all trace of hysteria gone from his voice. 'Tania, thank you. Thank you. From the bottom of my heart. I was—I admit quite frankly, I was so utterly lost I think I had given up all hope. And you have come to my rescue. You have saved me. Literally, you have saved my soul.'

'Yuck! Don't, Loz,' I said, embarrassed.

'I mean it.' He was steadier now, starting to sound more like himself. 'You could well be right about the hypnotism and the brainwashing—I hope and pray you are right. You have to be right. But that doesn't alter the fact that Dick and Turpin— They are no longer with us. And I don't want to try to evade any responsibility I might have about that in however limited a way. Even if it was under some sort of hypnotic influence, I must have let her into the flat, mustn't I, taken her back there—or even, if the place I thought I had gone to didn't exist, invited her into the flat in some way. I am morally responsible for what—what she did. And if charges are to be pressed—the policeman mentioned the RSPCA, I think—I am only too prepared to—'

'We can sort all that out later,' I assured him. 'When Randy comes home. Nothing can bring them back, Loz. There's time enough. I'll talk to her, I'll tell her how it happened.'

'I—I am truly appalled,' he said with a quiver in his voice. 'I will never forgive myself, Tania, and I mean that most sincerely, for— Dick and Turpin. And for what it will do to Miranda when she knows about them.'

'They're at peace, Loz,' I assured him gently. 'It's just a sentimental sop I suppose, but it's true. They are at peace. I know they are. Sally and Josh from Flat 2 have laid them to rest in the garden and they've had a—a little service, with prayers and—and flowers.'

I did not care whether I was embroidering the truth here, because I felt Loz needed all the reassurance and comfort he could get. So

266

far as I could see, he would be paying a lifelong penance, whether it had been his hand or some infernal hand of darkness that had actually wielded a knife to the cats—and that, realistically, was something we would never know now.

It was not so much that Loz was going to have to carry the disgust and loathing of Sally and anyone else who might hear about what he had supposedly done in the future. It was because, whether he was guilty or not, he would never be able to stop blaming and loathing himself.

'Let's concentrate on what to do about Opal,' I suggested in a brisker tone. But Loz obviously found this prospect even more disturbing.

'What can we do?' he asked rather fearfully. 'I—I don't think I would know how to face her—not now. Not after this. She—is truly terrifying, Tania.'

'Oh, come on Loz, don't be such a mouse. You're bigger than she is,' I pointed out grimly. Somehow the situation seemed to be spiralling off into what could only be described as black comedy. I had never really appreciated black comedy before, but I thought a little wildly that I'd view this aspect of theatre from quite a different angle after today.

He seemed too stricken to reply so I said more soothingly: 'Well, don't worry anyway. I'll deal with her.'

Assuming my most Wagnerian manner, I informed him: 'I am a woman too. And I assure you I can be just as dominant and terrifying if I have to be.'

I heard Loz gulp. 'Oh,' he said.

'Leave her to me. Just concentrate on getting yourself better and coming home,' I told him.

'Do you—um—do you really think Miranda will allow—?' he began humbly but I was getting a little tired of the Submissive Male scenario by now.

'Randy is not a monster, Loz. She'll understand, I'm sure she will. You're in trouble, you've been through a hard time. But you're part of the family, and that's what families are for.'

When I rang off at last, Loz was still sounding subdued, but expressing his determination to try and overcome what had happened. Though I sensed regretfully that the incident—whether it had really happened or he only thought it had—would be with him always now. Like any loss of innocence, the experience he had suffered was irreversible. The scars would always be there and Loz would never be young again.

* * *

I had sounded far more confident than I felt. I

took quick stock of the situation as reaction hit me now that the crisis was over. Exhausted, and with no idea at all of how I was going to deal with Opal-Ophelia—or if I was honest, deal with anything—

I nerved myself to call Randy in Austria, but she was not available—mention was made of 'the piste', which did not mean a great deal to me. She had, however, left a reassuring message in case I rang. She knew about what had happened and had everything in hand. Would talk later.

So that left me on my own at last. Very tired, very vulnerable. Trying to surface from black horrors that threatened to drown my soul as well as Loz's. Trying to convince myself that I was back in the real world, trying to find some joke I could crack, some way I could laugh it off.

A funny thing happened to me on the way to—

Food. I'd had no lunch, I needed food. But just as I was going into the kitchen to make myself a snack—trying to focus my mind in a new direction altogether and worry about all the Christmas cheer I had stuffed the previous day which was certain to have piled on several thousands of calories—the doorbell rang. Stiffly, I went to open it.

I thought I must be imagining things again. How could Rowan be standing there, on the front doorstep of my home on Boxing Day afternoon, with an overnight bag at his feet? It had got to be some sort of trap, into which I was determined I was not, this time, going to fall. After one look I shut the door carefully, and went back to the kitchen. Just because what I wanted most of all in the world was to see Rowan—

The doorbell rang again. And again. And again.

*   *   *

What did you do to protect yourself against the evil eye (maybe even the Evil One himself)? Visions of *The Crucible* flashed into my head—there had to have been a reason why that was the play that had been chosen for our school production, it was obviously going to come in useful in my future career as the Chosen One.

Should I run for a bit of garlic, I wondered as I mechanically grated cheese and piled it on some bread to stick under the grill? Not garlic for flavouring, but to hang round my neck and stretch across the threshold to prevent the visitation—whatever it was—from entering. Or what about repeating a few prayers—the only trouble was that after my conversation with Loz I was so traumatised myself by now that I didn't seem able to think of a single prayer I could gabble.

The front doorbell had stopped ringing and

I watched the cheese bubbling invitingly in the blessed silence, feeling very hungry suddenly. Minutes passed. I turned to fetch cutlery from the drawer, and as I did so found myself confronting a looming figure at the window, tapping preremptorily on the glass.

I froze. My mouth went quite dry. This was more than I could cope with.

The manifestation opened its lips.

'How long are you going to leave me out in here in the cold, girl? Apart from the fact that I'm ravenous. What sort of game is it that you think you're playing when I've taken the trouble to come all this way to see you?'

Then the ice that was paralysing me melted at last. I don't know whether I was laughing or crying or both, as I ran to open the back door with shaking fingers. This might be some sort of cunning demonic visitation but I just didn't care any more. I'd had about all I could take. A moment later I was in Rowan's arms in a bear-like embrace, being hugged hard against his chest.

*   *   *

'You—came, you came to me!' I gasped shamelessly, intoxicated with relief and joy. 'You knew—you knew how much I—needed you—'

'Not a bit of it,' he said cheerfully. 'What sort of sentimental mush is this, girl? I

271

happened to be finding myself in Sheffield over this festive season, among strangers, as they say, and I was feeling I'd like to see a familiar face. So rather than just head back for London I thought I would drop in on you on the way. I've had a run through the frosty Peak scenery this morning, wonderful, down through—what do they call those little places —Tideswell and Millers Dale—'

Somehow, he didn't seem to notice that I was by now crying hysterically, sobbing into the front of his parka. He just carried on in that slow, deep voice.

'—I think the bells were ringing in the Cathedral of the Peak as I passed. All the Christmas lights were everywhere, it looked just like Brigadoon—you know, the magical village that only appears once every hundred years. It was even seeming likely I might meet up with a raven-haired, apple-cheeked village maiden I'd have to fall in love with, and there'd be a tragedy when she had to leave me and disappear back into her own time. Though I'd have gone with her, I have to admit it, if she'd got legs like Cyd Charisse in the movie—'

I managed to laugh in a sniffling kind of way and he handed me a handkerchief that had appeared from somewhere. I blew my nose.

'But no such luck girl, it seems,' he continued regretfully. 'I wended my way onward with nary a raven-haired maiden in sight—through Buxton and over the moors—.'

I nodded. I had travelled that road many times in the past. 'Took the Macclesfield Road at Leek, and here I am. But when I finally run you to earth in your hidden valley, what do I get? No welcome, but the door shut in my face. I ask you, is that fair reward for a hungry traveller?'

He stopped suddenly, stiffening.

'What's the matter?' I demanded, freezing again.

'God, girl, did you have something on the stove?

Then I smelled it too, and rushed into the kitchen laughing uncontrollably, just in time to see my toasted cheese going up in flames.

*　　　*　　　*

Gran came home to find us feasting royally on deliciously fluffy omelettes. Rowan had whipped them up after he cleared away the remains of my burnt offerings from beneath the grill, since I was by this time in a state of near-collapse and unable to cope at all. Weak from crying and laughing, reaction to the various shocks I had just sustained of course, too much joy following too much fright and strain, I was unable to explain any of the details to Rowan but he dealt promptly and effectively with the situation by simply taking over. He sat me firmly down out of his way to recover while he donned the blue and white

273

striped apron that hung on the door and got on with the job in hand.

Within minutes, I was being served sizzling golden omelettes and the sort of classy salad that never materialised when I put lettuce and tomatoes and cucumber on a plate myself. All this as well as steaming coffee that seemed to have far more of a kick in it in than the instant powder in the jar—and I'm not talking about the whisky Rowan had added with a liberal hand, either, though what he had produced was of course, Irish coffee you'd have paid a fortune for in London. I had never suspected, but Rowan was obviously one of your natural cooks, someone who had the equivalent of the gardener's green fingers when it came to cracking eggs and opening tins.

'Eat up, girl. Nourishment is an effective cure for most problems,' he told me, his eyes laughing at me from across the table. Seduced by the delicious smell wafting up from my plate, I could hardly restrain myself and as I ate I realised he was right.

It was still difficult to comprehend that he was really there, at home in the kitchen I had grown up in, calmly lounging in the big carver chair as though he had sat there for years. His steady presence seemed to fill the room, though the disturbing effects I had noticed before when he was around—the coloured lights and silken-unguently-scented hands caressing me shiveringly inside, while music played and fountains burst in plumes of spray—had subsided to nothing more than a comforting sort of glow. I was beginning to feel much, much better by the time Gran arrived home.

She seemed remarkably unsurprised to see him.

'This is Rowan, you know I mentioned him, Gran? The Ghost of Hamlet's father. He—um—happened to be passing on his way back from Sheffield—he's just been telling me, he went up for an audition and he's had the most amazing offer for a new trilogy—. Actor-director, and they're planning to film the creation of the work for world-wide distribution—'

I was gabbling a bit because somehow it was vitally important that Gran should understand. I didn't want her to freeze Rowan out, as she had always been inclined to do in previous years with other boys I showed an interest in. But she was far from doing that this time. Again she surprised me by revealing a side of my grandmother I had never seen before.

She shook Rowan's hand with the greatest cordiality, saying in the most gracious of tones: 'I'm delighted to meet you at last, Rowan. You'll stay, I hope? The spare room's been kept ready.'

Well, I hadn't got as far as even thinking along those sort of lines myself but Rowan took it without blinking an eye.

'Thank you, Mrs Nicholls,' he said. 'I am honoured indeed. I would be happy to stay.'

So that was that.

Gran had already had lunch of course, but she joined us for a cup of coffee—Rowan serving it up while she sat in state like a queen—and I filled her in about my phone call to Loz. By now it seemed perfectly natural that Rowan should be there, and I was glad of his laid-back presence when I had to describe Loz's version of what had happened on Christmas Eve.

'I think he's all right now but he was in an awful state,' I said. It was unsettling even to talk about Loz, confined in his little space in the Unit. Under observation. Watched. Sharp instruments removed. In case he went off again. Loz the fastidious, the elegant, the untouchable. 'And Gran, it was you who gave me the clue about what to say to him in the end. You were the one who saw through Opal. Because she'd deluded him too, of course, hypnotised him into believing the most ghastly stories that nobody in their right mind would accept for a minute.'

Gran listened silently, her eyes dark with concern.

'The way he tells it, she contacted him and invited him to stay for Christmas. Well, we knew he was going to stay with somebody, but we didn't realise it was supposedly with Opal. It's no wonder he was so secretive after what had happened the last time she was around though, when I went to that restaurant with her.'

Still Gran said nothing but shook her head slightly. What was there to say, after all?

'And apparently,' I went on gamely, hating every minute of this, 'she promised to take him to some other kind of gathering or meeting—not a coven but something even more secret—where they could grant him miraculous wealth—and that's Loz's weakness, his Achilles heel. Oh, dear, it's all so terribly sordid and sad. Power and influence, what they can do to people. I felt as though I was listening to Faust explaining how he'd been persuaded to sell his soul to Mephistopheles.'

'The story of Faust is the story of Everyman,' Rowan's deep voice murmured somewhere in the background.

'I remember hearing once about—I think it was General Booth, the founder of the Salvation Army,' Gran said unexpectedly. 'He asked why the devil should have all the best tunes. Evil can seem so fascinating, especially to the young.'

'It made my blood run cold. He's convinced he went with Opal to some sort of black magic gathering and swore an oath to the Evil One, and killed the cats himself as a blood sacrifice,' I said baldly. There was no gentler way to put it.

A chill frisson ran through the room,

through all of us. There was a subtle shift in the atmosphere, and Gran amazed me by lifting her hand involuntarily and making a sign I hardly recognised. It was like something in a horror film, and got to me more than anything else that had happened that day, hurting me and making me suddenly very angry. Was even my wise, lovely Gran so frightened in the depth of her being that she had to cross her fingers against the mention of the Evil One?

We were not in the Dark Ages now. And yet I had lifted my own hand too in the gesture that was becoming familiar, to touch the silver fishes round my neck. Suddenly I was very conscious of Rowan's presence next to me, though he did not move and said nothing. Gran was looking distressed, old and frail, and I leaned forward to take her hand encouragingly.

'But it's all right, Gran,' I said, my voice strong, though I didn't know where the strength was coming from. 'Loz will be okay, I promise. And the cats are at peace. I told him that. Sally buried them in the garden.'

She shook her head a little once again. I suppose the events of the last twenty-four hours had been just as much of a strain for her as they had been for me, perhaps more so, for in spite of her courage she was an elderly woman. And though she had faced up to Opal-Ophelia, she had never lost her fear of what she had seen.

I reminded myself again that it was I who carried the burden now, I who was the Chosen One. It was not Gran but I, who must do whatever had to be done.

'I think I managed to reassure Loz that he— well, he wasn't to blame himself,' I told her. 'He seemed calmer when I rang off.'

Her eyes were warm now as they rested on me. She seemed to have gathered new vigour, brought herself back into focus, as it were.

'Of course,' she said rather cryptically. 'Yes, you need to take care for your people.'

'Rowan has seen Opal too,' I remarked without thinking and Gran merely nodded.

'Naturally.'

'Why naturally?' I asked and she looked from me to Rowan and back again, and then she smiled.

'Tania, Tania. Why do you think the young man is here?'

*   *   *

So I reassured myself that at least Gran and Rowan seemed to know what we were doing— or more accurately, what I was supposed to be doing. And I was not alone when, a few days later, I found myself standing consciously on the edge of the void, in one of the places where there were gates between the worlds. We had driven here together, Rowan and I, in the awareness that there was work to be done—even though what kind of work, or how we were to do it I still had absolutely no idea.

The site—half-hidden by trees—stood across a field high up where kestrels fly, over an unfolding view of the Cheshire plains. The Bridestones, they were called. These stones. Megaliths. Just one more of the mysterious reminders of the past that you stumble across so often in the hills round my home.

'For this is ancient country,' Gran had said, and added crisply: 'Thank goodness.'

*   *   *

I sat in Rowan's car lapped in warmth and fortified by his strength, summoning my courage to venture out into the bitter air and walk across the country road and up the short path to the stones. It was not my kind of scene really, and I didn't know what we would find here except that somehow, Gran had thought there would be answers.

I had heard of the Bridestones of course, since they were well known landmarks. But I had never visited them before, not actually being one of your brisk walkers whose idea of bliss was tramping the fells, or a devotee of trips to significant sites that were marked with helpful stars on the tourist guides. A little odd really when you came to think about it, since I had always felt the ghosts of the past and

280

magic of the countryside so very keenly. But maybe that was the answer. I was so used to the magic I had taken it for granted and never needed to go searching.

The Bridestones are very ancient, all that remains of a prehistoric monument that was originally built as a burial chamber—so Gran had rather surprisingly informed us.

'They are supposedly dedicated to the Earth Mother,' she said. 'Their name comes from Saint Bridget, some people say but I prefer the pagan Bride, the goddess of the Brigantes.'

'I had no idea you were so informed Gran,' I said, amazed. 'You never told me anything about all this before.'

She turned to me and smiled.

'There was no need to. Perhaps there are quite a lot of things about me you never knew.'

And since this had become blatantly obvious over the last few days—probably that I didn't actually know a great deal about anybody at all, I was beginning to think—I said no more but just sat quietly, waiting for her to continue.

'There are innumerable monuments and connections with ancient history in this area,' she went on reflectively. 'But the visions or whatever we experienced seemed to bring us all into conflict with horned warriors—Mother and myself as well as you, Tania—so there does appear to be some link with Scandinavia. And it was the places with Viking connotations that I thought might give us some clue about what action to take next.'

Because of course, we had to do something. Or I did. And the problem was very much in our minds over the days of the holiday break, between the times when Rowan and I walked, and Gran shopped, and we both did the tourist things for Rowan and lazed about in satisfied exhaustion afterwards. The three of us, like some kind of ancient Triumvirate, snatched time together to talk the more surreal aspects of the matter over between ourselves.

Gran, who had guarded the silver fishes for long silent years while she waited for her successor to take the burden of responsibility from her, assured me that she and the ghosts were with me all the way. Rowan said very little but I was immensely grateful for his presence.

*   *   *

The first mention of the Bridestones arose towards the end of a companionable evening lazing around with Belgian chocolates, Auntie Rosalie's potent and aptly named Celebration Punch and a video of *The Red Shoes*, the classic ballet film of Hans Anderson's famous fairy tale. I had insisted on getting it because of my visions of the Haunted Ballroom, and Rowan was quite happy to go along with me and watch it as part of dance history, while

Gran said she was only too charmed by the prospect of being able to view one of the inspirational movies of her youth again.

'Moira Shearer, ah, she was so young then, so lovely and such an elegant dancer,' she sighed nostalgically. 'It was a beautiful film. Truly beautiful. So civilised somehow.'

'They don't make them like that any more, Gran. Is that what you mean?' I suggested naughtily.

'Nothing seems very civilised to me these days, Tania. But then that's because I'm getting older and my era is passing. One has to learn to acknowledge gracefully that age brings its own rewards—the best of them being that one is able to leave all the effort and hard work to the new young generation,' she came back, smart as a whippet.

'Well, but even if I went to one of these ancient sites, what would be the point? What kind of action could I possibly take?' I wondered aloud after a moment, knowing what she was referring to even though she had not spelled it out.

'Frankly, I have no idea,' she admitted. 'But magic works in faith and very often it works symbolically. All the ancient myths and tales, even *The Red Shoes* will tell you that, Tania.'

So I was back to basics again, the bedrock where all the secrets lay. The hidden meanings and messages in old, atavistic lore handed down through the centuries. The dark archetypes that lurked within seemingly innocent nursery stories; the recurring patterns of aspiration embodied in the Grail Quest, terrifying journeys and voyages that took the soul into strange lands of enchantment, across alien oceans and seas. Ancient parchments that were dimmed with long-spilled blood and warned 'Heere beye Dragons' were what had guided those who undertook the quest to right wrongs. Shining talismans of truth and light had been what saved them in doom-laden castles, when they were trapped in the webs of evil. But they had still made the effort, they had gone nevertheless, whatever the cost, if they had to.

* * *

That night as I slept, I found myself wandering uneasily in the garish and imaginative nightmare world of Sven A. DeWitte's *Endtime Explored*.

'. . . *there always arises also a hero figure which takes upon itself the responsibility of confronting and doing battle with the powers of chaos and darkness. It is with the hero that all hopes for the future survival of the laws of ordered rightfulness must be placed.*

'*The destiny of the hero seems to be ordained and not necessarily of his own choosing . . . he is generally portrayed as flawed by human weakness . . .*

'But however difficult the hero's task might seem, however doomed to failure, the hero fights on, pledged to sacrifice even his life if necessary, rather than abandon his allegiance to the right and to his honour or allow evil to prevail . . .

'. . . the hero figures of our cultures . . . often we may not recognise the truly heroic. Even the everyday man or woman in the street . . .'

Right, get the message, no need to spell it out, I thought, as I was despairingly swallowed up in my dream into the depths of a deep, foam-flecked black vortex. It bubbled cauldron-like below the sheer walls of the castle that I had been attempting to climb to escape from the jaws of a mighty serpent—

Sven A. DeWitte and Sigmund Freud both, were they gently trying to point out to me yet again that I was suffering from fears of my blossoming womanhood—a longing to become an adult clashing with reluctance to accept the responsibilities and burdens adulthood would inevitably bring (in a sexual connection, of course)?

*　　　*　　　*

Prodded into action by this obviously highly meaningful dream, I speculated silently the next morning on the best way to try and find out more about the necessary symbolic acts which, performed in faith, would work the magic to prevent Opal-Ophelia and/or Loki the Shape-shifter from carrying out further horrors like the slaughter of the cats. My thoughts did not sit too well in the context of our breezy touristy day out, and in the end I was forced to seek help.

'Because I can't just ignore what's been going on, Gran. I wish I could, but I can't. I—well, it doesn't bear thinking of, what happened to Dick and Turpin. I have to do something. But what?'

Gran gave me a long look across the teacups.

'Why not ask the gods?' she suggested unexpectedly.

'Ask the gods?' I repeated, lowering my voice.

It was getting more and more crazy. By this time we were sitting having tea and teacakes in a coffee shop in Buxton, lapped soothingly in Victorian Spa town gentility. The most unlikely of settings to discuss the best way to try and deal with Loki, master of chaos, and the possible Ending of the World as portrayed in Scandinavian mythology.

Because apparently, according to what Rowan contributed to the discussion next, this was what Loki's master-plan was all about. The Ending of the World as recounted in the prophetic stories of Ragnarok, it appeared, was the Shape-shifter's eventual aim. Even more disconcerting though, was the fact that our objective seemed to be doomed from the start, because by all the rules of myth and symbolism, something that had been preordained (like the Ending of the World) was inevitably going to come about anyway and there was nothing you could do to stop it.

'You see,' Rowan explained, as we wandered a little later through the steamily exotic air of the conservatory in the Pavilion, breathing in the fragrance of heliotrope and hyacinth beneath the towering trunks of palms and the foliage of giant tree ferns, 'the Ragnarok—the Day of Doom—is fated. Sooner or later it has to happen, girl. It has been foretold in every culture and so like the Day of Creation, it must come into being. Inexorably. In its due time.'

'Oh, right. Well, that's that then, isn't it?' I said. 'No point in worrying about it, is there?'

Gran was more thoughtful. She stared at the golden shapes of fish gliding about in the pool as she enlightened me.

'I know very little about such things Tania, and I admit, I do not want to know more. But in the same way that we each had our encounter with the woman—with Opal-Ophelia—and it was actually with—'

'With Loki the Shape-shifter,' I prompted. Why beat about the bush at this stage?

'Apparently so, yes. In the same way that Mother and I—and now you—have experienced some confrontation with her—and in different locations—it seems to me that whatever action we have to take next will happen in the same way.'

'Mentally?' I asked. Sometimes I catch on very quickly. 'The will and the intent, you mean? Sort of apply ourselves to creating the solution to the problem in our heads?'

'They call it visualising, I think. Visualising the solution to a problem, making thing happen the way you want them to,' Gran told me.

The only thing was, exactly what was the problem we were trying to deal with? If Loki the Shape-shifter was in the early stages of his Ending of the World scenario, what new version could we think up to counteract it with? Particularly since it was going to happen whether anyone tried to stop it or not?

Because I now carried the silver fishes and all that went with them, because I was the Chosen One and had a role to play, then it was up to me to take appropriate action, okay, I accepted that. And after the revelation I had experienced beside the lake when I had come through that horrific personal dark night of the soul, I knew instinctively that I could face whatever I might have to face and do whatever I might need to do. If only I had some idea what that was.

Just as she had suggested in the coffee shop when we were eating our teacakes, Gran said again, quite simply: 'Why not just ask? For information. And for help.'

Obvious really, when you came to think about it. And again obvious that since we seemed to be dealing with ancient Scandinavian gods, we had to find a place with suitable (ancient and/or Scandinavian) affiliations to make contact.

'You mean I should go to Copenhagen? To visit Daddy and Ulla?' I queried slowly. After all these years, I found that rather a disturbing thought, though I could not have explained why.

Gran was looking at me consideringly.

'Do you want to?'

Did I want to make new and adult contact with my father? Re-evaluate my relationship with him and his partner? Go to Denmark? Some day I would have to tackle challenges like this of course, especially if I wanted to succeed in my own right as myself, as a successful actress. Today Daddy and Denmark—tomorrow, the world!

'Well, maybe some time,' I said cautiously. 'Yes, maybe I will go some time Gran. But he's away at the moment so there would be no point just now.'

That was when Gran brought up the subject of the Bridestones. And mentioned another of the ancient places in the area that had Scandinavian connotations.

'Thor's Cave,' she said.

Rowan looked up at the mention of Thor.

'Well, he was one of the gods too, wasn't

he?' Gran enquired brightly.

'Indeed he was. The most loved of all the Aesir, protector of Asgard, the god of wind and thunder,' Rowan told us after a moment, and as I listened to his voice I could feel the coloured lights and fountains begin to play again, realities shift and mingle, the earth quiver. The magic was there once more.

I hadn't actually been aware of it during the last few days while Rowan had been staying with us at Rudyard. The fact that it seemed to have faded hadn't bothered me though, I'd been content just to experience a warm, comforting glow of pleasure that he was there. Back in my own familiar territory I thought, it was natural enough that after our first meeting when I had thrown myself into his arms, he should merge into the background, almost seem like an ordinary person. But now I realised once again—with a thrill that ran through me like a powerful electric current—that he had been creating this illusion deliberately in exactly the same way he had been doing it throughout the last week or so of term.

For Rowan had his own methods of hypnotic persuasion and sometimes, I had begun to understand, it suited him very well to cloak himself in the solid, reliable image of a simple Edinburgh lad with theatrical aspirations, though he could do little to disguise the muscular grace years of dance training and fencing practise had given him. It provided a sort of inoffensive invisibility, took the pressure off, as it were. He had done this to make sure that I was given the space I needed during the holiday period, I suddenly saw with appreciative clarity. He had given me time to grow accustomed to his strangely fortuitous presence at Rudyard, time to gather my resources together after what had happened over Christmas, before any more emotional demands were made on me.

But now the mask was off. He was himself again.

Whoever he was—

14

It had by now begun to dawn on me that there had to be far more to Rowan's unexpected appearance on my doorstep than met the eye. Wasn't it highly unlikely that with loving relations in Scotland—even though they were eccentrics who ate and slept on piles of books—he would choose to give a visit home a miss at this festive time unless it was for some very good reason?

Now, just happening to pop by our rather remote little village (especially out of season) in order to seek out a friendly face didn't add up to half a good enough reason to me. I understood that the Scots set a lot of store by celebrating Hogmanay, piping in the haggis and all that. So it must have taken something quite earth-shattering to keep Rowan away from celebrating with his friends north of the border. And then when you came to think about it, Gran had behaved oddly as well, inviting him to stay at a moment's notice—the spare room ready almost as if she had been expecting him— Spooky, I thought.

Were they in some sort of cahoots? Impossible since they had never met before, and yet—

Gran's revelations about her knowledge of magic and witchcraft had revealed all kinds of previously unsuspected possibilities. In the delight of simply showing Rowan around the locality and enjoying his company, I had completely forgotten too that he was probably a Scandinavian god himself. Let's face it, this was not the kind of information any girl could be expected to take seriously when she was trying to enjoy herself innocently celebrating a quiet Christmas break.

'Thor was not a god of war, as is most commonly believed,' Rowan was explaining now, his voice evoking tiny shivers up and down my spine. 'With his mighty hammer Mjollnir, forged by dwarves, he defended the human race against the forces of evil. Tiny pendant hammers made of silver have been excavated all across Scandinavia, and it's thought that they were actually worn as amulets representing the magical hammer of the god. Thor was the deity the people called on when they needed defending, he fought famous battles with giants and other creatures of darkness.'

I roused myself resignedly from staring at the brilliant yellow stars of some lusciously petalled tropical flower I did not know. 'Right, well, then. Seems like it's Thor's Cave first stop if it's help from the gods that we need.'

'Go to the Bridestones first Tania,' Gran said enigmatically. 'I think that will be best.'

*   *   *

So here we were, sitting in the warmth of Rowan's car considering the situation. He had pulled up at the side of the country road, and I looked across the wide field to the right. In their dark stand of trees on the rising ground beyond, the ancient stones loomed, holding their secrets, particularly still and impressive on this wintry day.

The road was long and straight, the land gripped with frost, but unfolding ahead of us into a wide and breathtaking view. We were high up, nearly as high in fact as the hill called the Cloud, which had been an Ancient British Camp and which lay somewhere on our right. From Cloud Hill you could see nine counties.

Rowan, map and guidebook now open in his

hands, was regaling me with further information about the Bridestones.

'It seems safe to pronounce that this is all that remains of a Long Barrow . . . built by the Battleaxe-folk round about 2300 BC . . . opinion has differed as to whether the Bridestones was a prehistoric burial place of some chieftain or a place of Druidical worship . . .'

I was no archaeologist, no scholar of history. So what if the stones had stood here for thousands of years and knew the secrets of life and death? What interested me more about them this morning, actually, was that they seemed particularly appropriate for us, for Rowan and myself, because Gran had told us they were the ancient marriage stones where time out of mind the country people had come to make their vows and bind themselves to their lovers.

This was a place of those rites of passage I had long been so aware of in the shadowy woods and hills round Rudyard. Ceremonies celebrated to the strains of flutes and bells, with songs and flowers.

I could feel the presence of such rites now, hear their eerie musical rhythms—and yet it was not the place itself that evoked them. As I turned to look at Rowan I knew that I carried them within myself, that I would carry them for ever, those celebrations of joyous union. Not a making of vows, but a reaffirming of vows we two must have made long ago in some other life, some other time. Or maybe even before time began.

Or at least, that was what I told myself, for yet again Rowan was being blandness personified and I dared not make any mention at all about ancient pacts of union between us. I was coming to understand him a little better now though, and was content to say nothing.

'Indigestion girl, from the look on your face,' he commented, breaking off from his informative reading with a lifted dark brow.

'Maybe some sort of psychic indigestion,' I acknowledged, grinning despite myself.

'Ah! Roasted cheese has that effect I understand.'

I hit him with the guide book. 'Pig! If you are going to throw that in my face for ever. Just because you can cook—!'

We walked slowly up the drive past a high wall and found the wooden gate that marked the entrance to the site. The way lay through a darkly clustered yew hedge. I took a few steps beneath the trees, and there they were before us, two tall monoliths perhaps eight feet high, raked against the sky. Round their foundations lay more stones sunk into the earth, all darkly silvered beneath the ice-limned boughs of the gathered woodland that closed protectively in—

—Standing looking at the stones now, shivering in my thick coat, no wind to stir my hair. Far from the rest of the world, out of time and place.

It was very quiet. I went forward a few paces on my own, and touched one of the stones. I was very conscious of the silver fishes round my neck, concealed beneath my tawny fake-fox collar. Both they and the surface of the stone under my hand seemed to be humming, waiting, the energy leashed and in check.

I stood for what seemed to be a long, long time though it was probably no more than five minutes. There was still nothing but that watchful, waiting silence. No ghosts, no answers.

I thought of all the couples who had come here to be married, the even more ancient ceremonies that had been carried out here. For after all, this had originally been a burial chamber and there must have been solemn rites—something to do with fire and sacrifice, Rowan had said—

—Severing the links with the soul of the dead—whoever he had been—a warrior or person of great importance, people assumed— although some authorities thought the person who had been buried here had been not a man but a woman—some powerful goddess—

That was where the name of the stones had come from, Gran had told us. It was from the goddess Brigit or Bride—

An ancient earth goddess—
    . . . for this was anciently, before the time of

the other gods. Then Great Nerthus alone cared for her people and was known to them. She would come among them in her holy wagon, as a mother to her children, and all men laid aside their weapons and forgot their wars and did her reverence when she came . . .

I had a father then, and a mother. I had a name to which I answered. But I forgot them, forgot them all, forgot my name and my family and my tribe after Nerthus reached out to touch me . . .

*   *   *

I did not know why, but I found I was crying, tears starting to my eyes and trickling unheeded down my cheeks. I let them fall, making no attempt to stop them or wipe them away. I was aware of Rowan watchful behind me, glad of his strength and presence but even more glad of his stillness, his understanding of the mysteries that I sensed intuitively far surpassed my own.

There might have been tears, I do not know, when I left them. Certainly there was pride when I was called. The harpers began to compose songs in my name when the wagon left my father's hall. I was honoured for my calling. Yet I walked behind the wagon in submission, as befitted a chosen daughter of Nerthus, with my head bowed for I could not look upon my great Mother . . .

Must I undergo it once more, the destiny I had been aware of, that destiny of sacrifice and pain? How many times did the Chosen One need to hang from the tree in agony and give up all, possessing only the moment of terrible awareness?

I was lost, naked and shivering. The levels of the world were turned upon each other so that I was neither in space or time. I was an object, an abject dead flesh that had its only reality through the contact of the pain inflicted by the living flesh that lifted it, bound it with bonds that cut deep to bring forth the salt taste of blood—

There were voices keening in the wind that blew cold from the sea, the voices of souls lost and beseeching their way. The first heavy drops of the storm that gathered itself out there in the darkness stung my flesh like knives. And I knew without knowing how I knew that they were the forerunners, that even the grass was bending lower before the tempest that would come, crouching itself ever deeper and lower against the sand, blurring the line of the shore so that all was grey, all shapes in the mist, no substance, no difference between earth and sky, sea and land—

*　　　*　　　*

My tears were blinding me now and there was the salt taste of them on my mouth. I was shaking with a terrible despair, so weak and sick that I could hardly stand. Unable to take any more, I turned and fled from the place, pushing past Rowan as though he was not there, sliding, almost losing my footing on the wet frozen ground.

I wanted to scream out my pain, my frustration and my misery. For after all, they had failed me. They could not help me. The stones held no answers.

I knew nothing. I was nothing. I was the Chosen One and the need was great, and yet I was overwhelmingly aware of myself only as nothing. Less than a grain of sand. Nothing. Nothing. Nothing.

* * *

In the drive outside the yew hedge I stopped and stood trying to gather my senses and pull myself together while I waited for Rowan to join me. I was gulping down air, still choking on my sobs, when suddenly I turned sharply with the sensation that someone was watching me. A figure had emerged from somewhere further up the drive, from the private land of the farm perhaps. Because of the tears that still blurred my eyes I couldn't see her clearly, but she spoke and her voice was kind.

'Good morning.'

'Good morning,' I managed, feeling all kinds of a fool, trying to speak normally. I was embarrassed by my state of distress. 'I—I hope we're not trespassing. I—we came to see the stones.'

'Not at all. This is a public right of way. The path to the stones is free to whoever comes.' There was a momentary pause and then she said: 'The cave is on private land, though.'

'The cave?'

'Yes. This whole area forms part of the old Bridestones barrow complex, you know. The stones were moved, some of them taken away, some used to build. The cave is an artificial construction, it is thought to be made of the original stones, perhaps even part of an original entrance into the burial chamber. You might like to see it. I think you would find it particularly interesting. It is known sometimes as the Serpent Cave. Or else, people call it the Womb of the Earth Mother.'

Something seemed to happen, but so subtly and infinitesimally that I could not identify it. Did the earth shake slightly? Did the fishes stir of their own accord round my neck, did the very sky move?

'You are most welcome if you would care to come with me. I will show you the way,' said the woman.

I had to go. I knew I had to go and I glanced back over my shoulder at Rowan. He had come out through the gate by this time and

300

was standing quietly waiting for me, but somehow it was his figure now that had become unfocussed, lost in a kind of haze, and not that of the woman. He moved very slightly, making a gesture of encouragement.

'Come,' said the woman and turned. I followed her, round a curve in the drive and through a wide stone gateway that was square and battlemented like something out of a fairy story—

The castle portal of ancient myth—

—was it of the Castle Joy or the Castle Perilous?

The gateway led me into a garden that lay silent and still beneath its delicate frosting of ice. Trees rose in stately and spacious dignity, the dark of evergreen clustered thick in the copses along tall walls that stretched down the sloping vistas. Directly before me, riding the height of garden like a ship serene on high seas, was a house. An ordinary Victorian mansion I supposed, built, like the gateway and the walls and the outbuildings I could see stretching away on my left, of soft earth-coloured local stone.

Everywhere around there were ancient stones, old stones that were mute, withdrawn in their mystery. But the house was lit for Christmas and the lights twinkled and blazed, turning it into a place of magical enchantment.

As I followed the woman across the garden, I felt no curiosity about the cave I was going to see. I was only conscious of the most overwhelming sense of rightness. I did not need to ask who she was, or why I should be here. None of that mattered. All that was relevant was that I should go with her.

In one glance, as I entered beneath the gateway arch and stepped onto the path, the prospect before me had impressed itself indelibly on my memory, and I knew I would never forget it. The wide walk was graciously curved, the terrace of the house low and uncluttered, with simple lines. A stone-paved sunken rose garden where the bare stalks of the rose trees reached up delicate, yet sturdy promise of summer blossom against the earth, lay empty on my right. Beyond were sweeping lawns, perfectly trimmed, and in the middle of the lowest, standing in beautiful symmetry amid the other decorative shrubs, the silent shape of a cedar tree.

It was the sort of tree that might have shaded innumerable lazy summer tea parties, watched over the scrambling of babies on that velvet grass, the clicking of croquet mallets, the fluttering caps of maids and the starched prints of nannies. Lovely women in dresses diaphanous as the wings of butterflies would have mingled with their men, who smiled, rugged and tanned in their sporty whites. This might be ancient and sacred ground but the ghosts who greeted me here were not of ancient warriors. They were of families gathered in the golden days of an Empire on which the sun would never set, secure in their confidence of immortality, even though beyond them at the edge of the garden where the evergreens clustered thickly along the high walls, dark shadows waited, yet to emerge.

I felt a great sense of inevitability, of completion and peace as I walked through it all a pace behind my silent guide. We passed the house and turned down the slope of the hill, and then she led me towards the deep recesses beyond rockery and garden. I saw that there were thick, interwoven stems of two ancient, dead yews that rose like pillars, marking the entrance to a cave.

Something within me knew the place, and I could feel confirmation from the fishes, heavy about my neck. This was where my journey was to end, this was where my sacrifice would be made. This was the place of destiny. Here all would be resolved for me, all would be made clear.

A black hole, about the height of my breast, yawned open before me. I could see that there were paved stones leading into darkness, and that the passageway turned sharply to the left just beyond where the light ended.

'The Serpent Cave. The Womb of the Mother,' said the woman. She had stopped a little to one side and left me to go forward alone. I looked at her now. A plain woman with a sturdy, honest face. A woman who might have been any age. Or ageless. Her dark coat might have been a cloak. Or a rough black fur pulled about her shoulders with homespun under it, the sort of thing the unquiet spirits had worn in our play. Her long hair might have been braided. Might have been threaded with grey—or frost—. She might have been any woman. Or every woman. I could not see her clearly.

'Enter,' she said.

I had no torch or light. I did not know whether it was safe to venture into that dark hole, whether it led to a pit, a shaft from which I would not return, but there was no way back now. The rime had frozen in ruts where I left the path, and as I moved forward onto the patch of earth before the cave under the overhanging branches, the ice made a soft crackling noise beneath my boots. I placed my feet deliberately, careful not to slip as I bent my head and my back, and took a hesitant step onto the stone slabs.

I entered the passage. Hunched over, I went slowly forward. I felt the cold stone of the walls close around me. The walls of a tomb. For this was part of an ancient grave. A burial ground.

Terrors that were not my own but atavistic, the terrors of the grave that have haunted every questing human soul since the beginning of time, shook me and held me so that I thought I would not be able to force myself to move. Gasping now, I fought them off, shuffling deeper into the tunnel, feeling my way with my hands. I turned where the passage turned, and stepped blindly into the dark.

*   *   *

It was moments—centuries—aeons later that I stumbled forth again. I passed between the ancient yews and the garden received me in still and solemn silence. I had come a long, long journey, and I was disorientated and shaking with sobs. The woman had gone, but Rowan was there. I saw him standing just beyond the shadowy branches from which I emerged, and without a word I went to him and he took me in his arms.

I cannot remember my birth, but I knew in that moment what it had felt like to be born. Shattering, light-splinting, blinding brilliance lit the black and white of the garden, the sky, the Victorian country house with its aura of *aurora borealis* colours. The air sang, the very trees and grass were singing in harmonies I could not have described. My body was made of light made flesh. I knew this, and that I was no longer in the grave only because Rowan's embrace was hard as steel around me, and beneath my cheek I could feel the beat of his heart.

I had gone defenceless, sightless into the grave prepared to find worse terrors there than I had endured already. In desperation, I had been prepared to give myself up to hang for eternity from the tree if I had to, if that was what it meant to be the Chosen One. And I had found that death is not death but a new life, that the dark of the grave is but yet the more dazzling intensification of rebirth.

The tears on my cheeks were not because I had been granted the sight of such eternal verities, though. They were because, in surrendering myself to the relentlessness and awful power of the Earth Goddess, I had met instead the softness of my mother's arms, the touch of her lips on my hair. I had been comforted beyond all comfort, soothed by the voice that drives away all fear.

I was hers, I had always been hers, like the hound that knows his master but knows not the how of it . . .

My mother had not failed me. She had not forgotten me nor left me to struggle in the dark alone. She had been there at the last, when I could give no more and go no further, and she had given me all that I needed and more, placed treasures in my empty hands beyond my wildest dreams.

I tried to speak through my tears, to tell Rowan of the wonders I had seen, but he lifted his hand and gently brushed the wet streaks from my face.

'Easy, girl, all is well. Be easy. You are here safe with me and that is all that matters now.'

I would never be able to explain yet somehow I knew I did not need to. Rowan knew. He had always known.

As we left the Bridestones, our footsteps ringing out loud on the pathway back to the road where we had left the car, I could feel the dream receding. I tried to cling to it, but intuitively I knew that it was not possible. But I also knew that some day—some day far in the future—I would feel that awareness, that wonder and that joy again, and be reunited once more with those I had left behind me in the cave.

Rowan stopped before we got to the road and indicated something set into the long wall that bordered the garden. I saw that there was a low stone pillar, a standing stone that might have been there since the burial chamber was made, for the wall had been built carefully round it, making it into a small shrine set in an alcove. There was a cross—a Celtic cross, I recognised it as—roughly marked on the top of the stone.

'Shall we leave a votive offering? To thank her?' Rowan asked me and I did not need to know who he was referring to.

Wordlessly I nodded. Overcome, still swept by the sense of completion I had known in the cave, I reached to take the silver fishes from my neck but he stopped me.

'No, girl. They are yours, her gift for you and your successors to carry. For do not doubt, there will be need of them again. I will thank her for both of us.'

What he left on the tiny altar I did not see, but I was grateful and glad as we went on and emerged onto the long straight country road. Still lost in the glory of my visions. The warmth of the car was like stepping into another, less real world, and I shook myself as though I was waking from a long, deep sleep.

Rowan was watching me, a little smile on his lips.

'Food next for you, I think girl, and then we will go to Thor's Cave. There is one last thing for you to see.'

* * *

Well, a plate of steak and chips washed down with a pint of real ale soon puts a proper perspective on any problem. I had no idea at all what I was supposed to do when I got to Thor's Cave, and Gran's idea that I would find the answers when I arrived at these ancient sites did not actually seem to be working, because nothing had really happened regarding Opal-Ophelia and the sinister designs of the Shape-shifter—whatever these were—at the Bridestones, had it? Not so far as I could see, anyway.

What I had experienced in the cave had

308

been something intensely personal. It would make no difference to the forces of chaos and mischief whether I had encountered my mother—or the Earth Mother—or whoever it had been—there or not. But strangely, none of this bothered me any more, and I said as much to Rowan as we drove on.

Nothing seemed to be able to get to me now. I was just going with the flow, enjoying the ride. The whole excursion had turned into a fun day rather than some kind of serious cosmic quest. The concept that we were trying to come to terms with a dark enemy in another dimension was difficult to keep a hold on, since I was beginning to get high on an unexpectedly heady sense of well-being and *joi-de-vivre*.

This was no doubt partly the effect of what had happened in the cave—whatever that psychedelic experience had been, which I found difficult to recall in any detail now after our stop for a meal—but it was also in no small measure due to the real ale. The pint I had downed had helped me understand fully why 'olde England', where real ale was quaffed in huge amounts, was always referred to as 'merry'!

'You know, there's no problem really, is there?' I remarked glibly as we bowled along, Rowan's hands steady on the wheel, his eyes enigmatic behind the tinted shades he had slid on against the glare of the low winter sun. 'I can't really see what you or I or anyone else could possibly do about it, if somebody was determined enough to make the ending of the world happen. I mean if scientists exploded some sort of bomb for instance, there would be nothing anybody could do, would there? Nobody could stop a catastrophe like that, even if they did happen to be Chosen—and quite honestly I'm more than inclined to feel there's been some sort of mistake somewhere about that too. People like me simply don't get Chosen by ancient Scandinavian goddesses. It's got to be a joke, an interactive TV challenge we just don't know about yet. Somebody's been having us all on. I mean how could I possibly start trying to explain seriously to—well, to a person like Ted, for instance—that I had a mission to save the world?'

Rowan's lips curved briefly but he did not answer for a moment. He was concentrating on his driving. Then he said:

'Oh, you are in the right of it, of course, girl. I always knew there was sense behind that pretty face.'

I turned to stare at him, feeling as though I had been kicked in the stomach.

'But yesterday—when we were talking to Gran—you seemed to take it all so seriously. What happened to poor Dick and Turpin—and Loz—you agreed, *we* agreed that it was all caused by, you know, Loki the god of chaos—. And here we are now, heading off to Thor's

Cave because Thor was another of the gods, expecting to find advice and protection. Aren't we? Well, aren't we?'

In spite of my easy words, this was not what I had expected. Suddenly everything was very badly wrong. My voice sharpened and rose in spite of myself.

'Rowan, have you been stringing me—and Gran—along all the time? Don't you really believe in any of it yourself after all?'

There was a long pause. Then:

'Myths are not reality, girl. They are stories, fantasies, nothing more than that,' Rowan said mildly, but with such ruthless finality in his words that I was frightened into silence.

We had taken the road beyond Leek towards the Manifold Valley on the edge of the Peak District National Park now. Heading into the wilds. Soon we'd turn off towards the village of Butterton and drop down to join the Manifold Track, a paved footpath which follows the route of the former Leek and Manifold Light Railway, winding through this picturesque river valley beside the Manifold River.

Shaken beyond speech, I just sat looking dumbly out of the car window, watching the scenery as it unfolded. This was spectacular country even for someone like me, who was used to it. The Manifold Valley was rightly described in all the tourist brochures as nothing short of stunning, with its walks and tracks, its ancient woods and caves, its tiny villages and quaint industrial relics and abundance of lush natural beauty. In the early days of the Twentieth Century train passengers used to board the narrow gauge railway and puff their way for nine glorious miles through the hills and gorges, passing the villages and stopping at the tiny stations. Tourists came in droves, alighting from the train in summer with their picnic baskets, while in winter, when in my friend Will Shakespeare's words 'icicles hang by the wall and Dick the shepherd blows his nail', the hardy folk from the little farming communities travelled crammed into one single carriage for survival.

Ah, those were the great days. But eventually, as the local historians picturesquely expressed it, the line ran out of steam. The tracks were lifted and the old route was resurfaced. Now walkers and cyclists, ramblers and tourists, could follow the path where the railway tracks had once been.

As I told you, I have never been a great walker—probably spent the time others were exploring the countryside practising speeches from Shakespeare in the woods round Rudyard, or choreographing dance routines in the studio—but I was familiar with the Manifold Valley. I didn't need the map that lay open in my lap. And Rowan seemed to have an instinctive navigator's sense of direction.

'You know yourself that myths do not refer to reality, girl. That they are not factual,' I heard him saying now and I was stung into speech.

'You mean they don't happen? All right then.' Even though this struck at my whole sense of the inherent rightness of things. 'What you're telling me is that there was no Loki, god of chaos, no divine interference, is that it? You're saying that it really was Loz who had a brainstorm and went berserk and attacked the cats?'

Rowan seemed unmoved by my angry hostility.

'What do you think?' he countered with great gentleness.

And at that, I started to feel very uncomfortable. I recalled with a flush almost of shame, how I had sworn on my hope of salvation to Loz, that he had not been responsible for what had happened to Dick and Turpin. I could not believe it or accept it. But seriously, what other alternative was there? Did I really think some ghostly hand, a ghoulishly dark form out of a horror movie, had come into the flat, picked up a knife and plunged it into helpless bodies of our pets?

I'd been wilfully blinding myself to the truth, hadn't I? Because realistically, it had to have been a physical hand, only a physical hand could have picked up a knife—a three-dimensional kitchen knife—and spilled the cats' very real and physical and life-giving blood. Put like that, the thought frightened me more than I was prepared to admit. But I could not deny it.

Rowan turned the car and we went on. We were on the roof of the world, it seemed. Black-etched trees raised spectral fingers like witches' besoms against the pale sky, and we could see for miles across far distances where the rounded folds of the hills rose and fell. Everything was in shades of grey, though the red sun was faintly staining the horizon with its winter carmine. On now to the village of Butterton. Icy fields, distances. I shivered, my skin clammy and cold in spite of the car's warmth. It was a long time before I spoke again.

'Rowan?'

'Girl?'

But I stayed silent. What could I say? I was way out of my depth.

We went on through the twisting little narrowed roads, down through stone cottages and past the spire of the church. Lichen-encrusted dry stone walls, sheep lonely in the fields, crumpled hillsides with ruined buildings that, though we were not in Yorkshire, reminded me of Wuthering Heights. Old, old country in which I now felt very lost and helpless. Rowan stopped to check his directions once over the hill, then we were heading sharply down to where we would turn off and enter the dark of the former old railway tunnel. Here the little trains had steamed valiantly through into the river valley beyond.

As we were plunged into the darkness, I was vividly reminded of the cave. But there I had found peace, the consolation of arms that had soothed and lifted my burden from me. Now I was struggling as though in dark waters, all my visions and inspirations—all my aspirations for goodness, for enlightenment and some sort of wisdom—wiped out by a few cruelly accurate words.

I glanced at Rowan's profile but did not dare to break the silence between us. He was frowning, and there was something awesome in the set of his mouth. When had I ever thought this man was just an ordinary drama student? This man was immense, frightening in his power.

The further end of the tunnel was a point of light that flared like a beacon. We came out of the dark, emerging into gentle country, though there were high wooded slopes rising on either side. Out now into the river valley, the car followed the twisting road and we were heading for Wetton Mill. On the map this was a place for people, there were comforting amenities for human beings promised, but there were no human beings to be seen on this day. The valley was silent and empty. We might have been the only ones alive, all that moved. But for the ghosts.

I could feel them all around me, clustering close, drifting in towards the car and then withdrawing. But I was withdrawn too deeply now in my own despair to feel fear. I had to face the truth, the absolute truth. I had obviously got everything wrong. What did I know about realms beyond, about cosmic destiny? Who was I to assume in my arrogance that I—even my intuition, my willingness to learn, to give—counted for anything at all?

*   *   *

There was a car park beside the shallow-flowing river and Rowan pulled up, letting the car engine idle.

'Shall we stop here and walk to the cave?' he asked, indicating the sign that pointed to an access path. On either side the high hills and cliffs towered. We could not see Thor's cave, it was hidden from us in the depths of the valley.

I felt the fishes stir on my breast as he spoke.

. . . she who must hold the fishes and follow them across the vast worlds of water, the kingdom of Njord, and guide the lost mariners safely to land . . .

. . . and guide the lost mariners safely . . .

'Would you like to walk?' Rowan repeated

and again I felt the energy pulsing. Every nerve in my body jerked in tense awareness and anticipation.

'No. No, go on,' I said without conscious thought.

So he drove on, taking the narrow road that wound up the hill towards the village of Wetton. Trees closed in upon us, though their branches were bare. And then as the hill grew steeper, suddenly I could feel the wind and hear its low howl. I had not noticed the wind before. Thor, the god of thunder, was stirring.

The cave was visible now, and I pointed it out to Rowan. A dark gaping hole in the cliff. Serrated rock rose behind and above the entrance, tearing the sky.

The wind tugged at the car. We were rising above the valley floor, there was a steep field on our right down into the tangled woods and thick shrubs below. Tree ivy clustered thickly on ancient hawthorns, twisted by years of blast into sinister shapes that overhung a turn in the road.

And then with terrifying suddenness, there were shapes ahead of us on the empty road, shapes from the mist of nightmare, figures in the path of the car. Crowding over the top of the ridge on the left they came, the hordes with their animal faces and tall antlers, their snarling snouts and tossing manes and great hooves tearing up the frozen turf, the sound of their howling cracking and whipping against the red sky. They streamed down upon us, slavering jaws open, baying and yelling, yellow eyes bestial as they screamed aloud in an awful cacophony for blood.

Rowan had stopped the car. I did not know it but I was crouched down against him, and the voice that was screaming was my own. And then on the other side, striding across the steep valley and down from the high limestone cliffs to the right of us, I saw the giants. Their shaggy heads touched the sky, their feet trampled the trees like matchwood.

Great hordes of dwarves and strange spirits were flying and swooping on the wind, as they advanced up the hill to crush us. The Wild Hunt was almost upon us, its panting, desperate prey.

There was noise and movement everywhere. Shapes banged against the windsceen, rattled the doorhandles, lifted and jolted the car so violently that I thought it would overturn. I was whimpering. I was screaming. My heart was jerking, beating so hard with terror that I thought it would burst out of my chest. I could not breathe. I caught the flash of Rowan's eyes as he pointed, shouting:

'Look—the cave—'

Through the red mist that was blurring my sight now, I saw the shape of the god. I saw Thor with his mighty hammer held aloft, standing to his full great height on the threshold of the cave, roaring so that the very earth shook. And with each footstep the ground vibrated, as he came striding down towards us. He swung his hammer in awful arcs, and the beasts scattered. There was blood everywhere, and screams, and wet fur and entrails bright and steaming across the grey frozen grass and the silent leafless trees.

And then above the thunder, there was the sound of a horn, piercing as steel. From the cave came an army of white-clad figures with torches in their hands, bobbing like sparks in the grey afternoon. Their shrieks were audible even over the baying turmoil of the hunters, and the noise battered the car like a physical thing. Or was it the earth that was shaking, cracked by lightning forks sizzling down so blue and violent that I thought they would kill us outright?

'Rowan, who are they? What are they?' I screamed but my voice was lost.

Perhaps we were already dead. Rowan was fighting off one of the creatures that had wrenched off the car door. We were open to the elements now, and over and above the crashing thunder there was a roaring wind howling in, bitter with snow. Hail and sleet in it soaked us to the skin.

The cold cut knife-like, slashed jarring to the bone and the dark had us—

It was all dark, only the torches jerked like red stars in the blackness—fading—fading—into nothing—

I came to consciousness to find Rowan's arms around me. He was holding me clasped tightly against his warm body and tilting a flask to my lips.

I tasted brandy on my lips and thought rather wildly that I had probably drunk more alcohol in the last few days than in all my months in London. A ridiculous, irrelevant notion. Because—wasn't there—something far more terrifying to think about—? But when I remembered and started up with a cry, my heart banging painfully again, I found only a strange quiet everywhere.

We were still in the car, still at the same turn in the road where the tree ivy clustered thick round the twisted hawthorns. But—

'Where are they?' I gasped, pushing the flask away in my panic. 'Rowan, what's happened? Where are they? Where have they all gone?'

The rushing adrenalin, the high of battle readiness had blurred my senses. Dazed and confused me.

For there was nothing to be seen. There was no battle, no sign of a battle. Only the empty contours of the land. The untouched turf of the field that stretched down to the valley floor on the right, the hill reaching quietly up on our left. The cave loomed its dark mouth under the serrated cliffs, but the sky was clear. The red winter sun was setting on the spare and peaceful landscape.

'Rowan,' I sobbed, terrified again, not understanding, and he soothed me with gentle words, his hands roughly tender on my hair.

'Hush, hush girl. All is well. It is all over.'

And then as though he could not help himself, his hands were twined in my hair, I could feel their warmth on my skin and feel their urgency. He lifted me in his arms and bent his head and his lips were on mine. I reached for him with my whole being, clinging, offering, accepting, as the quiet land about us rocketed through time and space to bloom in the living silver of that far distant star. And then spent, I leaned wordlessly against him while he stroked my hair.

'You had to see it for you to understand, girl,' he told me, after a while. 'There is no Light and Dark, no Good and Evil, save in the balance, the maintaining and achieving of harmony. All is. All must be. Only the struggle to maintain the balance is constant. And the struggle goes on even now. It is eternal. It goes on in all time, in every place, but beyond the sight of those who cannot see.'

I did not really understand even now, but I knew it did not matter any more. Rowan had wisdom for both of us.

'Even the Chosen One cannot bring an end to the struggle,' he told me gently. 'There is no end. Yet sometimes the sacrifice is necessary to shift and maintain the balance, to redress it.'

'It isn't fair, though,' I protested weakly. Tears were blurring my sight. 'It isn't fair. You know it isn't. The cats are dead—and Loz will take a long time to recover—if he ever does—'

Rowan's silence was so awful that I trembled. I clung even harder to his body while I resigned myself within my heart to acceptance. I had been given the 'sight', the means to see true. I was the Chosen One. If I did not accept the truth, how could I use the fishes that had been entrusted to me wisely, how were they to guide the lost souls that in their confusion and weakness were unable to accept?

Life was not fair. All I could do was to recognise the truth and make the sacrifice I had already made at the lakeside. That was the limit of my power. And in despairing bitterness I recognised again how puny it was, that what I had to give was less than nothing.

. . . she who must hold the fishes and follow them across the vast worlds of water, the kingdom of Njord, and guide the lost mariners safely to land, must surrender herself to them as a servant of Njord and lose all sense of self . . .

It was all I could do, and I did it. But even as I recognised and accepted its nothingness, I felt Rowan touch my forehead gently with his fingers. With the touch came reassurance, blessing. And the certainty that though my sacrifice counted for nothing, yet in the making it had become everything.

I knew an immense peace, a great content. I could have stayed in that moment for ever. But the enchantment was rudely broken as Rowan stirred, gave me a big hug and then turned to start the car engine.

'Enough of these melodramatics, girl,' he said briskly. 'I thought that steak would have been enough to sustain you but I can see the occasion calls for even more drastic measures. Roasted cheese on toast, perhaps—?'

I wanted to reply, to laugh and challenge the bright gleaming blue of his eyes that were drawing me back to the familiar everyday, but I could not. Not quite yet. He reached for my hand and squeezed it before turning his attention to the narrow country road.

'Some more of the scenic route, girl. And then I will take you home.'

15

Meanwhile, back in the real world—

Enter the Player Queen the following evening. Costumed stunningly in a moss green velvet gown slashed low across the shoulders, with long tight sleeves and a sinuous bias-cut that as Gran pointed out smiling, 'make every move you make rather suggestively indecent, Tania dear.'

But that was the effect I wanted. One: because I intended to have a very physical and if, possible, entirely mindless night out tonight. I had had quite enough of deep thought and spiritual endeavour for the time being, thank you very much. And Two: because I wanted to make an impression on Rowan that he'd never forget as I sashayed down to where he was waiting to whirl me off to the ball.

It wasn't any kind of jealousy, don't get me wrong. I told myself virtuously that I was far above such petty emotions, especially where Rowan was concerned, but I'd seen the way he'd eyed Louise (attired sexily as Queen-Gertrude-of-the-cleavage) at the Civic Hall bash after *Hamlet*, and I had a shameful, secret urge to prove that if I really tried, I could do better.

When he saw me sinuously undulating down the stairs towards him, mysterious in gold and emerald eye-makeup with my Cretan hair flaming over my shoulders—and of course, my glasses nowhere in evidence—I have to admit smugly that on the whole, I was quite satisfied.

It wasn't really a ball we were going to but a New Year's Eve do at the Swan. Food, drink and dancing the night away with Genny and the Creepers. (The cointreau-smooth chanteuse Genny had somehow metamorphosed out of plain, freckled, bespectacled Jennifer who had been in my year at school). Other friends would be there too.

Not the full-blown Hogmanay celebrations Rowan was used to, of course, first-footing by a dark man and all that, but he seemed quite happy at the idea. Gran had produced two tickets that had miraculously materialised at the last minute (Auntie Bee had passed them on from young friends who couldn't use them) so as she said, why not take advantage of them.

'You deserve it, Tania. Enjoy yourself, let your hair down.'

I grinned, shaking my Cretan crimps at her.

'How can I let it down any more than this?'

'You know what I mean,' she said, unruffled.

It was true, though. I needed to run mad, be silly, chill out—let off steam—all the clichés that express a releasing of tension after unbearable strain. So why not go for it. Face the music and dance. Gran was right, I needed a break, something to convince me that I was back to being an ordinary girl again, to let me just enjoy being a human being in a three-dimensional world.

After all, I had been working hard just lately. Confronting the ancient shapeshifting god of chaos and mischief, not to mention staving off the End of the World—well, temporarily anyway. I deserved a bit of fun and frivolity. So I was determined to throw myself wholeheartedly into eating, drinking and being

325

merry tonight, before I had to sober up and think about putting my shoulder to all the grindstones that were waiting when I returned to London. Though all the prospects of tomorrow were suffused by a kind of background glow now, since one way or another, they were probably going to include Rowan.

We would lift our glasses tonight to drink to the future as the chimes of midnight rang out, exchange kisses in token of commitment to the year that was dawning, and sing Old Lang Syne in homage to the past—because already we had a past. And whatever fanciful notions I might have been harbouring about some sort of ancient and cosmic connection with Rowan, they didn't need to be aired because already, even in this life, we had a history together.

He had mentioned the possibility of taking me to Edinburgh when the next term broke at Easter. Whether he was back in London, or pursuing the dream career that would take him out of the Theatre School and into the wider world of theatre, it didn't matter. We'd be together whenever we could. And that was good enough for the moment.

I might have been ready to throw everything to the winds for him, might even have declared that was what I wanted to do, but I wasn't going to be allowed to do it. I had my own life to live, my own career as an actress, Rowan insisted on that. I owed it to the people who were waiting breathlessly to see, at some stage in the far distant future, my interpretations of the great roles—Juliet, Katharina, Lady Macbeth.

'You obviously have a many-aspected destiny,' he told me solemnly. 'And who am I to stand in the way of that? I could not deprive the theatre, girl. I'd not rest easy in my bed.'

'You think I am that good?' I couldn't help asking. I am of course as human as everyone else really, and flattery will get you everywhere so far as I am concerned.

'What is good? You belong to the stage,' he said in grave tones. 'In the immortal words of the Bard—. Er—what were they now?

*　　*　　*

We were walking together beside the lake. I particularly wanted to share this special familiar scene I loved with him, since soon we would both be gone from Rudyard, and I was building up a stock of memories. This morning there had been a fall of snow, a light fall, but enough to soften the dark of the trees and make it seem as though the lake floated upon itself. Children were feeding the ducks, shouting and calling, red bobble hats bright as berries, their dark figures vividly alive in the still landscape. Breath laughing in frosty shapes on the air.

'What immortal words?' I thought for a

moment and then spoke at random.

'Do you mean: '*All the world's a stage*
And all the men and women merely players?'

'*As You Like It*. The Seven Ages of Man speech,' Rowan identified promptly, with a snap of his fingers. It was a game we all played all the time at my Theatre School, trying to out-quote each other.

'I wanted to know whether you thought I was any good,' I reminded him, and he gave me one look.

'Oh, all right,' I said. 'So I'm going to be the new Sarah Bernhardt and all that. I should have known better than to ask.' Actually though, I was rather pleased, and pursued enjoyably: 'It's nice to think you don't regard me simply as *a poor player, who struts and frets his hour upon the stage and then is heard no more.*'

'Ah, but that's not a reference to acting, it's about life—what is life, is it merely an illusion?' Rowan retorted, smiling. '*What's Hecuba to me, or me to Hecuba*?' Does nothing matter? Is nothing really real?'

Suddenly sobered, I looked round. I could not escape my vision, the awareness bestowed by the 'Sight' even here. Was this scene before me actually as illusory as a stage set? I seemed to see beyond the images of the children playing, the dog trying to fetch a stick that had fallen on the icy lake surface, barking excitedly, splashing and half-slithering.

328

They were there, all real, it was true, but beyond them were the ghosts I knew so well who were just as real to me. And beyond those ghosts, there were other ghosts. Darker, more ancient ghosts. Layer on layer. Which was truly real? Or were they all real? Or all equally illusory?

I did not care. I was a part of them all, I belonged. I had a place, a role to play. That was all that mattered now. Whether it was as the Player Queen or as the Chosen One—or as any other aspect of my self, of Tatiana Forrester—all I had to do was to live each role I was given, in whichever world it happened to be, as fully and as faithfully as I could in truth and intent. That was all that would ever be expected of me.

*   *   *

It was New Year's Eve. The turning of the year. The inevitable progress of the earth's journey towards the sun. Though everywhere was still cold, the ice still patchy on the lake, I could feel that stirring below my feet. Life stirring, unseen.

The fishes on my breast did not rest heavy now but light, as though they were a part of me. They were quiet for the moment, their task done. And yet I was conscious, for all that, of the presence of the dark enemy still hovering somewhere unseen. Distant.

Menacing. Like the far-off sound of cannon-fire.

'There is a saying of Rabindranath Tagore that I particularly like, girl—and don't ask, he was a great Indian poet,' Rowan said unexpectedly, starting to walk back across the Dam. 'Let me share it with you.' And he quoted:

'Faith is the bird that feels the light when the dawn is still dark.'

As I followed him I considered this, finding it beautiful.

'Yes—' I said after a long pause. And then, because I was human I suppose, because I was compelled to voice the deep fear and acknowledge that it was still there, that I would never be quite free of it, I went on in a low voice. 'But Rowan, what if—what if there is not going to be a dawn. Never. Really never going to be any dawn at all.'

He didn't laugh or scoff at me. He stopped and looked down into my face.

'Watchman, what of the night?' he quoted inscrutably.

'I don't know. What about the night?'

'The Watchman said: The day cometh, and also the night. It's in the Bible.'

'Okay, clever clogs,' I said. 'But that's no answer really, is it?'

'There is no answer,' Rowan reminded me gently. 'That is why you hold the silver fishes.'

I looked up at the traceries of the bare

boughs above me.

'Rowan,' I ventured. 'Where did they really come from? The fishes?'

But I knew even before I spoke what his reaction would be. He smiled.

'Does it matter? They are here and you have them safe.'

And then he smiled a different kind of smile, and the coloured lights blazed all around me, and the violins struck up and the fountains leaped.

'Come on girl,' he said wickedly, striking a pose. 'I'll give you this one, it's Lord Byron.'

'On with the dance! Let joy be unconfined;

'No sleep till morn, when Youth and Pleasure meet

'To chase the glowing Hours with flying feet.'

Deliberately, he held out his hand. I laid my fingers in his. And I went with him.

AUTHOR'S NOTE

Background research for this book has covered a period of nearly twenty years.

My use of the silver fishes in the context of the story is based on references to the 'spaewomen' of ancient Scandinavian times, who were apparently gifted in unearthly ways—one of their reported functions being the ability to steer or navigate the sailing vessels of the period by means of mysterious objects whose usage was not commonly understood.

I have assumed that the easiest way to carry such objects would probably have been strung round the neck, and that since they concerned sea voyages, the shape might well have been that of a fish or fishes. Also that they were probably made from some kind of precious metal.

In recent conversation with Kevin Kilburn FRAS, I learned that new theories regarding the use of the stars in ancient times confirm that the ancients may have navigated by means of a 'plumb-bob' that was worn round the neck and taken off to be held vertically when needed.

The battle in the Manifold Valley between the forces of Light and Dark would, like all such battles, have drawn on whatever resources were at hand. The Scandinavian connection was assisted here (though Tania was not aware of it of course), by the ghosts of Twentieth Century Druids who did historically meet in Thor's Cave under the leadership of the impressively named Ralph de Tunstall Sneyd. Though so far as I know there is no record of any of their ghosts haunting the valley, I feel certain the Gorsedd would have joined enthusiastically in any struggle that was on-going there against the powers of darkness.

I am indebted to Basil Jeunda's excellent *Rudyard Lake 1797–1997, The Bicentennial History* (Churnet Valley Books), for topographical and historical details about the Rudyard area.